Learn to Howl
Jennifer R. Donohue

<u>Praise for Learn to Howl</u>

"It's not often someone pulls off a coming-of-age thriller, but this smartly-paced story does so beautifully. 'Learn to Howl' showcases a tightly-knit pack dealing both with its newest member and a raft of family secrets—not to be missed." — Premee Mohamed, Nebula award-winning author of 'Beneath the Rising'

• • • •

THE ONLY THING BETTER than a heist adventure is a heist adventure with werewolves who can smell your fear. – Julie Reeser

• • • •

"LEARN TO HOWL IS PAGE-turning must-read for any werewolf fan. Donohue's got a knack for creating captivating characters, and here, she keeps the action moving deftly and swiftly through werewolf lore and family rivalries, through the New Jersey Pine Barrens, and into menacing corporate lairs. A thrilling, entertaining, and wolfishly wonderful read." — Maria Haskins, author of Wolves & Girls and Six Dreams About the Train.

• • • •

DONOHUE HAS DONE IT again! Learn To Howl is another immersive experience into a
fantasy world written so believably that the hairs on the back of your neck will stand up. This

novel incorporates such relevant themes along with master storytelling that I could picture it on
the big screen! — Wendy Cartwright, author and columnist

. . . .

A RELATABLE STORY ABOUT self-identity wrapped inside high octane action. This hair-raising tale keeps the stakes high without sidelining complex family dynamics. An excellent introduction to an exciting new series, we can't wait to see what Donohue has for us next. — Fiction Fans podcast

. . . .

"THIS ONE HOWLS STRAIGHT from the heart. It's a dark heart, but there's a lot of it!" — Matt Wallace, Hugo Award Winner and author of the Sin du Jour and Savage Rebellion series

. . . .

FOR READERS TIRED OF grizzled alpha males, Donohue portrays her werewolves as an intimate, close-knit family—one that you just might wish you were a part of — Gwen C. Katz, author of *Among the Red Stars*

. . . .

"IN LEARN TO HOWL, DONOHUE gives us the family we always deserved: full of love, eventual acceptance, and finding ourselves. A found family book full of the best dogs (and the best werewolves). Donohue's wonderful razor sharp narrative voice is perfect for this novel of razor sharp wit and perfect comedic timing. Loved it. - Jordan Kurella, Nebula Finalist author of "I Never Liked You Anyway"

Author Note

The werewolves in the Learn to Howl trilogy are different from typical movie werewolves; they are people and they are wolves, with no bipedal werewolf form in between. They're a little different from common pop culture urban fantasy werewolves; they're normal sized wolves, they don't communicate telepathically, and their social structures are based on familial pack dynamics. I had a lot of fun with canine body language in the course of the trilogy, and maybe you will too!

Triggers for Learn to Howl include:

Threat of sexual assault

Kidnapping

Medical experimentation

. . . .

For Jim

. . . .

THIS IS A WORK OF FICTION. Names, characters, places, and incidents either

are the product of the author's imagination or are used fictitiously.

Any resemblance to actual persons, living or dead, events, or locales

is entirely coincidental.

No AI/LLM was used in the creation of this work.

Learn to Howl © 2024 by Jennifer R. Donohue

Cover art © 2023 by Nora Fraser

eBook ISBN: 978-1-945548-26-0

paperback ISBN: 978-1-945548-28-4

I was thankful for the sapling; it kept me from falling while I puked. Mama always told us to count our blessings. I leaned back and tried to catch my breath, wiping my mouth with the back of my hand. It hurt, and my hand came away sticky. My scalp prickled, my knees felt skinned, and I couldn't say where my jeans got to. I held onto my sapling and tried to get my bearings; I had to be in the woods out back, and I knew those blindfolded. I hadn't thought I was quite so drunk.

I stopped trying to think so hard about it and let my bare feet get to walking. My mouth tasted like pennies and throw up, and was gritty like I'd taken a mouthful of dirt. I had a deep down ache in my joints, like I'd caught a fever. It took forever, it seemed, but then the neighbor's dogs started barking and hound hollering and I knew I was almost there. I could see the porch light.

Mama waited, hugging herself against the dew. She came off the porch and took me by the shoulders, stared me in the face. "Alleluia, what happened?"

"I drank at the football party." I was shivering by then, the evening on us and the cold dew in the grass around my ankles. I waited for the 'I told you so.' For her to say I wasn't going to that school anymore, I'd had my chance at the experiment but home was better.

"Let's get you inside." I almost fell when my feet caught on the first step. "Watch now." Maybe she wasn't going to beat me for drinking 'til I was sober.

She set me in a straight backed chair and pulled a picnic quilt out of the cupboard to put around me. "Mama, I'm sorry."

"Are you hurt?" she asked. I looked down at my hands. Dried blood was in the creases of my knuckles, and my palms were skinned too. Under my ring, my thumb had an angry red weal like a burn. I pulled the ring off, and it slipped from my fingers and rang when it hit the floorboards. I watched it roll under the kitchen table.

"I don't think so." I thought. "There was a boy."

"Did he hurt you?"

I licked my split lip. My eyes felt prickly and too warm. "I might have hurt him."

Mama poured a cup of coffee from the pot on the stove, then pulled a square bottle down from the shelf above and poured a dollop in. I watched her in numb surprise. "Drink this." She pushed the mug into my hands and I did as I was told, the coffee stinging my raw throat and the warmth curling up in my stomach like a cat in my lap. Mama filled a basin and got a washcloth and washed me down. "You're okay," she said when she was done, relieved. "Just skinned hands and knees. And your lip."

"Am I in trouble?" My brothers had to be sleeping. Daddy too. The three of them sawed logs all night long, and Mama and I frequently found ourselves in the kitchen together. My roaming gaze found the clock on the wall; it was almost one in the morning.

"No, baby." My head lolled, drowsiness wrapping its arms around me. "Let's get you some clothes."

"You're not going to yell at me?" She wasn't going to let me go back to school. I shouldn't have gone to the football party.

"No, Allie." Mama went away for what seemed like a long time. Maybe it was only a couple of minutes. She helped me stand, and I dropped the quilt on the floor as she helped me into underwear and a fresh pair of jeans. I slumped back into the chair, all my joints relaxed. Mama got my torn shirt and bra off me, helped me wriggle into a bra and another shirt. She knelt in front of me and got my feet into boots, tied them for me like I was little. "Let's get you into the car now."

"Are we going to the hospital? Did you call the sheriff?" My tongue felt too big for my mouth.

"You're going to be safe." We almost fell down the back stairs, and I started laughing, or crying. Mama propped me in the front seat, fastened the seat belt. "I need a couple things from inside, I'll be right back."

"Mama, it was a boy from school. What if he comes here for me?" I tried to sit up, but my head was too heavy and I hurt all over.

"He won't, Alleluia." Mama went away, leaving the smell of her hand lotion. My eyes fell shut and I heard the car doors slam when she came back, but I was too far gone at that point. I dreamed, but it was all blurry and wrong, flashes of images, flickering light, the smell of the woods. Laughter, mean laughter. A fist wrapped in my hair and the breath knocked out of me. My knees scraped, dirt under my nails.

I woke up sweating, my face pressed against the glass of the passenger door; the air conditioner in Mama's old car had long been broken. My head pounded, and my scalp felt too tight. We were on a four lane highway, no road signs in sight, and by the clock in the dashboard, it was seven a.m. and the cross hanging from the rearview flashed little daggers of light in my eyes. I looked in the back, and a suitcase and my guitar case were on the seat. "Mama? What's going on?"

"We're going to see your aunts." She didn't look at me. Daddy's Thermos was in the drink holder between us, dark smell of coffee filling the car.

"Aunt Lucy and Aunt Sarah? Why?" My father's sisters were older than him, spinster sisters living in a lavender and lilac scented duplex up north of us. I couldn't imagine what they had to do with anything.

"No. Your aunts in New Jersey."

"I have aunts in New Jersey? Mama, what is going on?" I was almost seventeen and this was the first I'd heard of Mama's sisters. "Does Daddy know?"

"He met them a few times before we were married."

"That's not what I mean. Does Daddy know you're taking me there?" I wished, not for the first time in my life, that I had a cell phone.

"He'll agree with my decision, when I tell him." Wasn't that always the case. Mama agreed with Daddy and Daddy agreed with Mama, forever and ever amen.

"I have a whole family I never knew existed." The cut in my lip was rough, scabbing over. "Why are we going there now?"

"They'll be able to best handle what you'll go through after last night."

"I thought you were taking me to the hospital or the sheriff's. You said I was safe."

"And you will be. With my sisters."

It finally dawned on me. "You mean you're leaving me there?"

Mama glanced at me. "Don't start."

"But Mama—"

"Enough." The next answer would be a slap, and then she'd talk for hours about how Godly children minded their parents. Daddy was the preacher but Mama set the rules. The drive to New Jersey was a long one, maybe we wouldn't even get there today. I turned my head and stared out the window. We drove in the quiet, the rising sun burning away the dew and throwing heat shimmers off the highway. I saw a red sneaker lying in the shoulder, laces trailing.

After an hour, I tried again. "Mama, I don't know what I did."

She kept looking forward out the windshield, and I would have given anything to know what she was thinking. Then she sighed. "It isn't your fault. It's just how God made you, and that's that."

"I don't understand." Mama looked at me then, brown eyes distant, and it was like looking at a stranger.

"It's too hard for me to explain. Your aunts will be able to."

"I don't know how you could just hide an entire life from me. Are your parents still alive?"

Mama was quiet for a long time, and I thought she was just going to stay that way. "My mama died a long time ago," she said.

"And your father?"

Another pause. "Wasn't around."

"Why did you leave?"

"Alleluia, you're just going to have to wait for them to tell you."

"Sorry, you haven't gotten rid of me yet." I kind of wanted her to slap me. I wanted something.

"My sisters are different. They'll tell you how different. But I'm not like them, and I hoped you'd be like me. I hoped how your daddy and I raised you would be enough."

"Well I guess I'm just a big disappointment."

"I didn't say you were a disappointment."

"No, but you did always say actions speak louder than words." Mama looked at me, but what kind of argument could she make? Other than being disrespectful, I was right. "Does Daddy know?" I asked again, my final slim hope.

"He'll trust me."

"Why would he agree to just dump me all the way in New Jersey with strangers?"

"Your daddy has always let me take charge of you," she said evenly, and my stomach dropped. I'd heard a lot of tones out of her, but never that one.

"I just don't see how you can," I said, a few tears dropping. I wiped them off my face; I didn't want to cry. If Mama could turn her heart to stone, I would too.

"The Lord doesn't give us any more than we can handle, Alleluia."

"Amen," I said, staring at her. She kept her eyes on the road, jaw set.

At one point, we made a stop for the restroom and I wandered into the wooden general store and glared at the array of candy. I didn't see a pay phone anywhere. "You want a Coke?" Mama asked when she came in. One last treat; I wouldn't give her the satisfaction. I didn't know how much longer a drive it was.

"No." Mama got a Coke for herself, and a Hershey bar she handed to me. It tasted bad, sour, and I folded the wrapper and stuck the rest of it in the glove compartment. It would melt there, or Kevin and Jason would find it and fight over it. My final gift to my little brothers.

"Alleluia," Mama said, and then stopped. She and Daddy said they chose my name as a parenting tool. It was hard to be angry, or impatient, when you started out praising the Lord. It didn't always work, of course.

"What, Mama?" I asked. I didn't smile so much as bare my teeth. She just shook her head. She just drove. It was a lot of time to ride angry and sad in that hot car. It was a lot of time not talking to each other. Mama didn't read directions at any point, not even when we were into the pines and none of the roads seemed to have signs.

The sunset clouds were orange like wildfire when Mama turned onto a dirt track I hadn't even seen, close pine branches grasping for the doors on either side and whipping against the windows. There was a clearing with room enough to turn around, and Mama put the car in neutral and pulled the emergency brake; she left it running. She looked at me until I got out. I took my guitar. Mama set the suitcase at my feet, and then turned to the trees that leaned in close.

"I hope you're happy, you bitches!" she shouted as I stared. She paused for a moment, tears beginning to fall, then took another breath. "Now come take care of her." She broke off with a small sob, hand over her mouth. Mama, who said "sugar" and "darn." The trees declined to answer. She got back in the car, slamming the door. She didn't look at me again. I watched her tail lights disappear. Howls started in the woods.

I did what I was supposed to do; I waited. So much of the time, I did what I was supposed to do. Panic tried its teeth on me, and my vision wavered a little at the edges, but I bit my cut lip and stood still, the pain lending me some focus. I could hear the rustle in the underbrush now, see the occasional branch shifting, and then six dogs burst clear of the trees and circled me like I was a treed bobcat, baying but keeping their distance. After a few moments, three women also came out of the woods, and the dogs went silent and sat.

"Was that our sister I just heard?" the tallest one asked, head cocked towards the others. She had a shotgun broken over her arm and a red bandanna in her long tangle of black hair.

"I think it was," the shortest one said. They all wore jeans and t-shirts, boots, and they hadn't looked at me straight, just sidelong glances.

"She didn't stay to say hello," the middle said sadly.

The tall one sniffed. "Did you expect her to?" Their eyes were pale blue like mine, just as their hair was my hair, and I knew if I looked at their hands we'd have the same narrow palms, long tapered fingers, and hitchhiker's thumb. These strangers were more like me than my mother.

"You're my aunts," I said.

The tallest nodded. "I'm Rachel Culver. You must be the preacher's daughter." I couldn't read the gleam in her eyes. They moved through the ring of hounds. I could smell them, a wild scent of wood smoke and moss and broken pine needles.

The middle smiled at me warmly. "I'm Dulcie, and that's Sela." Dulcie's face was the most like Mama's of the three. When she stepped in close and hugged me, I let her, wanting to cry.

"Alleluia. Or Allie."

"You're with us now? Something must have happened." I got the sense that they were caught off balance as well.

"Seems that way." I took in the guns, and the dogs. Everything was too strange. Mama left me. Daddy would listen to whatever she told him. I wish I knew what she'd tell him.

"There'll be a few ground rules," Rachel said, and I nodded. Every house had its rules. "Take that cross from around your neck." My hand went to the silver cross I'd worn since baptism. My whole life.

"What? Why?"

She looked me over with a critical eye. "Those earrings too, if they're silver." I tried to think about it; my small hoops were silver. I took out my earrings first and held them in one hand as I debated the necklace. I wasn't wearing any other jewelry.

"Now, please." I sighed and undid the clasp, coiling the chain in my palm.

"What have you got against crosses?" I asked. She held her hand out, expectant, and I dropped the necklace and earrings into her palm.

"It's silver we mind. We'll get to it." Before I could question, or think to take it back, she turned away from me and threw the cross and earrings out into the woods.

"Hey, why'd you do that?" I stepped in that direction, like I'd ever find anything, and Dulcie took my hand.

"Let's go up to the house. What did your mama tell you about your family?"

"Nothing," I said, pulling loose and picking up my guitar. Sela picked up my suitcase.

Rachel sniffed. "Then you have a lot to learn."

Chapter Two

The walk to the house was shorter than I expected, but it was hard to gauge distance in woods I didn't know. I couldn't decide what to think of them, with their weirdness and their pack of dogs, and their house in the woods. It was a big clapboard house, suited exactly to its space. There was a well to the side of the porch, and a chopping block. At least two other smaller buildings were around back. No power lines, that I could see. The dogs stopped ranging around us so closely. Three of them went up on the porch and settled, others went off on some sort of doggy missions. One of them was white, with a black ear, and stuck close in to Rachel until she went inside, then looked at me with a question in his face that I didn't know how to answer. We'd never had dogs at home, no matter how much I begged.

I followed them up onto the porch and inside. It was woods quiet, full of branches shifting, the occasional liquid birdsong. I wondered if anybody knew they lived back here. They weren't in a hurry to enlighten me, but if they could be quiet, I could be quiet. I'd just had almost a whole day of practice. It wasn't as dark inside as I'd expected; there were skylights. Wooden stairs led up to a second floor balcony that squared the walls, and there was a doorway straight back to the kitchen. I could smell coffee on the stove, just like Mama made, fresh every morning and cooking down stronger as the day went on.

There were so may bookshelves; at a glance, I saw cookbooks, plant guides, survival manuals. There were easy chairs and old leather couches, woven blankets thrown here and there on the backs of them, and a big river rock fireplace with the front half of a black bear reaching out over the mantle. The floor was honey-colored wood, polished, and had rag rugs in a few spots and sheepskin in others. A doorway to the left, showed me a long dining room with table and chairs, and windows enough to make it bright as outside. I wonder who built this house, and when. I knew how to make those kinds of rag rugs; Mama and I did it at home.

"You must have a lot of questions," Sela said. Rachel put the guns up in a glass-fronted cabinet.

"I don't even know where to start." I looked at them, watching me and waiting. Still looking around. I've never been in a place that didn't have pictures of family all over the place, but I didn't see any here. No crosses either. "I never knew you existed before Mama told me in the car."

"Your mama never said anything?" Dulcie asked. Her eyes seemed the kindest, smile lines around them. It was easy to smile when she did.

"No, nothing." None of them said anything for a few minutes, and I cast about for a way to continue.

"So what happened?" Rachel asked.

"Problem is, I don't really know what happened." I stopped again. This time, nobody threw me a rope. "Last night, I was over at the school for a football party. There was some drinking. I was coming home through the woods, and there was a boy." I thought hard, back to the feeling of a hand in my hair, but that was as far as I got, skin prickling on the back of my neck. "I can't think of who. I remember parts of it. Getting knocked down. And then I woke up with my clothes all torn up and my face in the dirt, but I wasn't hurt at all." I wasn't raped, was what I meant. I didn't even want to say it, it just made me feel so sick and scared. Didn't want to explain the fights that I had with Mama and Daddy until they let me go to real school, the high school that was practically in our back yard. I tried so long to be so good, but especially after my little brothers were born, Mama's focus on me, and control, had loosened, and with the high school right in our back yard, I'd got too many glimpses of the world to stay satisfied with homeschooling.

"Then what?" Rachel prompted again. Other women would have been comforting by now. Not Mama last night. And not her sisters now.

"Then I went home, and Mama gave me coffee with brandy in it, washed me up and put me in the car. I fell asleep. And now here I am." If I was normal and had friends at school, they'd be freaking out that I was missing. But I was the homeschooled church girl, and my church friends weren't much talking to me either, after I started going to the high school.

"Just like that?" Dulcie asked. She bit her lip and cut her eyes away to Rachel.

"Just like that."

"What about your daddy?"

"He was sleeping. So were my brothers." They had to miss us by now. They had to have missed us when everybody got out of bed.

"Brothers?" Sela asked, eyebrows up. All three of them looked at each other, stiff, blinking.

"Yes. Kevin and Jason." I sighed. And Mama had a heck of a time having each of them, lots and lots of appointments where I sat in the waiting room with my homeschool lessons. Lots of prayers in church, the whole parish circling up. Lots of church ladies coming over with casseroles, because Mama was on bedrest both times. Doing all the house chores myself. But I was sure they didn't want to know all that. If Mama hadn't left, they'd've been there to help her. "Are you going to tell me what's *happening*?"

"You want the short answer or the long one?" Rachel asked, still studying me, still not smiling. Something about her set me on edge, made me tighten my shoulder blades and stiffen up.

"Looks like we got time," I answered. I picked an armchair and finally sat. Sela and Dulcie settled on the couch.

Rachel, still standing, cleared her throat. "Our family is different. Only ever women. Your mama was the first not to be like us, even though she and Dulcie were in the womb at the same time. Not identical twins, whatever you call that."

"Fraternal," Dulcie said.

"Fraternal. And well, your mama, she grew up knowing she was different from the rest of us. She doesn't even look like us. When she was twelve, thirteen, she started going to church. Tent revivals, when they were around, that kind of thing. Eventually, she met your daddy and ran off with him. She fed him some line, that we were all devil worshippers out in these pines, something like that. He bought it, and took her away. We could've found her if we wanted to, tracked her when she left, but she wasn't happy here. There wasn't any point."

"Different, how? I don't understand any of this."

My aunts exchanged looks. "We haven't had to do this before," Sela said. "It's going to sound very strange."

"With the time I've just had, I guess you just need to try me," I said. Mama would have slapped me for taking that tone. Rachel looked like maybe she wanted to, and crossed her arms instead.

"All right, then. The women of our family are werewolves. Most of us come into it a little before puberty, at ten or eleven, and all of us have been able to turn into wolves by the time we're fourteen. Except your mama, and she must've thought she had a way to keep you from changing that just didn't end up working out."

I stared at the three of them. I waited for somebody to snicker, or crack a smile, or for the camera crew to show up. Back home, there would be a clock ticking away those awkward seconds, but in that cabin, there was only silence and the woods around us, a distant dog barking

"You've got to be kidding me."

"No joke," Dulcie said, watching me with an anxious frown.

"Turn into wolves? All of you? Us? By ten or fourteen? What could keep that from happening, then? It's not like Mama constantly prayed over me or messed with chicken bones or whatever. And why not Mama too?" I wanted to laugh, but really couldn't. Somehow, it didn't sound crazy. Somehow it sounded like the answer.

"No, she might have put it in your food, but whatever it was gave out, or the threat was stronger. It could've been a lot of things, we don't really know." Rachel didn't seem like the joking type. I wanted to argue, I really did, but there was that burned-out part of my memory. The aches and the blood. And I had vitamins that Mama gave me every day, the kind you swallowed not the kind you chewed. I looked at the burn on my thumb, from my silver ring; it was probably still on the kitchen floor. Oh what the hell, Mama. "We don't know why your mama ended up different. She wanted it for so long, like a girl waiting for her period, and then when it didn't come she grew to hate it instead, and finally fear it. We thought she would come back, Culver women always do."

"So what, you're saying last night, when that boy came after me, I did what? Turned into a wolf just like that? Killed him? Ate him? Is that what Mama's afraid of?"

"You fought back." I thought Rachel seemed proud. "It might never have happened, except for that boy. Or it would have happened later, after you got married and had kids and had to lift a bus off of one of them. There's no way to tell."

"So it might never have happened, and I might've just ended up with a normal life?"

"Alleluia, I don't know what you think a normal life is, but from where I stand, it isn't anything to hope for." Rachel was starting to color in her cheeks. That was one of the warning signs Mama was getting mad, too. Not so different after all. "She knew you wouldn't be normal from the time you were born, she just had to take one look at you."

"Your Mama isn't afraid of you killing that boy. Your mama is afraid of your change," Dulcie said.

"Into a wolf." I shook my head.

"You don't believe us." Dulcie turned her head.

"Did you think I would, just like that?"

"I think you know, in your heart."

"My heart is awfully confused." And my head and everything else.

"It's a lot, for one day." Dulcie reached out to pat me, and I shrugged her off.

"It's a lot for one life," I said.

Rachel shook her head. "She should have brought you back sooner, if she wasn't going to raise you right. If we'd known, we would have come and gotten you."

Like witches in a fairy tale. Except we're the wolves. This is like a bad dream. "So what does all this mean? What's different?"

"Well, smarts and looks, you get what God gave you. You'll be stronger. Better sense of smell, better hearing, better balance. Your taste buds won't improve, might dull some. Your reflexes can get better, but not on their own." I wonder how the aunts had decided that Rachel was the explainer. Maybe Rachel was just the mean one. She seemed like it. Dulcie and Sela nodded agreement once in a while. Maybe Sela just didn't talk a whole lot.

"Silver?"

"That's a truism. Sometimes it's just itching, like an allergy. Other times it's like that," she nodded at my thumb. Of course she noticed. Or maybe she'd smelled it. I liked this and hated it and wanted to cry and throw up. A whole family I'd never known existed. A whole werewolf family. Who wanted their daughters.

"What else?"

"Well, you'll have family responsibility. Everybody here works, does chores, cares for the land, which amounts to this patch of the pines. Upkeep on the house. Feed the chickens. Garden or gather the plants we use and sell. Make grocery runs into town, but you won't be doing that for a while."

"Figures," I muttered. I was supposed to go along with all of this? Mama had kept me away for so long, and then rolled over just like that. I didn't get any say? "You got a phone?"

"Nope. They got a payphone at the bowling alley in town." Rachel sized me up. "Somebody you need to talk to?"

"Yeah, sorry, I'm not thrilled to be initiated into my supernatural bloodline of hillbilly freaks. I'd really like to just call my Daddy." Rachel, who I'd kind of meant to hurt, smirked. Sela turned away, and Dulcie just looked sad again, and I immediately regretted it.

"Your Daddy isn't going to change anything," Dulcie said softly "This is your Mama's blood and her affair."

"It might be okay, if I talk to him before Mama does. She'll be driving for a while." I sounded so stupid. She probably already called him.

"Sweetheart, his blood don't carry in you. Part of the benefits of being a supernatural freak. They test you, you ain't his.

That isn't your life anymore." I looked from Dulcie to Rachel, and she nodded.

"It's true. Our blood carries. Father's blood gets choked out somehow. We've checked." Rachel hesitated. "That, and we don't have boys. Never have."

"He wouldn't think of a paternity test."

"He would. Plus, he has two boys of his get, however they came about. He'll let you go, once he hears her story. What's that sticking out of your suitcase?"

"I don't know," I muttered, because honestly fuck the suitcase. I didn't know what all Mama had packed, except probably not my vitamins, but I turned to look. The corner of a manila envelope stuck out of the zipper. I crossed the room to get it, and pulled open the flap. My birth certificate and social security card. I'd never seen them before, hadn't gotten my learner's permit even once I was in the high school. Mama made some excuse about losing them, said we'd had a fire in the apartment we lived in when I was little, before the church caught on the way it did. Said she'd get around to getting new ones, but hadn't yet, even though so much time had passed. The papers said Alleluia Culver. For the father's name it said "Unknown." There was also a single piece of paper that said Petition for Appointment of Guardian of Person on the top of it, all filled out in Mama's round hand, with Rachel's name and mine in the blanks.

"What is this?" I turned and shoved the papers at the closest aunt, Sela, who flinched a little. She took them and looked, then handed them to Rachel, who glanced them over.

I couldn't read her face or her posture, not at all. Couldn't *smell* anything either, if that was true.

"You never knew?"

"Of course I never knew! How could everyone not have known?" Our church community was small, close-knit. With Daddy in charge.

"Or your daddy kept it quiet, but really, it reflects him in a good light, taking in somebody else's bastard. But your mama had it planned all along, looks like. Just in case. Maybe that's how she got him to take her away so young; she told him we summoned a demon to put a baby in her belly and that way he'll still forgive her and you're stuck with us." I stood in front of the fireplace and stared at her, actually shaking. "You might hate me for that, and I'm sorry, but that's the way things are. Dulcie and Sela are nicer than me. This is about survival, though, for all of us. You'll get used to it, and you'll learn."

"You think I'm just going to stand here and listen to you talk about her like that? My mother isn't like that. Maybe you think you knew her, but that was years ago."

"That inclined to be loyal, after she dropped you off like a stray at the pound?" Yeah, I was on my way to hating Rachel all right.

"What if I left? If I don't want to stay here, I'm more trouble than I'm worth." Dulcie, red-eyed, took a breath to say something, but Rachel plowed on.

"Think you're going to learn how to be a wolf all by yourself? Your mama hasn't told you anything, and spent your life burying your instinct. You don't know how to survive on your own."

"Won't I just figure it out? Isn't that what instinct means?"

"You could if you were raised in it, changed on time. You're ignorant and sixteen."

"Seventeen in February." Sullen was not my best face, but they were right. I was ignorant, and I hated that too. There was so much I didn't know "So no more school?" Like I was even used to public school, to the world outside the church.

"You can get a GED if you want. We'll teach you what you need, and there's plenty more to learn. You can go to college if you want. Or not, if you want to stay home. School isn't everything," Sela said cautiously.

"Home," I said, shaking my head.

"That's right. You're home now," Rachel said, her tone just a little bit kinder. "How about we get you settled some before dinner, get you into a bedroom. We weren't expecting this either, remember."

"Yeah, all right." I thought again about just running, and went back to the door, where my stuff was. I guessed I could find somewhere that would take me in. Strangers were strangers, after all.

"Alleluia?" Dulcie said, from a little behind me.

"Yeah, Dulcie?" I stared out the screen door, into the spring green pines, the sandy soil so different and so like what I knew. I should call them Aunt, I thought, but just couldn't do it. If I ran, would they come after me? They let Mama go, but Mama wasn't like them.

"It might be hard for you to believe, but we're glad you're here."

And so I couldn't go. "Thanks."

Chapter Three

I woke up sometime in the middle of the night, the house quiet, with fever and chills. My joints ached like nothing I'd felt before, and my muscles were all cramped up. I sat up against the wall, wrapped in my grandmother's quilt, and listened to my teeth chatter. I didn't think I could navigate the dark house and stairs, but at some point in that long dark night, Dulcie came in with tray and an old wooden rolling pin. First she had me drink a tall glass of cold water, and then she had me lie on my stomach, and rolled the pin up and down my back, and down the backs of my legs.

"Why do I feel like this?"

"You're changing and didn't have the luxury of doing it as you grew."

"How long will it take?"

"I don't know. Nobody's done it like this before." I could hear her worry, her voice so like Mama's. After a while, she had me sit up, wrapped in the quilt again. "All right, I'm going to give you something that doesn't taste so good, but then something sweet."

"Okay." I opened my mouth dutifully as she offered me a spoon, and her warning was the only thing that kept me from spitting out the spoonful of thick, acrid stuff. "What is that?"

"Onion syrup. Now here's willow tea, with honey and cinnamon. It might help."

"Thank you." The mug warmed my hands, and I thought of the brandied cup of coffee Mama had given me. It seemed impossible that she had done that, but so many things seemed impossible. The tea was good, herby and sweet. Dulcie sat with me until the mug was empty and my chills subsided. I was starting to feel drowsy again.

"Better?" she asked, taking the mug from me.

"A lot better, thanks." I laid down, and she tucked the quilt in around me again.

"Try to get some sleep," she said, gathering up the things she'd brought. I was almost asleep again when I realized she hadn't brought in a light, or turned on a light. But then I slipped away into dreams of the woods, the woods back home, the woods I knew, not the woods where Mama abandoned me.

There was a knock on my door right around dawn, and I knew it was Rachel. The sun was just coming up; the light at my window was pale gray. When I opened the door, she looked me over. She was already dressed, jeans and t-shirt and work boots, and had a mug of coffee. "We get an early start here."

"I see that," I said, rubbing my eyes.

"I was thinking we'd have a family day. Tour the property, run in the pines, get to know each other a little. Maybe we'll put a history lesson together for you."

"Okay." I couldn't read her face at all, I couldn't read her posture, I didn't know what she meant by run in the pines. They didn't really seem like jogging people.

"We'll see you downstairs, then."

I shut the door and made the bed on autopilot, then looked at my suitcase of clothes and the dresser, but decided

I'd unpack later. Tomorrow. Sometime. There was a carved wooden toy I hadn't noticed last night on the broad windowsill, a little animal on a platform that you held, with a ball that swung underneath. I picked it up, and realized it was a wolf, sitting back on its haunches, and when the ball swung, the arms moved as though it was knitting the little wooden stocking in front of it. I swung it for a second, lost in the click click click of it, then finished getting dressed, braided my hair and tied on a bandanna.

We got outside and the dogs came from all sides and stood around us, tails wagging when there were tails to be had. As we headed off into the woods, they fell back and went back to porches to sleep. "You're awful quiet, Alleluia," Rachel said, as we started at the first blazed tree.

"Sorry. I just don't know what to expect right now, I guess."

My aunts didn't follow a path as I could recognize it, winding through the pines, occasionally pointing out tree growth or damage. There were blueberry bushes, a copper moonshine still. After I'd completely lost track of time, we stopped. I could hear a creek nearby, and when I looked I saw a big old weeping willow tree stooped there. There was kind of a clearing, but not really, trees hedging in from the sides, and then I saw why we'd stopped: white marble headstones. They were closer together than I would have expected; I guessed we cremated in this family. I walked around, read the dates. Meredith was born in 1952, died in 1990. Ivy was born in 1945, died in 1980. That wasn't reassuring. I moved to Lydie's headstone; born in 1919, died in 1960. And each one back.

Not a single one of them had dates spanning more than fifty years, and a lot were more like forty. Not a single one said anything other than their first name, and the dates.

"Why was everybody so young?"

"We all have our time," Dulcie said after a moment, after they passed glances around. "What happens to us, it isn't easy on our bodies. You've noticed that, and you haven't caught up yet."

"It isn't like wolves live all that long," Rachel muttered.

I looked down at the headstones. Fifty years, give or take, mostly take; that was a sobering thought. I wasn't a good judge of age, but it seemed like Rachel was probably pretty close. Maybe it was enough of an excuse. Maybe not.

"So what now?" I asked.

"Take your clothes off," Rachel said.

"What? No." My aunts looked at me and waited. Dulcie had a sympathetic look on her face; Sela looked like she wanted to say something, but also didn't want to fight. Rachel just looked expectant, and when she realized I intended to wait them out, she sighed.

"It's just easier if you don't have to worry about your clothes. We'll all do it, all right? We won't watch you. It's not a trick."

"What's easier?" Rachel curled her lip, just a little bit. I shifted my weight, but didn't really know what to do.

"Living out there with your mama hasn't done anything for you. Changing is easier. When you're wearing clothes, you get distracted, and worried about getting caught up in them.

If you're not, you can concentrate. Especially for your first time. Or your first on purpose time, I guess."

"We're going to do that *now*?" I was terrified and relieved. I had this thing, I was a wolf, and the more I could talk about it, inhabit it and acclimate, the better.

"You need to learn sometime," Dulcie said, soothing.

"You keep saying easier."

"Yes, as opposed to harder," Rachel said impatiently, kicking her boots off and unbuttoning her jeans.

"Sorry if you're strangers, no matter how much we look like each other" I said, and I looked away and undid my belt buckle, slowly. Sorry if I was attacked by a boy two nights ago. Standing naked in the woods was never something I thought about doing. I never even went skinny dipping at the swimming hole. I kind of wished I had, now, because I was feeling pretty shy. Another thing Mama would've striped my hide for. Letting me wear jeans and go to the high school was one thing, but modesty was another thing entirely. I'd had so many rules and it seemed like pretty much all of them were ones I could just forget.

"We can thank your Mama for that," Sela said, surprising me, but it wasn't like I could argue the point. It was the truth. Mama had made me a freak among freaks.

In the end, I hesitated until it seemed like they were all undressed, not looking at them. I took my clothes off. I folded them as I went, but didn't have anywhere to put them. The dogs that had come with us were gone, I noticed. They must not like sticking around for naked wolf time. I somehow managed to stop myself from snickering. "All right, now what?"

I turned back to my aunts; it was easier than I'd thought it would be.

"It's a hard thing to instruct on. We've been talking about it since you got here," Sela said. "It's just a second nature, after you've gotten over the initial phase. You might not be able to do it today. Or it'll be really easy. Normally we don't watch each other change, but we're here to teach today, so we're breaking that rule."

"Just don't get stuck," Rachel teased. Maybe she didn't realize just how abrasive she was.

"Can that really happen?" I asked, staring.

"Don't listen to Rachel," Dulcie said, looking as though she'd like to swat her sister. "Close your eyes, that'll probably help. Think about how you feel. And then think about how you felt that night in the woods, before you went home to your mama."

"Doesn't this need to be at night or something? On a full moon?"

"No. We told you it doesn't." Did they? I didn't remember already. Rachel didn't sound like she was amused at all. I'd already closed my eyes, and didn't risk looking at her.

"Doesn't that break the rules? I thought werewolves only turned on the full moon?"

"This isn't movies, we can change when we want. Does it matter?"

"I guess not." Not like I'd seen many of those movies. We didn't even have a TV in the house, or a computer.

Think about how I felt. For starters, I felt naked. I knew Dulcie meant more, so I thought about it harder. She meant how human felt. Upright, arms and legs, shoulders. The wind was like water on my skin. My braid hanging down the length of my back. Pine needles underneath my bare feet, spreading gently between my toes.

I thought back a few nights, to my last night home. The woods there, the different trees, the way they smelled. The taste of the dirt in my mouth. That was different from dirt here too. How would I feel if I wasn't human? I drew a complete and perfect blank. Other than getting knocked down, and waking up, I really couldn't remember that night. I sighed, and took a breath to complain and Dulcie said "No, you're thinking two legs. Now think four legs. Keep trying." Because it was Dulcie, I did.

I thought about being outside my school, at the football field. I thought about walking away from the school, and walking towards the woods. I thought about the way the light changed, there under the trees, filtered green through the branches. I thought about the dirt, the way the dust would cling if it hadn't rained in a week, the way your hands got powdery if you stopped to pick up a rock or a stick. I thought about how birds sounded, startled off of branches by your passing, or rabbits sounded, bolting through the underbrush. I thought about the roots on that path home through the woods, sometimes more exposed or less, depending on the rain. I thought about how the woods felt at dusk instead of in the afternoon, because it must have been dusk when I entered them, or early evening. After the game, after the after-game party. I thought about how the path felt if somebody else was there, instead of being alone. I thought about the feeling of somebody coming up behind you.

The woods smelled different. The varied green scents of the moss, and the pines, all swelled into my nose and made me sneeze. The wind felt different. I could hear the creek rippling against rocks, and the shush of the water against the leaves of the weeping willow that hung low enough to take a dip.

"Okay, open them," Rachel said, and she sounded pleased.

I opened my eyes, and the world was so strange I shook my head, hard, in reflex. I could hear my ears flap. The pine trees around us, boughs so green, were gray instead. The sky was still blue, but muted. I could see far off on either side of me, so much it was disorienting, and I whipped my head around to watch a bird's flight, wings fluttering fast. I looked back at my aunts, and laid down. I could feel my tail, and I turned around to look at it, brushy and kind of tucked in, the flag of my emotions. I didn't think wolves were black, but I guess I just didn't know anything about wolves. Like how I didn't know anything about werewolves either. I licked my lips nervously; I didn't know how my tongue fit in my mouth. It seemed too long. I could move my ears separate from one another, and they flicked about of their own volition, catching birdsong, and car engines off in the distance, and a plane flying far overhead.

Then my aunts were black wolves too, musky and wild scented, and they circled and nosed me. Rachel was bigger than the rest, with some silver hairs on her muzzle. Sela was a little shorter than the other two, just like when she was people. Dulcie was leggy, and her tail seemed less like it was bushy and more like it had a fringe. We all had pale blue eyes.

After a while, I was able to stop panting and stand up. My stomach didn't feel so great, and I could hear it gurgle. Rachel took a few steps out of the cemetery and then looked back at the rest of us over her shoulder. No talking now, and no telepathy, but even a puppy could read her body language loud and clear. Come this way.

I thought too hard about walking forward and got tripped up in my feet. Paws. Dulcie and Sela went ahead of me, and then looked back as well. I looked down at the ground and stretched my legs, watched my toes spread. Then I looked up at them and tried not to think much at all. It worked out better after that, but it was still hard to believe this was happening. How much I smelled, how much I heard. The way my balance adjusted running up an incline, my tail doing whatever it was that it did. Feet spreading on rocks, powerful leg muscles, big breaths filling my big rib cage.

They were easy on me. We ran out through the trees, jumped the creek, and then looped back around. Rachel kept up the lead and set the pace, and she didn't run me ragged or go anyplace where the ground was too difficult. I didn't see any of the dogs, but I could hear them and smell them. A bird flushed out ahead of us as we got back to the cemetery, and I looked up. When I looked back, my aunts were on two legs again. In a way, I was disappointed; I wanted to explore this a little more. I wanted to know what the house smelled like, and what you could hear from there. I wondered how things tasted, as a wolf.

"Allie, honey, now just switch back," Dulcie said, smiling but smelling like worry. That was what worry smelled like. The three of them weren't even breathing hard, after that little bit of running; it was embarrassing that I was. I thought about two legs again. My whole life up to this point was on two legs, walking in the woods, wearing shoes, going to church, riding in cars. My senses dulled, and I felt the air again, cool on my hot skin. I was trying to think of something snappy to say to Rachel when I bent over and threw up instead, hands on my knees. I took stock, saw I'd missed my clothes, and then heaved again.

When I was done, I was shaking, I was cold, and my head spun. I was nauseous and hungry at the same time. I got my clothes back on unsteadily, piece by piece. Dulcie moved to help me, I think, but I just kind of shook my head.

"Can't say I expected that," Rachel remarked, once I looked at them. All three waited; I didn't know what I thought. Throwing up wasn't something I liked doing for an audience.

"I'll try to warn you next time," I said, and tried to smile. Rachel didn't make a wisecrack back, but the look she gave me seemed like it was one of approval. That was something. First steps.

The dogs joined us when we were partway to the house, tails wagging. They smelled us all over as they fell in step, sneezing as we went. You haven't really lived until a pack of dogs sneezed all over you. I stumbled a lot on the walk back, but I gritted my teeth and kept up. The sun was lower in the sky than I thought it would be, throwing long shadows through the trees. My vision wasn't quite back to normal, it seemed. Sometimes, I'd see all the greens and golds right, and other times, things would gray out on me. I'd always wondered if dogs really saw in black and white. Another wave of nausea hit me when we got into the dooryard, and I ducked into the outhouse for a round of dry heaves.

When I came out, the white dog sat watching the door. He looked at me expectantly, and I let the door swing shut behind me. "What?" I said, and walked past him to the back door. Rachel had emptied her cigarette butt bucket at some point, but the smell of it still almost knocked me off the porch, and I put the back of my hand to my nose to protect it as I went inside.

"How are you feeling?" Sela asked, grimacing a little in sympathy. "I hate throwing up."

"Yeah, me too. Thirsty, I think, more than anything. Achy. Real tired." I poured a glass of water from the pitcher and sat at the kitchen table.

"Think you can stand to eat?" Dulcie was already at the stove, and she paused, spatula in hand.

"I'll try, anyway. I'm starving too. My stomach's all confused." I laughed a little, and drank some water. It was cold and a little mineral tasting, and it soothed me as it went down. "Where did Rachel go?"

"Had a phone call," Sela said. "She'll be gone for a while."

"Not scared off by vomit, then?" They didn't have a landline and I wouldn't've thought there would be cell service out here worth mentioning.

Dulcie, facing the stove, laughed a little. Sela smiled. "You'll need to come up with better, if you want to scare Rachel."

"I'll keep that in mind. Who called? Where did she go?"

"I didn't ask. We get called sometimes, to help with things."

"What kind of things?"

Sela just shrugged. "Things Rachel's good at, I guess. It varies."

Tired as I was, even after eating, I wasn't ready to go to bed before sunset. I got out my guitar and sat on the front porch, messing around with it. I didn't have to play church songs anymore, and so I just couldn't settle on what to play. The guitar felt like a foreign thing in my hands, or it was my hands that felt foreign. Sometimes I hummed along with what I played; if I concentrated too much on one, the other would get messed up, and vice versa.

The birdsong changed as sunset played out, and the crickets had some overlap in airtime. There were little frogs that sang too, or maybe it was just another kind of bug. I needed some time with those nature books inside, I thought. Needed to learn about the Pine Barrens. I'd set my guitar back in the case and fastened the hasps when the dogs nearest me perked their ears and ran off into the woods. I watched them go and wondered if I should say something to Dulcie or Sela. They already knew, probably, but I was firmly back in the range of normal human senses, other than my skin feeling prickly. A few minutes later, Rachel came out of the wood line.

"Feeling better?" she asked.

"I guess, but real tired. Goodnight," I said, getting up with my guitar case. I realized I'd wanted to be sure she was back before I went up to sleep.

Chapter Four

I wished that spending the day together in the woods just made me feel at home and put me at my ease with the aunts, but of course that wasn't true. I was still shocked at Mama's abandonment, at my whole life being blown open like that. I still didn't remember what happened in the woods, and nobody seemed eager to talk to me about it further. I guess maybe they, we, hoped I'd be able to just forget it completely and move on.

Something about Rachel especially grated me the wrong way almost every time we were in the same room together, and that was a lot. I was unwilling to take everything she told me just because she was the one who told me, and she hated having to explain everything. She wanted me to listen and trust her and learn in context. When I thought about it, I figured it was hard to teach something that was just her nature, and showing rather than telling was a better way. But it was hard to pause and think about it. We just butted heads. Dulcie especially tried to make me as comfortable as she could, but by acting like I belonged with them and had always been with them. Sela did a lot of the same, maybe a little less comfortably.

Dulcie was the one who gave me the basic family history lesson one day while she wound yarn over my hands which sounded totally made up, but she also had the hand written diaries from the 1800's on up to prove it, nestled right there next to the family Bible with all the names and dates. The first one of us to change was Mary Culver. Her husband was accused of horse thieving, and even though the supposed stolen horses were never found, with the Culvers or otherwise, he was hanged at a crossroads for it, and they left his body just dangling there as they went and burned his house. Mary took his pistol and his hunting knife and hid in the woods, and by the moonlight crept out to his body and cut a strip of skin from his back. A wolf strap, it was called, and whoever wore it could turn into a wolf. Funny thing is, they had the diaries, but the strap was never mentioned again, and nobody found it since.

But, Mary Culver was pregnant at the time all this happened. She went and found a place in the pines and a new house got raised up for her, in time for her little girl to be born, who had black hair and blue eyes just like her daddy. Martha Culver learned midwifing from her mother as she grew up, and when she was ten or eleven started having what Mary took to be growing pains, and fevers in the night. She'd wake up in the yard in her nightgown. One night, Mary went to check on her, and found a wolf in the bed instead of her daughter, sleeping curled up in the blankets, and though Mary was a Christian woman she'd also known enough to cut a wolf strap. She sat in a chair and watched and waited, and when the sun came up, the wolf turned back into her daughter, and Mary knew using that wolf strap with Martha in her womb had changed her daughter in a way she never expected.

After that, right up to Mama, the Culver women had daughters, the Culver women always came back to the pines no matter how far they roamed, and those daughters were always wolves. I didn't have a whole lot of school biology, but I guess sooner or later there was going to be a mutation, and that was Dulcie and Mama being twins, and that was Mama being just a normal person. Is that how she had Kevin and Jason? She was just different enough on her own?

The next time I was sick in the night, Dulcie didn't come. I got as far as my bedroom door, quilt wrapped around me, and then stopped. I could hear somebody talking. I clenched my jaw to stop my chattering teeth, closed my eyes, and tried to open my ears. It worked, for the first time.

Dulcie sounded like she was downstairs, maybe in the kitchen doorway. Rachel sounded like she was on the steps. "She'll be all right," Rachel said.

"She's sick, Rachel. We've never seen this before. There's no harm in giving her a couple of remedies. Sleeping seems to be what's best, but she can't sleep for the aching and the chills." Dulcie sounded angry. I wondered if my aunts argued much, or if Rachel just won every time. I wondered if Mama argued with her about Daddy, or if Mama just left.

"I don't know that you want to coddle her, Dulcie. Lord knows nobody coddled us."

"No, and we grew up the way we were supposed to. We didn't have this problem. Help isn't coddling."

"Depends on the help."

They were quiet for a few minutes. I wondered where Sela was, and what she thought of the matter. I wondered if there tended to be a tiebreaker in disagreements. Maybe they just didn't have a whole lot to disagree about until I came along.

"Are you going to let me bring this to her or not?" Dulcie finally asked.

"Not."

"You're acting like a child."

"You're letting her be one." I heard Dulcie sigh, and then turn around and go back into the kitchen, setting the tray down on one of the counters none too gently. The syrup spoon rattled.

"Are we welcoming her here or not? We should be treating her like one of our own, not somebody who needs to prove something. We know she's our blood"

"She's of our blood, but she isn't of a mind with us yet."

"So stop fiddling around then. Remake her into what you seem to want her to be. She isn't your daughter."

"I know." Rachel muttered something I couldn't quite catch. Did Rachel have a daughter? Did any of them? That wasn't in any of the family lessons just yet.

"Then stop acting like you're already disappointed. You don't know Allie."

"Neither do you. She isn't your daughter either."

There was a long pause after that, a tender spot even I could sense from here, and then Dulcie said, even more softly, "No, and that's why I'm treating her right."

There was a rustling, and then Dulcie came up the stairs briskly and went to her room. She closed the door with a firm hand; I would have slammed it. I stood and listened, and after what seemed like a long time, I heard Rachel sigh. Then she continued down the stairs, and out the front door. I put one of my sweaters on and got back into bed, under all the covers. I shivered and chattered until I fell back to sleep. I didn't dream.

Without any good way to tell unless I carved hatch marks in the wall, I stopped being preoccupied with the days, and with what time it was. I woke when it was time to wake up, ate when it was time to eat. It was just the beginning of fall when Mama brought me here, and I saw the shift of season as it happened, out there in nature instead of through a window. I spent a lot of time not thinking about what life was supposed to mean anymore, grateful for the chores as I learned them. They took my mind off just about everything.

Sometimes Rachel gave me a different task instead, especially after we'd clashed over something, like the three days in a row I split wood, my hands blistering, weeping, and reblistering, while I refused to say anything about how much it hurt. Sometimes I learned family history from Sela or Dulcie, sometimes I read the family books. I helped tend the still, I gathered kindling, I got up on the roof with Rachel and fixed shingles and weatherproofing. This last one was tempting fate, I thought. The two of us with tools and height to throw one another from could have been disastrous. We made it through the day without raising our voices, in fact, in part because most of what we said was "pass the hammer" and "is this the spot you meant?" We cleaned mildew. We plugged squirrel holes (though those squirrels must be the bravest squirrels in the barrens, gnawing into the rafters of a werewolf den to scrabble around and cause their havoc.) We left birds' nests alone.

I learned the woods. I found the property lines, and was building a map of the family land in my head. It was pretty big, and I wondered how much the taxes must be every year, and how we paid them. If we paid them, and if anybody official knew we were out here. I guess it was possible nobody did; I never accidentally found a neighbor's land, or even sensed another person nearby. I don't think I ever gave New Jersey credit for having woods like this. But I didn't know. I didn't know anything. Sometimes, when I was out alone, I practiced being a wolf, but not often. It excited me but it scared me, so doing it alone really scared me. I really didn't want to get stuck and then have to face Rachel.

One day, I was walking through the woods, on two legs not on four, I found a paved road. I stopped on the shoulder and stared at it. I hadn't really been thinking about where I was going, and hadn't noticed leaving the property. Not as smart as I thought. I looked over my shoulder, to see if anybody was there. I didn't see or hear anybody, not my aunts, not even one of the dogs. I paced a little bit on the shoulder, thinking about it, and then I picked a direction.

There wasn't much of a town north of where I'd broken the wood line, but it was enough. Gas station, drug store, tiny library, and I could see the neon sign for the bowling alley at the end of the drag. I was sure there were houses in along the main road too, but I didn't explore. I went to the library, figuring that was far enough, and then I'd go home. There were newspapers there, and they had a single computer with dialup internet hooked to it, that you could use even if you didn't have a library card. I got a guest pass, went, and uncomfortably sat. The computer was in a corner, and put your back to the rest of the room, including the door. I tried to shrug it off, just imagined turning my hearing behind me.

I went to my hometown newspaper's website, clunky and ad-riddled thing that it was. No black banner mourning a high school football player; so far so good. The date on the web page put me almost at the end of October, and it was the beginning of September when it happened. So I hadn't killed him then, whoever he was. I didn't even know why I thought he was a football player; practically the whole school was at that party. I tried not to dwell on it. If I thought too hard, the memory got away like a fish slipping its hook. I went back through the news archives, the baseball games, the river bottom parties busted up, the church socials, and prom pictures. Then I saw it: "Local Quarterback Animal Attack. "It was a wolf!" Dodd Swears, Sheriff Skeptical."

I clicked on it and sat back in the chair, watching the page load, color by color. The flickering of the monitor bothered my eyes, and I looked away at the rest of the library to give myself a break. Nobody else came in while I sat there, and the librarian was doing something behind the desk. I wondered where the school was. And the jail. I looked back, and saw Kyle Dodd's bloody face. They must have gotten the picture when the ambulance got him to the hospital, or he got himself there and it was a cell phone picture. He wasn't even torn up that bad. His arm, his leg. It looked like he hit his face when he fell down scrabbling away. He said he didn't get a good look at what attacked him, just that he'd stepped into the forest adjacent to the school after a function, and heard growling. Doctors said they were canine bites, that was true, but not consistent with any Alabama wolves. Not consistent with most domestic dogs, either, to head off the anti-pit bull sentiment. I didn't kill him, though. That was important.

I searched my name and only came up with a tiny article on how proud Mama and Daddy were that I'd gone off to be a missionary in Kenya, digging wells for villages. Did Rachel have to be right about everything? I cleared the web history, and closed everything out. The librarian didn't look at me again as I left. I sighed and rubbed my eyes; the fan in the computer had sounded like a field of june bugs.

I found where I'd left the woods, no problem, and headed back through the woods. It seemed like a good idea to have something to show for the afternoon, but I didn't have any-thing to carry berries in, or anything to try and catch a fish with, so I just kept walking. I could smell bread baking and the pot of coffee that was perpetually on the stove. Some of the dogs came from the woods as I got closer, falling into step around me.

The dogs went their separate ways when I went up to the cabin, and when I went inside, all three aunts were in the kitchen. Rachel had a cup of coffee in front of her, cream no sugar, and cocked her head as I came in. I could see her nos-trils twitch. I saw Sela and Dulcie exchange a look, tension in their shoulders. Dulcie checked on the bread, and I went to get a cup of coffee. Supper was on the stove, in a big bubbling pot, but I'd gotten enough raps on the knuckles from Mama to know better than to peek. Sela went out the back door.

Rachel was still looking at me as I sat down. "So, how was your day?" I asked. She rarely seemed pleased with anything. I didn't know what else to ask her, though, or maybe it was truer that just small talk couldn't really be made with Rachel. She was quiet, or there was something of merit to be said, and that was that.

"Where were you this afternoon?"

"Out in the pines," I said. Not a lie, but not the whole truth. She sniffed.

"Where else?"

"I went to the library," I said; I hadn't even noticed the library's name.

"What made you do that?"

"I wanted to look at my town newspaper."

"You didn't email anybody? Call anybody?"

"No, just used the internet to look at that newspaper." I didn't know anybody's email. Who would I call, anyway, I was in Kenya. I didn't have the kinds of friends that I called, I barely had school friends. Church friends I couldn't count on; they just wanted to be close to me because of Daddy. I drank some of my coffee. Rachel was still looking at me. "I wanted to know if I killed that boy."

"Did you?" Rachel's voice was as flat as I'd ever heard it; I knew, right then, she'd already checked. She'd already checked, and knew who it was, and hadn't told me, wouldn't even talk about it.

"No. I didn't." I stood up, knocking the table with my knees and making my coffee slosh out on the old oiled wood. I couldn't be in the room with her anymore. I'd go up to my room, or out on the porch, something. Rachel's hand closed on my wrist. I pulled, but she was far stronger than I thought she'd be.

"You do not leave the property without telling us you are going. You do not leave without permission. You do not have contact with anybody you knew before coming here." I tried again to yank my arm free.

"Look, I didn't ask for this. You can't make me stay here." Maybe I should've pressed this conversation when I got here. When I thought about running. Why was she yelling at me for coming back?

"You didn't ask for it, but it's what you've got. It's not like we were expecting you, either."

"All the more reason to just let me leave."

"Your mama left you here. You can leave when you're eighteen, if you hate it that much, but you can't just go off on your own. So far as your papers say, you belong here."

I wanted to undo everything that happened, to be able to say Mama wouldn't have done such a thing, or Daddy wouldn't have gone along with it, but not so long ago, I would've said Mama would never have spiked my coffee with brandy after I came home thinking I'd been raped in the woods, and then driven me across eight states and left me with strangers she'd been too terrified to stay with herself. "Why would I want to stay here?" I spat.

Dulcie interceded then, gently. She interposed her shoulder between Rachel and I, and reached down to take my wrist out of Rachel's hand. I'd stopped yanking; we were at an impasse, staring into each other's eyes. "Alleluia," Dulcie said in a soft voice. I licked my lips and looked at her. "We know this is overwhelming, but we do want what's best for you. We've got rules because it's what works to keep us all safe, not to make you feel like a prisoner." Tears stood in her eyes, and in trying to hurt Rachel, I hadn't thought about Dulcie. Sela was still outside, but she had to have heard me.

"I guess I overreacted. I'm sorry." I looked at Rachel, then looked away, feeling the smallest in spirit I ever have. "And I'm sorry for going to the library. I should've asked you."

Rachel was quiet for long enough I was ready to get mad again. "Apology accepted," she said right before I was ready to open my mouth and step in it again. She pushed off from the table and went out the back door, screen banging shut behind her.

Sela came back into the kitchen, a nervous smile making her eyes too bright. "Supper, then?" she asked.

Chapter Five

The next morning, Rachel wasn't at the breakfast table. Sela and Dulcie were there, frying bacon and drinking coffee and talking. "Morning," Sela said. No trace of what happened yesterday in her voice.

"Morning," I said cautiously. I wasn't willing to make a guess at how to occupy myself, not after yesterday. I got a cup of coffee, slid in at the table.

"How do you want your eggs?" Sela asked. She and Dulcie glanced at one another, and Sela turned away to hide a smile.

"Scrambled is fine, over easy if you feel fancy. Thank you." I moved to get up and help, maybe get more water, and Dulcie held up her hand to stop me.

"We need you to have your breakfast and then go pick up your cousin," Dulcie said.

"My cousin? I have a cousin?"

"You've got a few. This one happens to need a bailout." Sela coughed, and Dulcie shook her head, just a little.

"Wait, what? She's in jail? A few cousins? Where are the rest of them?"

"It wasn't anything major," Dulcie said. "Just a misunderstanding, more likely than not." Sela coughed again, definitely laughing.

"Well, okay. Where is she?" I smiled too, not really getting the joke.

"A little more than an hour away. We'll give you directions." Dulcie went and rummaged in the sideboard. She came back with a folded up road map, and a pad she started writing on. "Oh yeah, keys. Come on." I followed her to the front door, and she plucked a key ring off of the pegboard; it was one I hadn't seen before, with a big chunk of rock for a keychain.

"I thought I wasn't supposed to be leaving."

"Without permission. You've got it now."

"And Rachel knows?"

"It's her daughter." Dulcie gave me a second to digest. "It'd probably be better if you and Rachel had a day away from one another, and it'd probably be best for Morgan if her mama isn't the one who picks her up. She just gets into mischief sometimes." Sela coughed again, and then banged out the back door. I heard her laughing to the chickens. Mischief enough for jail. Rachel must be so proud. I sniffed, wondering if she was still in the house; maybe I had time to rub it in a little before going. Better not.

"I don't have a driver's license."

Dulcie pushed the keys and directions into my hands. "So what? You know how to drive don't you?"

"Well, yeah."

"Well, all right then. Your cousin's name is Morgan Culver, it's a little enough jailhouse, they'll be friendly. Probably. Here's the check for the bail, and then come on back."

"That's it? I didn't think bailing somebody out of jail worked like that."

"That's it when you're talking about Deer Tree, Pennsylvania, anyway. Every place is different, I guess." Dulcie hustled me out the front door, and Sela was still laughing out back. When I was on the porch, I heard one of the bedroom doors slam. Rachel had heard everything, obviously. "The Jeep is down in the clearing, just follow the directions, and you'll be fine."

"Dulcie, I don't know, why don't you come with me?"

"Sorry, Allie. But hey, it'll be good for you to get to know your cousin. I don't imagine she'll stay long, but you never know." Dulcie gave me a hug and then made a shooing motion at me. If she was wearing an apron, she would've flapped it. I headed away from the house, looking back once as I got to the path that led down to the clearing Mama'd dropped me off at, but Dulcie had already gone back inside. I looked at the check; it was made out to Cash.

I tried to think of what Morgan might be like and couldn't; even with the starting point of 'drives Rachel crazy', I couldn't form enough of an opinion. It certainly would be better for her, Rachel not being the one to bail her out. The Jeep was a Wrangler, black, and old enough to be respectable but new enough it would run. I got in the driver's seat and barely had to adjust the mirrors. It was stick shift, but Daddy taught me how to drive so I could help with church stuff.

The drive was about an hour, like Dulcie had said, on twisty, sun-dappled roads. I pulled over and took the soft top down about twenty minutes in, put my hair in a braid; it was nice to have the sun and wind on me. I looked in the center console for the title and insurance card, and the Jeep was in

Morgan's name. Yeah, that seemed like Rachel, to drive two hours round trip to recover a vehicle but leave the owner to think about what she'd done.

There was a big panel sign as you came into town, "Welcome to Deer Tree," next to a tree that looked in no way like a deer. Maybe it was, say, the deer hanging tree after the hunters came back. Or the tree the settlers first saw when they arrived, and a deer happened to be standing there too. Can't call your town Tree.

The jailhouse was small, and maybe used to be a house, which was kind of funny. I thought a jail was one of the first things people built when incorporating towns. The sign was there, though, and the parking lot, and some parked squad cars, though I couldn't imagine Deer Tree needed six or more police officers.

There was a lady in normal office clothes at a desk when I walked through the double front doors. She was typing, squinting a little at the screen, but stopped and looked at me. "Help you?" The fluorescent lights made it sound like there was a beehive in the dropped ceiling.

"Yeah, I'm here to bail my cousin out, Morgan Culver." I dug the folded up check out of my jeans pocket and put it down on the desk. She picked it up between two fingertips and squinted at it. I hoped she wouldn't ask me for ID. She looked up at me and smiled a little, then picked up the phone on her desk.

"Bring Morgan Culver up, we're cutting her loose. Yup, I'm holding the check." She listened for another minute and I held my breath and wondered if I was supposed to have brought a money order instead or something. Then she hung up and went back to typing.

"I'll just...wait then," I said. She glanced at me, and nodded. I stood in front of the desk for a few more minutes, listening to her type, and listening to a clock tick someplace I couldn't see, then I went to investigate the picture frames on the wall there. Some of them were patches with other police station insignias on them. People went back and forth through the door, and the phones rang a bunch of times. The water cooler bubbled somewhere, though I didn't even see it from where I stood.

I turned when I heard voices, and looked towards the back of the building. The floor plan was pretty open, lots of desks, no cubicles, and there was another higher counter by a door in the back. An officer came through the open door first and said something to the man at that counter, and then a girl a few years older than me came through. I thought they brought the wrong person at first, because her hair was so blonde it was white, but then I saw it was only the top layer of her hair that was bleached. It was still black underneath. She was wearing jeans out at the knees with a studded belt, and a t-shirt with the sleeves cut off and a band name on the front, bra straps showing.

She got a manila envelope from the officer at the counter, then cocked her head, listening to something he said, and threw her head back to laugh. She opened the envelope and slid a phone out, fiddling with it as she crossed the room, the untied ends of her bootlaces clattering like buckshot on the linoleum. I could see her nostrils flare, just a little, and then she looked at me, pale blue eyes just like her mother's. And mine. She sniffed, and then finished crossing the room, arms open.

"Hey, cuz." I hadn't expected a hug, and though she looked rail thin, she was all corded muscle. She hustled me out the door without looking back, envelope crackling in her hand, and the officers said something that I couldn't quite hear about trouble and making bets.

"I thought only thugs and Shakespeare said that," I muttered.

"And hillbilly freaks. We're taking it back." I couldn't help but laugh, but I wondered who told her I'd said that about them. Us. "You hungry?"

"I guess. I think I'm supposed to bring you right back, though. Rachel—"

"Yeah, she ain't here and I don't mind putting off the reunion. Let's get burgers. Keys?" She put her hand out and waited.

"Well, what's it going to hurt," I said like I thought she would've actually gone along with anything else I chose. I handed over the keys, and she hopped in and started it up, in gear before I had my door closed. Her nails were painted at one point, black I thought, but it was more chipped away than not. Her nose was just slightly crooked, like it had been broken at least once.

Morgan turned the music up loud and drove fast. It was some kind of bluesy electric rock, the guitar fuzzy and the vocals ragged, and she sang along happily, not ever really looking at me. Sometimes, I could've sworn the voice on the speakers was her, other songs it wasn't. It was so new to me, and I kind of liked it. A relief, after all the other new stuff that wasn't so great.

The diner we pulled into didn't look fifties style so much as somebody brought it here whole cloth from the fifties, all neon and chrome and red leather seating. I imagined for a few minutes some tall tale involving not only werewolves but also time travel, and then shook my head. It had probably just been open for sixty years. The hostess that seated us when we went inside did look like she'd been born during one of the world wars.

I just wanted coffee to drink, and the waitress, a lot younger than the hostess, brought me an entire pot. Morgan ordered a vanilla milkshake. Morgan also ordered two bacon cheeseburgers and a separate order of chili cheese fries. Then I felt bad, ordering just coffee, so added fries. I tried to think of when else I'd ever been in a restaurant. Morgan fiddled with her phone, and looked around, and when the food came, set right in. "Didn't they feed you in jail?" I asked. She wasn't the slightest bit messy, just fast and methodical. All right; I'd seen Rachel eat that way before.

"You're kidding, right?" she asked with her mouth full. I just stared at her. I wondered how much she knew about me, or if she cared. She finished chewing, drank some milkshake. "Look, I'm hungry a lot. Like, aren't you? It's kind of the way of things."

I had been more hungry, but chalked it up to the physical labor. I'd only had one 'your body is going through changes' talk in my life, and Mama was pretty short on the details. I apparently still needed more of the werewolf version, bad. Morgan ate, and texted, and at one point got up to talk to some young guys sitting at the counter, blowing straw papers at the waitresses. I finished my food, and when the waitress came by with the check, Morgan was gone. I scrounged in my pockets and came up with the money, but the tip wasn't something to remember fondly.

I got out into the parking lot and Morgan was leaned back on the hood of the Jeep. She'd gotten sunglasses from somewhere, and was smoking a cigarette. I wonder if Rachel smoked first, and Morgan stole them from her. Probably. Probably we didn't have to worry about lung cancer, anyway, with our lifespan. "That wasn't cool," I said.

"I'll get the next one," she said. Her phone buzzed across the hood, and she held it up to her eyes to read it, squinting. She hit two buttons on it, then threw it in the nearest garbage can.

"We're going back now, right?" She wanted me to ask about the phone. I wouldn't ask about the phone.

"Wow, Rachel really has you toeing the line, doesn't she." Morgan sat up and looked at me over the tops of the sunglasses.

"Not exactly."

Morgan laughed. "Yeah, me and Rachel have our problems too."

"It's kind of weird that you call her Rachel."

"She's not really a 'mom' or 'mama' kind of lady, you know? It works for us, if anything could be said to work for us."

"I've got to say, I was pretty surprised she had a daughter." Morgan smiled.

"Right? Two, actually. Frances is older than me by a couple of years, she's a *doctor*. Sela has a daughter in suburbia. Sidney, her name is, she's doing the husband and college thing right now. Or wait, no, she graduated. She's some kind of therapist now." I should know this kind of family stuff already. Sure the history was important, I guess, and maybe it was safe. Those people were dead, didn't have messy feelings and likes and dislikes to stir things up with.

"But Dulcie doesn't?"

"No. Dulcie doesn't." Morgan yawned, and stretched, "Did they give you my room?"

"No, I don't think they did."

"What, you don't know?" She looked at me over top of her sunglasses.

"I think they gave me Mama's old room. At the end of the hall."

"Oh. Yeah, that is." Morgan stretched again, then slid off the hood. She scraped her hair back in a ponytail and looked off to the middle distance. "Well, I guess we should get this over with."

"It won't be that bad," I said. Then I thought about how I'd feel, if I'd been in jail overnight and Mama knew. "So all right, maybe it will be."

"Not like it's the first time," Morgan said. "Probably won't be the last. The benefit of being arrested close to home is you got family to bail you out." We didn't say anything for a while, just watched the scenery go by.

"What did you do, anyway?" It was hard to think of something big enough to get arrested for, and small enough a few hundred bucks bail would be enough for.

"Mailbox baseball. There may have been substances involved."

I laughed. "What, really? Alone?"

"My compatriots did not have family close by. But, Rachel bailed 'em out anyway. I'm the only one she left in overnight."

"So it wasn't some kind of werewolf gang, out causing malicious mischief? Or is that a felony?"

Morgan grinned at me. "Nah, it was other people in my band. Mostly."

"Band?"

"Oh, Rachel didn't tell you? I'm the lead singer in a band. She disapproves. *Especially* since Fran's a doctor."

"I can't imagine."

"What, the band, or Rachel disapproving?"

"Your mama disapproving." Morgan looked at me for long enough that I got nervous about the road, and then we both laughed.

"So what's your band name?"

"Howling."

"Real subtle. You're not worried that with a name like that, somebody's going to find out?"

"That might be part of what Rachel's been so mad about. But lots of bands have names like that. The Pack A.D. Wolfmother. Umm....Wolfsun. Just plain Wolf. Wolf Alice, though she might be, I haven't met her."

"And what, you go on tour and everything?" I'd only ever laid hands on an acoustic guitar, had no idea what you even did to an electric guitar to make it sound like the ones on the tapes Morgan played when we drove.

"Yup, we're signed with a little indie record label, have CDs and shows and merchandise and everything. There's probably a million guitar picks in the middle thing there, if you want one." She said it like it was no big deal, but looked when I opened the console and rummaged down to the bottom. I hadn't seen the picks when I looked at the registration, and I took one out, stuck it in my jeans pocket.

"Thanks," I said.

"Yeah don't mention it," she said kind of gruffly, but also kind of smiling. Being a big cousin was something she was having to get used to, I reminded myself. Not everything was just what I was having to handle.

Chapter Six

We didn't realize anything was wrong until we were close to the house. The Pine Barrens smelled like smoke a lot of the time; controlled burns, campfires, forest fires. The aunts had already told me all that, that fire was just a fact of life here. It rejuvenated the woods, and the house had lasted for all this time even though it had been close once in a while, Sela told me. But the smell of smoke only got stronger as we got closer, and Morgan punched the button to turn off the radio. When we made the clearing, she pulled the emergency brake and got out of the Jeep up and over, didn't get out the door. I pulled the keys out of the ignition, jammed them in my pocket, and trailed her through the pines.

Smoke filtered through the branches, shot with fingers of sunlight, and no dogs came to meet us. Morgan crashed through the brush ahead of me, yelling the aunts' names. Her voice cracked on 'Rachel'. I'd thought I was pretty fast, getting in shape, but Morgan had me far outmatched. I felt the heat before I reached the dooryard, and put my arm up to shield my face. There were ashes in the air, big and fluffy like snowflakes, And though some of the trees smoldered, the pine pitch starting to pop, the fire hadn't spread far. There were shell casings on the ground, and even under the smell of fire, a cordite reek hung in the air. I tripped and looked down; one of the dogs, the one with the black ear, a feathered dart stuck in its flank.

I didn't see Morgan but I could still hear her, and the screen door was off the hinges. Eyes watering and nose running, I went in. Flames crawled across the floor and up the walls, eating up the rag rugs and the curtains. There was a slick of blood on the floor. Too much blood. My mouth filled with the coppery odor, but I didn't see any of my aunts, couldn't smell them, just blood and burning pine and dust. I stumbled to the stairs, but Morgan came down and banged past me, and through the smoke I could see all the doors were off the hinges there too. She went out through the kitchen and somehow through the roar I could hear the whispering crackle of broken glass under her boot soles. There was no way we were saving the house, but I had the urge to save what I could of the family history. It couldn't all burn up before I even knew it.

I grabbed up one of the quilts from the back of a couch and threw some books in it, the handwritten diaries, the Culver family Bible, a book I'd seen Rachel writing in, some others, and carried them out the front door. I dropped the bundle in the dooryard, by the dog, which seemed far enough from the immediate fire. He lifted his head and looked at me blearily and I crouched for a moment, took his big square head in my hands. I couldn't make myself go back into the house, and I left the dog and went around the side instead, gulping the fresher air, the smell of singed hair crowding my nostrils. I patted myself and my hair wildly, afraid I might be on fire. I saw one of the redbone hounds cringing off in the bushes and hoped more of the dogs were out there. I didn't see anybody, not Dulcie, not Sela, not Rachel, and definitely not Morgan. I made a couple of passes back and forth into the tree line, trying to smell or listen or something, but I couldn't. My senses were saturated, all I could smell was burning, and all I could hear was fire. I saw some tracks, older ones that were my boots and Rachel's boots, some I figured were Morgan's, others.

Then I found drag marks, and parts where the pine needles and sandy soil were kicked around, and tried to follow them, my heart in my throat. The trees were thicker, and thinner, and then there was another almost clearing that somebody had gotten a truck into, and the ground was all torn up with tire treads and tracks, and the smell of diesel and blood. Something glinted in the dirt and I picked it up; it looked like my silver cross necklace. I jammed it in my pocket and started to follow the truck tracks, but I didn't make it very far before there was thrashing in the trees and Morgan reappeared, breathing heavily and pissed off. "They got away," she said. "Where were you?"

"In the cabin." Had I really taken that long?

"What'd you get out of it?"

"The Bible, a quilt, a couple of other things."

"Well that's great," Morgan said. "Glad we saved the books."

"I didn't know what else to do."

Morgan wiped her nose with the back of her hand, smearing soot across her face. "I was trying to catch the bad guys. I guess it's good you stayed out of the way." She shoved past me and back up to the house.

Half the roof fell in while we stood there, sending sparks up like confetti or fireworks. Morgan watched it, feet planted and arms crossed, fire reflected in her eyes, mouth a hard line. I hung back and watched the woods line, looked for more dogs. The black eared one came and stood next to me, leaned his shoulder into me, and I wondered why he didn't go to Morgan. Maybe 'cause she was so mad. Then there were sirens; even I could hear them. I bent and picked up the bundled quilt, and pulled Morgan's keys out of my pocket. She cocked her head towards the jingle, and then looked at me. I offered the keys and she took them. "What about the dogs?" I asked. "The chickens?" I didn't even think of the chickens 'til right that second.

"Neighbors will feed what's left of the chickens," she said. "Take in the dogs. We'll be back." She snapped her fingers and the black eared dog went to her, and she rested her hand on his back for a minute, then led the way back to the Jeep, her fingertips still occasionally brushing his spine as he walked next to her.

"Neighbors?" I hadn't seen a single person around in the woods other than my aunts since getting there. They'd said there were other people around but nobody close enough by to just drop in for the sake of it.

"Yeah. You'll see one now. We need to pick up some stuff." I had a hard time keeping up with Morgan, in a number of ways. "It's where Rachel leaves her car. Closer to the paved roads, and they got a phone."

"Morgan, we need to call the police or something." I don't know why it hadn't been my first thought. "We need to wait for whoever's coming, fire department or whatever, and tell them what happened."

"They can't help us," she said. "And it's stupid to try and stay here during a fire."

"They can't help us? That's what they're for! Somebody just burned our house down and kidnapped our aunts. Well, my aunts and your mama."

"They can't help us," she repeated, and she had that Rachel look on her face.

We got in the Jeep, the dog hopping into the back and curling up on the little fold-up seat there. Right after Morgan got us on the road, a state park Range Rover blew past us, blue bubble flashing on the dashboard. A fire truck followed a few minutes later, and the siren with its piercing echo left me grabbing at my head. Morgan didn't seem to care. Fifteen, twenty minutes later, we made a turnoff, and then went down a twisting gravel driveway. Morgan honked twice before making the final turn, and when we pulled up to the white clapboard house, so much like the one we just left burning, a man in jeans and a flannel shirt stood on the porch, shotgun over his arm.

"I saw the smoke," he said. "Seemed to be from out your way." Morgan didn't even answer him, just jerked her chin in a nod. I got out of the Jeep after her and she turned to me.

"Wait outside, I won't be long. Dio, come on."

She went up the porch, the dog at her heels, and the man glanced at me, gave a nod, and followed her inside. "Who's she?" I heard him ask as the door banged shut.

"Cousin."

It was quiet there, and didn't smell like burning or blood or cordite. I felt like my nose was never going to be the same again. There was a cat on the porch, staring at me, and I put out my hand. The cat's eyes dilated to blackness and it puffed up to twice its size, hissing, and swiped a claw-laden paw at me. I jerked my hand back in time to avoid being scratched. Morgan came out of the house then with a duffle bag over one shoulder, and clomped down the steps. The neighbor stayed in the recesses of his home, and so did the dog. I guess they knew each other.

"Cats won't like you anymore. Depending on the dogs, them too. We're lucky there aren't horses around, or cattle. Wolves, they decide whether they can take you or whether you just belong. Coyotes run, but they typically run anyway."

"Wait, you're saying I'll have to fight wolves?"

"Well, I guess you don't have to. You probably want to live, though. I guess you could run. Nobody told you this?" Morgan turned her gaze on me and I kind of squirmed.

"I'm not exactly real used to this yet."

"Oh, are you fucking kidding me? I'm surprised they let you off the leash so soon."

"I think Rachel was going to strangle me."

"I could see why." Morgan spat on the ground and turned towards the Jeep.

"Oh, fuck you, Morgan. You could say thank you or something."

"Thank you?" she raised her eyebrows and I squared my jaw, stared back at her. I'd never said the word fuck out loud.

"I could've left you in jail, cashed that bail check and gone home again."

She turned around and grabbed me by the shoulders, shook me a little. It felt unreal, like we were doing a scene in a movie. There was still soot on her face. "Do you still really not get it? That isn't home anymore. They don't want you. Home? Home is the house that's burning up out there in the pines. Your family? Their blood was on the floor. Assuming they're alive, we have to find them. You show up in sweet home Alabama, your mama will run you off with silver rounds. She dropped you off and she meant it." We stared at each other for a few minutes, breathing hard. I didn't have anything to say. And if she knew all that already, why was she so surprised about what I didn't know? Finally, she let me go and opened the back of the Jeep, shoved around a bunch of equipment that was I guess music stuff before she stuffed the duffel bag in there too. "Okay come on."

"Where are we going?"

"Bowling alley."

I rolled my eyes. "Because that makes sense."

"I just ditched my burner, and the pay phone's there. I saw tags on the vehicle."

"You didn't tell me. You didn't even tell me you saw a vehicle."

"Gotta keep up. It might lead us to the people we're after. Probably not. But it's worth trying." Morgan swung onto the road without using her turn signal, heading back north.

"Wait, how do you figure? You're not police, you can't call tags in."

"You're right," Morgan said. "Lucky for me, and for you, I'm not calling the cops. I've got somebody else I think can help us out."

"Are they a cop?"

"They are not."

I didn't really know what to say to that. It'd been a few months since my life made any kind of sense. I'd just started to feel comfortable, maybe. Just started to maybe reconcile what happened that night, whatever it was. I could guess at it, put the pieces I knew together into something that made terrible sense, made me feel sick to my stomach, so I guess it was right. "Well maybe we should think about what Rachel would do? Who would she call?"

"I think it'll be better if you don't talk about Rachel to me." We passed the turnoff for the house in silence. Smoke hazed across the road like a ground fog. I didn't see any of the emergency vehicles that had passed us; I wondered if they took an access road or something I also didn't know about. Or if they'd realized there wasn't actually a road up to the house and they were going to have to call in a helicopter or planes or however it was they fought fires out here when they happened. "Do you know how to shoot, at least?"

"Yes, I do. Daddy liked hog hunting when he could. Ducks sometimes."

"All right, good." We drove through the no name town, past the library, and the gas station, and then we pulled into the bowling alley. From the look of things, it was the only place really set up to be the local teen hangout, a big smooth parking lot, flashing neon sign, long white flat roofed building. There was a single payphone on the side of the building, out of sight of the front door. Morgan dug in the center console and came up with quarters and gum wrappers and a jackknife. More guitar picks.

She dropped some quarters in the phone and punched in the number. She listened, and her head bobbed to a song. Then she stopped, head up, and licked her lips. "Yeah, hi it's Morgan, I know she's probably grounded or whatever but can I talk to Hunter? Please? Thanks."

I didn't know what I was supposed to do and stood a few feet away, kind of looking around. Nobody was on the street, and I probably should've just stayed in the Jeep. I would've heard her from there either way. A fire truck screamed down the street, and I shuffled my feet. "Morgan," I said, and she held up her hand.

"Hey Hunter. Yeah I ditched my phone and didn't know if you replaced yours yet so I called the landline, sorry." I'd known Morgan all of two, three hours, and she didn't apologize. Morgan clenched her jaw, and a muscle there fluttered. "Yeah, can you think of anybody offhand who drives a big blue pickup truck, probably a Ford? Veteran plates? Bill Ward? What the fuck...yeah, not right now. When I get a phone I'll text you. Yeah I know where that is. And I have a map." She paused again, finally laughed. "Nope, still no GPS. You know me so well." She hung up with a ghost of a smile still on her face, and the quarters clunked down in the phone.

"You know who that is?"

"Bill Ward? I guess I do. Not personally, but I know who he is. Not what he would've been doing here, or why he would've burned our fucking house down." She was so angry she was practically shaking as she lit a cigarette, exhaling smoke in an aggressive cloud. Like she wanted to breathe fire.

"Okay but—"

Morgan slammed the Jeep door and fastened her seatbelt. When I just waited, she half turned and looked at me. "All right. The Ward family and the Culvers haven't always gotten along. The Wards are all spread out, some of them are out in Pennsylvania, in the mountains, some are in New Jersey, some are further south. I really thought Rachel got them to some kind of truce, so I don't know what would make them come here now, and after us, but there it is."

"So what are we going to do, just knock on their door?"

"Eventually. But right now we're going to go to Middletown."

"Middletown? Why? I don't know where that is."

"It's where Sela's daughter is. Sidney might've heard something. She's been keeping a low profile, but it doesn't mean she's out of the game."

"What game?"

Morgan sighed, loudly. "It's an expression. But you didn't think we were the only family like this, did you?"

"I kind of had," I said, my cheeks heating up. "So the person you just called? Hunter?"

"In another family, yeah."

"Nobody told me." Like so many things.

"Well. I guess all of this is just really eye opening." She didn't say if she meant that for her or me.

Chapter Seven

I wish I could say Sidney looked happy to see us. Maybe it had to do with the fact it was ten o'clock at night and her house was dark when we parked outside. She was on the porch before we'd made it up the walk, pulling the front door silently shut. She wore glasses with square, dark frames and her hair was tamed into loose waves. "Morgan," she said in a tight voice.

"Hey Sid. What's it like, being civilized?"

"Just fine, thank you. Aaron is sleeping, so keep your voice down."

Morgan raised her hands. "Like a church mouse," she said, but I could see the smirk. Sidney looked at me.

"I'm Alleluia," I said. "Sorry to barge in on you like this." Mama had never been a hugger, but I guess that was the whole family and not just one of her particulars. It made Morgan's initial hug at the jail that much more mystifying, but I guess it was a threat display.

"We won't be long," Morgan said. "Or at least I don't think so."

"What happened?" Sidney asked, tensing. The wind had changed a little, and I guess she smelled the smoke on us, other than cigarette smoke. Or knew Morgan wasn't much for paying visits. It looked like a nice neighborhood; newer, and all the houses were built in that plastic siding, two-story style with slickly paved driveways leading up to two car garages. Manicured lawns and lots of spindly new trees growing up between stakes to keep them straight. Hybrid cars and white mailboxes with little red flags, and the across the street neighbor had a basketball hoop.

"Somebody came up to the house, set a fire, and took Dulcie, Sela, and Rachel. Shot at least one of them."

"Took them?" Sidney narrowed her eyes. "*Shot* them?" her voice scaled up.

"They were hurt, there was a lot of blood, but I don't think they killed them. Yet, anyway. The dogs were okay, they tranqed Dio."

"Why would anybody do that?" She looked behind her at the house, but I didn't hear anything.

"The truck I saw was registered to Bill Ward." I listened to distant traffic as Sidney mulled this over.

"I wouldn't have thought Bill would do that," Sidney said finally. "Everybody just sticks to themselves, you know?"

"What's the deal with this Bill Ward guy? Is this a Hatfields and McCoys sort of thing?" I asked. They both looked at me. "Sorry, it's not like we got to politics." But we sure fixed that damn roof.

"They seem to've left a lot out of the crash course," Morgan said. Sidney considered a moment longer.

"They probably thought they had more time, Morgan, and wanted to give her space to breathe and cope."

"Sure," Morgan said.

"I'm standing right here," A lot of the time, I couldn't tell whether I wanted to scream or to cry.

"Sure," Morgan said again, and sat down on the porch steps, lighting a cigarette. Sidney made a face.

"How did you find out?" I asked.

"Mama called me on a burner not long after Joyce dropped you off. I guess Morgan was out of touch at the time, or she would've known all the details."

"I guess I thought only Rachel had a phone," I said. I'd never heard of a burner, but that was the only thing I thought it could be.

"If you need a hug or something, I can do that for you. But we gotta figure out what to do," Morgan said. To my surprise, Sidney laughed.

"You're worried about Rachel. I never thought I'd see it," she said.

Morgan tensed up and turned square to Sidney, her eyes hard. "Yes, I'm worried about Rachel. And Sela, who's *your* mother, in case you need reminding. And Dulcie."

Sidney looked away. "Okay, okay. If it's the Ward family, you know—"

"I know where they are. Well, whereabouts. I don't know why would it be them, after all this time?" Morgan stood up and dropped her cigarette on the sidewalk, scuffed it out with the toe of her boot. There was a hopscotch grid chalked nearby but I didn't smell any other people in the house than Sidney and her husband. There must've been a lot of kids in the neighborhood.

"Could be new blood, wanting to pick fights. Could be a government contract. Could be anything."

"Government contract?" I asked.

"The Wards are military folks. God knows why they'd take the risk, but there you go."

"So wait, Bill Ward? I thought only daughters were were-wolves."

"In our family. In the Ward family, I guess it's the sons. Though I guess they can still have girls? But it's the boys who change, Rachel says. Wouldn't that be a genetic experiment, seeing whose genes won out?" Morgan grinned at Sidney, who licked her lips and shook her head. "Anyways, the point is there are families other than ours, and everybody's rules are different."

"Well how did the Ward family get that way?"

Morgan sighed impatiently, and Sidney tilted her head towards the house a second before answering. I still didn't hear anything. "They came to America that way, I've heard. Maybe somebody did the same thing Mary Culver did, I don't know. But they've been that way in the old country, wherever that was."

"Well whatever, right? What it comes down to is we need to drive on up there and see what them Ward boys think they're getting themselves into," Morgan said.

Sidney raised her eyebrows and looked from me to Morgan. She put her hands up and stepped back from us. "Oh no, I'm not part of your 'we.' I can't just run away from my life here, I could never explain it to him."

"That's not an excuse and you know it." Morgan climbed the porch steps and she and Sidney got nose to nose. I don't know what else she meant to say, but I heard her sniff, and saw her cock her head, just a little. Sidney nodded, just as minutely. "Okay. Well. Guess it's fine to leave him in ignorant bliss a little while longer," Morgan said, and backed off. "Let's go," she said to me. I watched her go down the walk and get in.

"Nice meeting you, anyway," I said weakly. Sidney nodded, arms crossed again so she was holding her elbows.

"You too. I just can't come right now. You can call me if you really need me and I'll...well I'll try."

"I don't know what Morgan's plan is. Take care, though," I said. Sidney raised one hand and waved a little.

I went and got in the Jeep. Morgan already had it running, and pulled away as I fastened my seatbelt. "What was that?" I asked. "You were ready to drag her off that porch and throw her in the Jeep and instead—"

"She's pregnant," Morgan said, eyes forward. "We won't be calling her."

"Oh." I watched suburbia go by, and we got back on the highway. "Where now? Other cousins? Your sister Frances?" I didn't know how many more free questions I could ask her. I didn't know how many first cousins we had.

"No, I think we might be on our own."

I waited for her to roll her eyes and say something like 'but you don't know anything so of course we're fucked.' When she didn't, I looked over at her. I could see the glitter of her eyes in the street lights, but I couldn't read the expression on her face. I wondered if feelings had smells. "So we're going to, where'd Sidney say?"

"We're gonna have a look at the Wards, yeah. They're by Lakehurst, where the Navy base is. I never met any of them. Most families tend to keep to themselves, though there are some business arrangements, lines of communication. Mediation. Rachel does some of that work, if you can believe it."

"I don't even know what I believe anymore. But this is a little like the Godfather." Mama would've skinned me alive if she knew I saw that movie, but some club watched it after school one day and didn't mind me hanging around. I told Mama I'd been getting extra study help, for math.

Morgan laughed. "I guess. Code of silence, family honor, that kind of thing. There's one family, the Coutards, who have always been neutral. If there are disputes, they mediate. If folks keep calm and think to call them, that is. Like, we don't really have a police and a court, but I guess Rachel and the Coutards are the closest we got."

"Are we going to call the Coutards?"

She paused just slightly. "I think we need to assess the situation a little more first. The Coutards are supposed to be neutral, and can't look like they're picking sides if this is a two-family dispute, especially with Rachel's relationship to them. It'd fuck everybody's trust." She paused again. "They might be okay, this might not be what it looks like."

"Do you really think that?" I didn't know much but, I didn't think that.

Morgan was quiet for long enough I thought she just wasn't going to answer me. "Hard to say. It depends on who has them, where and why. That was an awful lot of blood."

"Was it from just one of them? I didn't see if there were dogs inside too."

"None of the dogs were hurt, it didn't seem. Just a couple darted." She gave me a sidelong look. "You couldn't tell?"

"All I could smell was the smoke."

"It wasn't just one of them, but it was mostly Dulcie's." It was my turn to be quiet. The mile markers flicked by for a while before Morgan said anything more. "I guess we work on the who. Then the why, because we don't *know* anything, which I'm sure is part of the point," she said, staring straight ahead, everything about her coiled and ready to take action. Maybe if she hadn't thrown her phone away, somebody could've called it. If this was all a misunderstanding and everything was fine. I didn't think that, and neither did Morgan. "And then we get them back."

Chapter Eight

M organ drove until she was playing ping pong between the lines, and then I took over for a while. Every time we saw a cop, I was afraid of getting pulled over. Not for any real reason; I was a good driver. Just another thing to go wrong. Finally, we rolled into a big rest stop on the last fumes of the tank. I'd never really thought New Jersey was big enough to get tired driving around it, but of course it was. Morgan reached over and cut the engine, took the keys.

"I'll get a gas can and pump some," I offered.

"There's a can in the back," she said, getting out. She grabbed the bright red plastic gas can and a clear plastic tube, then started off towards the line of idling trucks.

"What are you doing?" I asked. I kept my voice low, though I didn't know who would hear me but Morgan.

"We need gas."

"I have some money," I said. I had fears of truckers with tire irons taking exception to making a gasoline donation. I didn't have anything that would be near enough money.

"So do I. One of the many delights in that duffel bag. If we need to, we'll use it. Money buys other things, like milkshakes and hotel rooms and cheeseburgers." She picked a motor home that was towing a pickup, and stepped up on the running board to peek inside. She sniffed, and then hopped down and moved to take the gas cap off the pickup.

"Morgan," I said, looking around.

"Either help me or go back to the Jeep," she said, barely audible. I stood off a little bit, still in the shadow of the motor home, and watched for movement. I tried to open my ears. I could hear the nearby rigs idling. I could hear some drivers, either sleeping in their seats, or in their narrow compartment beds. I could hear men talking, women, the clink of silverware on dinner plates, the flick of lighters by the door, the ding of the cash registers. Places like this never closed. I heard the gas going into the can, and smelled it. Nobody interrupted us.

We walked back to the Jeep and fueled it. "Sleep first or food first?" she asked. Honestly, I had to think about it; so much time had passed since the last time I'd done either.

I considered. My stomach seemed pretty quiet. My eyelids were ready to fall down and never open up again. "Sleep."

"All right. You take the backseat, I'll sit up here."

I crawled into the back and curled up, arm under my head. I slept fast and hard, no dreams, no chills, no fever. I woke up, hours later, when I heard Morgan rustle some papers. I sat up, and she glanced at me, and then looked back down at the book, cloth bound with a blank cover. I looked over Morgan's shoulder, and the page she was on looked like it had a list, and a few addresses. "Did you know what this was when you took it?" she asked.

"No, it was next to the Bible, I guess. I don't even remember taking it."

"It's Rachel's address book. It's got names and phone numbers, anyway, of a lot of family. Some acquaintances."

"So that's good, right?"

"Yeah, it's good. It's better than I thought. We can try to call on Ivy's kin." It took me a moment, then I remembered: Ivy was Grandmother Meredith's sister. So she'd left the pines for her own family. I wondered who brought her back to bury her beside her sister. Daughters, must be. That was the entire family story.

"Do you think they'll help us?"

"Maybe. Maybe with information on what the Wards might be up to. They might have had earlier contact."

"What are we even doing? Why didn't we just call the police?" I asked. "Or the Coutards, like you said? Why would this be up to us?"

"Breakfast first," Morgan said, and got out of the Jeep. She was partway across the parking lot before I caught up with her. The camper with its pickup truck was gone.

The diner at the truck stop was nice enough, more red vinyl booths, dark wood, a counter with stools, window back to the short order cook. The waitress nodded as we came in and pointed at one of the booths; she was waiting for a man in a screen backed hat to pick what kind of pie he wanted to take with him.

We slid into the booth and picked up our menus. I righted my coffee cup in its saucer; I definitely needed coffee. Morgan flipped through the menu and then closed it and set it on the edge of the table. I was still looking at mine when the waitress came over and set a pot of coffee on the table. "I'd like three eggs, over easy, a side of bacon, side of home fries, and a blueberry muffin, grilled. Coffee. Orange juice."

"And what do you want, honey?" the waitress asked me, still writing the tail end of Morgan's order.

I stared at the menu and couldn't make myself focus. The plastic was sticky from the syrup of those who had come before. "Just give me the same thing she's having," I said. "Please."

"Coming right up."

Morgan poured herself a cup of coffee and shook down three sugar packets at once before ripping the tops off and pouring them in. She clunked her spoon around to stir, glancing around at the other patrons, and then set it down on the table, puddling coffee around it. "Okay," she said, switching her gaze to me. "We need to figure out who took them. We need to figure out why they would want to. We need to figure out where they went. We can't call the police because it's kinda important to keep that whole werewolf thing a secret, you know? And like I said, Rachel's kind of like what we *would* call, in conjunction with the Coutards. The few times anybody calls." I think about the first time the aunts taught me how to turn into a wolf, and how Rachel left after, because 'she got a call.'

"Well then, what's the deal with the Wards?" I asked. "I keep asking and you keep not saying."

"Because it's a pain in the ass, it's not like it's just been one problem. They've got a long history crisscrossing with us. One of the old Wards thought our families should unite. That way, boys or girls, whatever babies we got would be better."

"Better?" Ward girls didn't change, she said. If Ward girls existed. It couldn't just be as cut and dry as that, could it?

Morgan frowned and took a sip of her coffee. That made her frown more, and she added another sugar packet. "Yes, better. We hardly ever even use any of the 'w' words but you know what I'm saying."

"Now I'm following." Being able to turn into a wolf was only useful if you were inclined to turn into a wolf. Heightened senses were nice. A shortened life wasn't. How was that better? "I hadn't been thinking about it like that. Better than human?" I must've sounded a little too shocked for her taste. The waitress came right then with our plates, so whatever Morgan opened her mouth to unload on me was delayed for that split second. She eyed me, and then started in on her food.

"I do think I'm better," she said after a few minutes, in an urgent, low voice. "I can't imagine living life as a normal human. I can't imagine not hearing how I hear, or having the sense of smell I do. I can't imagine being weak, or slow. I can't imagine just being boxed in a boring little human life because I can't ever do anything."

"You've had it a little different from me."

"Yeah, so you have to catch up. I was early, I started when I was nine, so at this point, I've lived longer with it than without it. And I knew about it the whole time. I knew how awesome it was gonna be."

"Everybody's expecting me to just kinda catch up, and I really don't know how I'm supposed to do that. I don't know how to make any of this go faster, like if there's a mountain I can climb and come down changed." I didn't figure Morgan would much get any religious references I made, and with high school, I was used to watering them down. The other kids spent a year asking if my daddy handled snakes and then forgot about me when the next new kid came in. And now I wouldn't ever see any of them again.

"Yeah, we're out of luck on that count. No holy mountains, and I'm not exactly the Kung Fu movie mentor type."

I'd never seen a Kung Fu movie. "I never would have guessed."

"Right, now that we got the touchy feely stuff out of the way, we should probably go to the gift shop. Places like this sell burners, we should get a couple of those and—"

"Oh yeah, a burner is a phone, right?"

"Yeah. Prepaid cell phones." I think Morgan had more patience than she gave herself credit for. "We should be able to call each other, if we split up. We should also get you a driver's license."

"Do we really have time?" Morgan closed her eyes for a moment.

"Cuz, pretend for a moment that legal thoughts rarely cross my mind," she said.

"Got it." For some reason, a fake ID seemed more risky and dangerous than the duffel bags in the back of the Jeep that were apparently full of guns and money.

The waitress came by to clear the plates, and set down our check. Morgan picked it up, looked at it for a moment, and got up. She pulled some bills out of her pocket and dropped them on the table, then headed for the door. I finished my coffee, and followed. We bought two prepaid cell phones, and some cards to add minutes with.

Outside, the sun threw up heat shimmers off the asphalt, and more trucks were coming and going already. We got back in the Jeep, and Morgan activated both phones and loaded the minutes in what seemed like no time at all. "So, where do we get me a license?"

"My bass player can handle it for us," she said.

"From your rock star days, I'm sure."

"What, jealous? And don't talk like my rock star days are over, that's weird. This was just an unplanned interlude and now…"

"No, I'm not jealous. I never dreamed of being the lead in a band." I waited, looking at the sunlight flashing off the trucks. There were a lot of things I never dreamed of, actually. Or never really dreamed past somehow leaving the church. "So, what else is there?"

She sighed loudly, and handed me my phone. "What do you mean?"

"Well, we're werewolves, apparently. What else is true? Vampires?"

"No, Alleluia, there aren't vampires," Morgan said, like it was the stupidest thing she'd heard me say yet.

"I don't see why not. It isn't like we make sense. What part of 'skin from a dead man's back' translates into 'turn into a wolf when you feel like it'?"

"I think we make a little more sense than a person who drinks blood to live forever. Nothing lives forever."

"Especially not us." I thought about that a lot. Nobody knows how much time they have, but seeing the headstones in the family cemetery, I was pretty aware of how much I didn't.

"I guess it's just the price we pay."

"Nobody asked me. I don't think I like the tradeoff."

Morgan patted me on the shoulder. "Better to burn out than to fade away, cuz," she said. She only sounded a little bitter, a little ironic, and very much like a rock star.

Chapter Nine

The meeting with the fake ID guy went much the same way the meeting with the neighbor had gone. Morgan parked in his driveway and got out, expecting me to follow. The guy on the porch wasn't in flannel, but skinny jeans and a black t-shirt and a studded belt like Morgan's, and instead of a gun he had a beer, but that was it. Morgan said "This is Al," and we went inside. I stood against a white portion of wall as the salt air came in through all his open windows, and he put the camera to his face, waited, waited, and then took the picture. Then he went to his desk, plugged the camera in, and started tapping on keys and clicking around with the mouse. I went and sat on the couch while Morgan rummaged in his refrigerator, smoke wreathing her head before she stubbed the cigarette out. An electric bass was leaned up in the corner, with an amp that looked like somebody had attacked it with a hatchet. Maybe it was part of their stage show. I'd never been to a rock concert. I'd never been to any kind of a concert.

Morgan came and sat next to me, eating a bologna and cheese rollup and carrying two glass bottled sodas. She handed me one and leaned back, putting her feet on the coffee table. The couch smelled kind of like popcorn. I could hear a clock ticking somewhere, probably in the kitchen. The soda was vanilla; not vanilla cola, or cherry vanilla, just vanilla.

The sound of the printer made me jump, and Morgan grinned at me, but didn't laugh. Al ran the card through the laminator and tossed it to me. I stared seriously at the camera, and really looked like I'd just spent an hour in line at the DMV to be helped for thirty seconds. "Thanks," I said.

"Not a problem, I owed Morgan a favor," he said. "You sticking around?" he asked, turning to her. "We need to—"

"No, we gotta get going," she said, and stood up. "Family stuff." I didn't want to just leave our empty bottles on his coffee table, which was empty and completely clean, so I took them and set them in the kitchen sink. When I came back, Al and Morgan stood together by the door. He looked abashed, or maybe irritated, and Morgan looked amused.

"Nice meeting you," he said to me, and then went back to his computer.

"Yeah, you too," I said, though we'd said less than twenty words the whole time we were there. And we left.

We drove for a little while, through suburbs, and then got on another highway. It was like Morgan had to drive to think, and a lot of New Jersey went by out my window while she was doing it, suburb and small town, diners and strip malls, and long swathes of green. She constantly changed the radio, every once in a while just popping one of her tapes in for a play through before channel surfing again. Pressing 'seek' here wasn't like how it was in the South; it stopped at pretty much every station, rock and religion and country and classical. Talk radio, rap, Spanish. "So, Ward first or should we call other family?" she asked.

"It's not like we can show up at the Ward homestead and ask why they took our kin," I said. "I mean, I guess we can, but I don't know how productive it'll be."

"Our kin," she said, like she thought it was funny. "It'll prove whether they did or not, anyway. If they're there, we'll know. Or if Ward was around them." Morgan glanced at me. "Well, I'll know."

"Thanks." She didn't say anything. "You think they didn't do it?"

"I think it's possible whoever knew about us knew about the history with the Wards and would benefit from us going off half-cocked and burning their house down."

"I hadn't thought of that." Frankly, it surprised me that Morgan had. Another reason not to call the Coutards, I guessed. We drove a few more miles in silence. We passed a blue 'Rest Stop 5 Miles' sign. "Who else knows the history?"

"How the fuck should I know? This is hard," Morgan admitted with a laugh.

"It's not the sort of thing you expect to have to deal with." Add it to the list.

"It might be strange to take this from me, but I actually don't want to cause unnecessary trouble. If Bill Ward and his *kin* had nothing to do with it, I don't want to spark a full on brush war that'll be killing our grandkids. Hell, it might benefit everybody if we warned them."

"You really think it was like, an actual contract or whatever, like Sidney said?"

"I don't know. You still think the idea of the government wanting werewolf super soldiers is stupid?"

"I never said it was stupid, it just surprised me. And I can see how we'd be of interest to the science community. Genetics. Gender maybe." Not like I knew much about either of those things.

"Is it still animal testing if it's done on a werewolf?" she asked, and then snickered.

"Morgan, seriously."

"Yeah, I know. But think about it." She stared ahead at the road for a few minutes, and then gave me a sidelong look. I couldn't help it, and cracked up. I felt guilty laughing, and laughing was a relief.

"You're a bad influence. Maybe that's why they didn't tell me about you."

"Oh, I'm definitely a bad influence, but I was fighting with Rachel is all. I otherwise make the pines my home when not on tour."

"So what, you tour with the band when you fight with Rachel?"

"Yeah, more or less. We're on hiatus right now. Record sales weren't exactly astronomical, though weirdly, they picked up once we weren't touring. So we're letting that ferment a little while."

"Do they even call it records anymore?"

"Gotta call it something. And actually vinyl is making a comeback, which I guess you probably wouldn't know."

"I guess that's true."

"All right, so look up one of our other cousins in there, and we'll get off at this rest stop and find a payphone, if they still exist at large in the wild. I think it's community service that the bowling alley still has one. Cell service still isn't the best down there."

"Do we know who any of these people are?"

"By we meaning me? Only a few. Hopefully one I met will be in there with a phone number. Me, if one of Ivy's granddaughters called me, I'd go help stage a riot. But I'm not sure it's reciprocal. Ivy and Meredith had some kind of falling out, way back when."

"Seems like we kind of all have trouble getting along." I thought back to my small amount of time with the aunts, overbearing Rachel, sweet Dulcie, Sela sometimes the moderator and sometimes just removing herself from it. But they loved each other the way I've only seen sisters love each other.

"Just the way family is, I guess. Grudges carry. Who knows, though, maybe that Ward thing would have worked out." There was a blue rest stop sign, with pictographs of a picnic table, restrooms, and a phone. Three miles.

"Do you think maybe you should call your sister?"

"Fran? I guess I should. I don't know that the good doctor will be able to help us. She probably isn't pregnant, but she has more professional entanglement than Sidney does, anyway."

"Maybe she'll have insight?" With the clock ticking the way it was, she had to have gotten to that doctor thing as soon as she could. I wonder if it was to study wolves more and she was a geneticist or whatever, or if she was a hospital doctor.

"Yeah, maybe. Fran tends not to get involved with any of it. Comes home on holidays." Morgan seemed, to me, strangely noncommittal on the topic of her older sister. "Well. Some holidays."

"Are you...jealous?"

"What? No. Jealous of what." Morgan gave me a hard look, and I grinned.

"Jealous that Fran is a doctor and you're just an on hiatus rock singer?" She reached over and slugged me in the shoulder, and the Jeep swerved just a little.

"I play guitar too. If I wanted to be a doctor, I could've worked on that."

"Or an astronaut. Or a bush pilot."

"Well if you're so fucking smart, what did you want to be?" She looked at me again. "A lot less funny, huh?"

"I wanted to get old," I said. We looked at each other for a long time, probably longer than we should have with the Jeep moving, Morgan's eyes invisible through the sunglasses. Then she nodded.

"Yeah. Why don't you see if you can find a phone number for Ivy's people?"

I reached for the books that had the family tree and names and addresses in it. Ivy had three daughters, Hanna, Lorraine, and Betty. Hanna had two daughters, Suzanne and Terry. Betty had one daughter, Louisa. It looked like the group of them lived in the same neighborhood, in Ohio, but there was only a phone number listed for Betty.

Morgan pulled off at the rest area, another big huge parking lot with a million gas pumps and then a reddish cedar building with bathrooms and fast food restaurants. The pay phone was just in a steel box bolted to the side of the building, near the picnic tables on a sorry patch of grass. "All right, what's the number," she said. I read it off. Morgan dialed, listened, and then counted out the change.

"Wait, didn't we just buy those burners?" I asked.

"I like using payphones, it makes them seem wanted. Besides, I don't really like cell phones." I shook my head. Of course not.

There weren't any other cars or people nearby, and I strained to hear any noise at all that wasn't tires on the highway, out of sight between a slim little line of bushes. There was the arc-sodium lights at the gas pumps. Timers and stuff inside, at the fast food places, and those people yelling to each other. I could hear the phone ringing too, from where I stood, but my sense of it faded by the time anybody answered. "Hi, may I speak to Betty please? It's Morgan." The voice Morgan used was somewhere between her regular speaking voice and one that would've made the church ladies think she was just sweet as pie. "Yeah, hi Betty. It has been a long time, hasn't it? I hope you and yours are well." Morgan rolled her eyes. This was going to take a while.

I tuned her out and wandered past the picnic tables, across the grass. There were some decorative bushes there that I didn't know the names of, and some potato chip bags and plastic cups caught up in the tall grass. I picked them up for something to do. When I threw the stuff into the garbage can next to Morgan, I heard her say in a voice like barbed wire "Well, now, that's a shame. Family is family, and I thought you'd be willing to help. I thought you'd realize how dangerous this is for all of us, whether you're over there in Ohio or not. No, I'm done, go fuck yourself." She hung up the phone, and looked at it for a second, as though she'd like to rip the whole works off the wall, clenching her fists, knuckles white except where scars stood out

"No Betty, then," I said in a neutral tone. I didn't want her to turn that anger on me.

"No Betty. Nobody from Ohio," she said.

I considered what else to say on the matter, and picked what I thought would appeal to Morgan the most. "Well, fuck 'em anyway." My second f word.

"Yeah," she said, turning from the phone with a grin of grim bravado. "Fuck 'em."

"So, the Wards?"

"Yeah, do we want to drive on down there, or call?"

"If we call, and it was them, they'll know we know," I said.

"Maybe you're right."

"I'd like to think I'll catch on sometime." Or, the real secret was that everybody's faking it all the time.

Morgan shook out her arms and exhaled loudly, looking up at the sky. Then she looked around; lots of cars, still not a whole lot of people. "We need to get away from the highway and go for a run, I think," she said, leading the way back to the Jeep.

"In jeans and work boots? Yeah, that'll be fun for both of us."

"As wolves, Allie. To blow off some steam. I'm not used to having to spell everything out."

"Sorry, I'm not used to, well, anything." I had never yet thought of it as something for fun. It was something I fretted about from the first, especially when I thought I'd killed somebody.

"Yeah. Your mama didn't do you any favors, raising you the way she did."

"I'm getting that," I said, frowning.

"I mean, you know how, right?"

I could feel my face getting hot. "Yes, I know how. They covered that, anyway."

"But nothing else."

"What do you mean, nothing else? I don't even know what else I need to know. I can tell you part of the family tree, I might remember seven generations or something. I might be able to moonshine now. And make soap."

"How to fight," she said. I could smell her impatience.

"No, we didn't have werewolf fighting lessons. I don't even know where to start with something like that." I tried to imagine me and Rachel squaring off and...what? If we were people, somebody would show me how to throw a punch, which I didn't really know how to do either. And I guess if we were wolves, I'd figured out already how to bite somebody, so long as I was already freaked out and scared out of my mind.

"Really, I'm just trying to get a feel of how much I'm going to need to babysit you."

"I can take care of myself," I said, far more firmly than I felt. Though I actually felt safe with Morgan, like she wouldn't hurt me, like she'd try her hardest for me to not get hurt. I couldn't say why exactly I thought that, it wasn't as though she'd been terribly kind.

"Right." Morgan pulled off the highway at an exit that didn't really look like an exit, took a turn down something else that seemed like maybe a service road, except there wasn't much in the way of buildings or anything. She pulled over and stopped finally, got out. "Well, you coming or not?"

"I'll come." I followed her into the tree line, where we kicked off our boots and then undressed with our backs to one another. Nervously, I closed my eyes and tried to think four legs. I didn't want to get stage fright. I knew when it worked, but still wasn't relieved until I opened my eyes and my vision had changed. I turned and looked at Morgan, and if I'd known how to laugh as a wolf, I would have. The dye in her hair worked out as a white blaze on her head and down the back of her neck,, and it looked kind of skunky.

She must've known how I was thinking, though, as she bared her teeth at me and then bounded off. I ran after her. She was just a little bit taller than me, and in better shape. My little bit of practice wasn't enough, though, and I had a hard time keeping up. Morgan ran harder and longer than I would have chosen to, but I wasn't going to give up early. When she turned back, I didn't expect it, and I dodged out of the way so that we didn't just pile into one another. I never gave canine body language much of a thought before a few months ago, but Morgan was definitely laughing at me. So that's how it was done. I clenched my jaw and chased after her. I could feel the heat in my paws and in my ears, and in spite of myself, my tongue lolled out as I tried to keep up. I didn't lose sight of her, but the space between us widened. When we got back to our clothes, it was hard not to just throw myself on the ground and pant. She looked at me a moment, head cocked, and then turned away. I did the same. That was the rule.

I heard the jangle of Morgan's belt before I'd gotten back to two legs, and I was still panting and flushed, even as I put my clothes on. My pulse beat crazily in my ears, and I fought with the nausea that still happened to me every time. The last thing I wanted to do was puke on my boots in front of Morgan. When I met her back at the Jeep, though, she seemed a little more relaxed, and gave me a crooked smile. "Not too bad, cuz," she said. "You could be a lot worse."

We got back in the Jeep and headed south again, back to the pines but further west. Morgan and I were clearly not diplomats; I both looked forward to and dreaded meeting any member of the Ward family. I really expected them to have Rachel's blood all over their hands by the time we got there. It would save the guesswork, anyway, because I knew if I had to choose, I'd kill Rachel first. It was *awful*, it made me guilty to think that way, but there was no sense lying to myself.

Morgan drove and I dozed, and my thoughts circled the problem and worried at it. How do you actually contain people that can turn into wolves? Silver, if they knew about the silver. Maybe it was just guessing, from the movies. The why of it, though, that was something else. If it was the Wards, the reason could very well be for breeding, and I tensed up, miserably angry at the thought. My own changing saved me from getting hurt, I was sure; the idea that my aunts' changed existence was the reason for them being in the same kind of situation had me sick. Not knowing made me sick.

I woke up with my face pressed against my window, and the memory of my mouth tasting like dirt. I'd dreamed what happened that night, but as soon as I tried to put it in words, it was gone, just like that. I sat up and rubbed my cheek. I wondered if Morgan had stopped again for gas without waking me up. Looking outside the car we didn't seem to be, well, anywhere. There was a two lane road, and a field that had once held a house but only had an ivy covered chimney. More fields beyond that. "What's going on?"

"You hungry?" Morgan asked, glancing over. Her cigarette hand hung out the window, her new burner balanced on the steering wheel. I was surprised the smell of smoke didn't wake me.

"I was sleeping." I yawned and rubbed my eyes.

"You were."

"I take it you're hungry?"

"Yeah, I felt bad stopping someplace and just letting you bake in the car."

"Well, I appreciate it. There isn't anything here, though."

"Well, no, but we're going to be coming up on a bunch of places. Besides the fact that we're almost there."

"Already?"

"Yeah. A few miles left, anyway."

"Any idea how we're actually going to go about this?"

"Knock on their door?" Morgan grinned at me. "Look, there's a buffet." Just like that, the road widened into a four lane through a town, strip malls galore, and we were in the freshly tarred parking lot of some kind of non-branded country buffet, yellow plastic flags snapping in the breeze.

It looked like they just opened, and no other customers were inside. We were pointed at a table, ordered water and coffee, and she headed for the buffet to pile her plate up. I got a plate and followed Morgan. We both loaded up and dug in. I couldn't think of anything to talk about. When we'd made our third trip to the buffet, the server brought us our check, a pair of mints perched on the green paper. Others had come in by that time, a group of construction workers and some sun-pinkened tourists.

Morgan went and got an ice cream cone and sat licking it while I finished a plate of crab legs. "Should we bring them anything, you think?"

"If we were going to bring them anything, it should've been moonshine from the still, that's the right way of doing things, according to Rachel. I don't think they'll want hours old buffet takeout."

"Damn, the still. I have a jug in the back of the Jeep, though, I think. I've got a lot of crap in the back of the Jeep."

"You do?"

"Yeah. I know somebody who wanted to try and see if he could make it work like ethanol in gas. Turns out he got sent to jail, though."

"Oh, you mean like you?"

"I was just detained," she said with a sniff. "He went to actual prison." She looked at the bill and dropped a pair of twenties on the table. "You ready?"

"I guess."

We got back in the Jeep and when we got closer to the Ward's town, Morgan had me pull out a map and hunt up their address. "It isn't often that I wish I had GPS," she said.

"I wouldn't imagine. You don't like phones either."

"What can I say, I'm an old-fashioned girl."

"With an electric guitar and amp in the back of her jeep."

She laughed. "Yeah you're right, I need a hurdy-gurdy or harp or something instead. Adding that to the act would really fuck with people, I love it."

Chapter Ten

Really, it wasn't hard to find. Lots of land, rick rack of mailboxes next to the road, wire fences. Forest hemmed the fields in, and scrubby pines came up almost to the back of the house, which was a freshly blue painted affair with big stretches of green lawn that somebody had mowed recently. It clearly used to be a farm, though it was hard to tell what crops had been raised in those fields. I thought of every movie that had backwoods folks killing people in it, from The Texas Chainsaw Massacre to House of 1000 Corpses, that Mama and Daddy absolutely did not know that I had watched with the movie club at school and would've put me in a closet for a week's worth of penance if they did. We turned into the gravel driveway, kicking up dust, and a couple of hound dogs came baying from underneath the porch, jowls flapping. Next step was going to be a guy on the porch with overalls and a shotgun. When nobody appeared, I looked at Morgan. She pulled the Jeep up and cut the engine. There was a flagpole to the side of the house, flying an American flag with a black VFW-POW M.I.A. flag under it, and well-tended rosebushes grew up around the porch.

"What do you think?"

"Well, I don't see that truck," she said. There weren't any cars here, or trucks, or anything.

"What does that mean?"

"The hell if I know. Let's go say hi." She opened the door and hopped out. She was about ten feet away from the dogs by the time I caught up with her. The biggest and loudest one looked mostly bloodhound. "Hey buddy," Morgan said easily. "Go get a grown-up." The dog stopped barking and cocked his head at her. She gestured at the house with a jerk of her chin. "Go on." Once the big dog stopped barking, the others slowly dropped off. They still stood there, staring, but they were quiet, and none lifted a lip to growl. After a moment of consideration, the bloodhound mix turned and loped off to the house. He nosed the screen door open and went inside. It slammed shut behind him, just missing the end of his tail.

"I didn't think that was going to work," I said.

"I had my doubts."

"You know, sooner or later this wing and a prayer stuff isn't going to work, and then what?"

"You should believe in the power of prayer, shouldn't you? Anyway, you sound like Rachel." Morgan grinned at me, and then the screen door banged again. We both looked up.

Instead of overalls, it was jeans, but I was right about the shotgun anyway. A boy my age, maybe a little younger, stood on the porch with the dog. His t-shirt was wrinkled, and he had some bad bedhead. "You're trespassing," he said. The wind was just right, and I could smell him from where we stood; detergent, cut grass, lemons, and wolf.

"I didn't see no signs," Morgan said with a smile.

"What do you want?"

"We're Culvers."

The boy's scowl deepened, and he flexed his grip on the shotgun. "Culvers? What do you think you're doing here?"

"Yeah, I know it's weird, but you see, one of your trucks was on our land a couple days back. And see, it was the same time a few of us disappeared. Being our only lead, you can maybe understand why we're here."

"Disappeared?"

"Well, not like alien abduction disappeared, more like had a bloody fight and got dragged off to parts unknown disappeared. You know something about that?"

His eyes got a little bigger, and he tried to keep up the tough guy act, but even I knew that he didn't know anything. "You think I'd tell you if I did?"

I looked at driveway, the channels in the gravel. It looked like there had been at least three or more trucks here at some point. I couldn't hear anybody else around, and I didn't think that if the Ward family was present in force, they'd just send this one kind-of-scared boy out. Or maybe they would, as an insult. I couldn't smell anybody else, anyway.

"Where is everybody?" I asked, before the pissing contest got any further. "You look like you're here alone." The boy screwed up his face a little more, and I realized he probably looked so sour from waking up coming into the bright sunlight from the dark house, and maybe a little from trying to look tough.

"Aw hell," he said, and relaxed the shotgun, exhaling. "You want to come in? Want lemonade?" Morgan raised her eyebrows at me and I shrugged just enough for her to see.

"Sure, lemonade would be nice. We can sit on the chairs out here if you'd like."

The dogs parted, and Morgan and I walked up on the porch. The boy went inside, and I heard the clatter as he leaned up the shotgun and walked down the hall. A few minutes later he came back with a tray of glasses and a pitcher. We all sat down in the white wicker chairs with a glass of lemonade and stared at each other for a few minutes. "Well this is kind of uncomfortable," the boy laughed. He was brown-haired and brown-eyed, and he was a lot friendlier looking without his face all squinched up. Not really how I expected the big tough military Wards to be.

"That it is," Morgan said. "So what's the deal?"

"They left this morning to go hunting," he said.

"What, everybody but you?" she asked, glancing at me.

"I'm the youngest, so I don't get to go every time."

"So the whole family cleared out to go hunting?"

"Grandma went to a baby shower." We sat there for a time, drinking the lemonade. "So, your people? What happened?"

I'd say we gave him the short version, but there really wasn't a long one. "We came back from a trip out of town, and the house was on fire. There was a lot of blood, some of the dogs were shot with tranquilizer darts, and when Morgan chased down the trail, she got sight of a truck and its license number."

This made the boy sit forward in his chair. "What did the truck look like? We had one stolen a while back. Like, a few months ago, maybe more."

"Big Ford, blue, diesel."

"Did it have mud flaps?"

"Yeah, your garden variety girlie ones." Morgan rolled her eyes. "Surprised your grandma isn't mortified to ride around in that kind of truck."

He kind of sniffed and nodded. "Well yeah, that's the truck. I can find the police report, if you don't trust me. But that was stolen out of the American Legion lot when Grandpa was there watching Sunday football."

"American Legion?"

"Yeah, he's a Navy veteran. Radio man in Vietnam."

Vietnam ended a long time ago; Grandpa Bill either went as a teenager, or the Ward family had some longevity to it that the Culvers didn't. That hardly seemed fair; weren't women supposed to live longer than men? But, every family has its rules. "So, what's your name, anyway? I'm Allie, this is Morgan."

"Joe. Nice to meet you." He set his glass down. "So you two seem nice enough, even if you did come here to kill us for taking your family."

"Well aren't you the sweetest thing," Morgan said, rolling her eyes. She wasn't looking at him, didn't see the sudden surprising blush, but I did. "What are we doing?"

"I don't know. If the truck was stolen when Joe says it was, then we're at a dead end, right? Somebody knew enough about us, and knew about the Wards, and bet that we'd waste our time fighting with them instead of following the real trail."

"Well, joke's on them, not only are we not fighting with the Wards, but we don't have a real trail." Morgan got up and paced the porch, her empty rocking chair knocking against the wall behind it. "Fuck."

Joe watched her with mild interest, or maybe it was apprehension. "Well, I could radio the hunting cabin, see if Bill or somebody can come down and help. Maybe they know something?"

She stopped pacing and turned on him. "I don't see why they would."

"I don't know why we wouldn't help. It's been a really long time, hasn't it? Plenty long enough to lay whatever that feud is to rest."

"That's true, but Rachel's never had kind words for Wards that I know of. And that makes me think she's run into Bill, and others, a whole lot more recently."

"Does Rachel have kind words for anybody?" I muttered, and Morgan glared at me. Oh okay we only got to badmouth Rachel when it was just family. I should've thought of that.

"Well, you don't know until you ask." Joe got up and went to the door. I looked at Morgan, shrugged, and followed him. Morgan came along, letting the screen door bang shut behind her.

The house inside was neat as a pin, the hallway a straight shot back to the kitchen, lined with photographs and daguerreotypes of generations of the Ward family. Nearly every man's likeness was in a military uniform of one type or another, right back to the Civil War. The house smelled a bit like lemon furniture polish, but also leather and gun oil and home cooking. Whoever the matriarch of the family was, she must have run them with an iron fist. None of the family portraits in the hall had daughters in them, but there were more framed pictures on tables with men and women, and a couple of little girls. The Wards didn't seem to just make copies of themselves like the Culvers, there was more variation in everybody's faces than there was between me and Morgan and Sidney, but I thought one of the girls looked a lot like Joe Ward, and wondered if Morgan noticed. There were no dogs in the house, but there was a fluffy pure white cat that regarded Morgan and I with disgust before sashaying upstairs. If I had to bet on it, I'd say that cat was Joe's grandma's.

"Radio's back here," Joe said, and there was a small room off the kitchen, built on the back of the house like an afterthought. There was a big radio and receiver on a table there, and also a couple of computers, and maps of the United States on the wall. A little low bookshelf, with big thick military histories and a couple smaller books with plain black spines, no lettering. I wondered if there was a satellite dish and antennas and stuff for all this hung off the back of the house, or if I just didn't know to look for them out front. Joe sat down at the radio and picked up the microphone, licked his lips, and glanced at us a little self-consciously. "Pack One, this is Wolf Den, come on back," he said. I heard Morgan sniff, and I looked at her; she was biting her lip to keep from laughing.

I leaned over. "You named your band Howling," I whispered. She scowled and turned her back, went to look at the map on the wall.

"Yeah Wolf Den, I copy. What're you up to?" crackled through the speaker.

"I got a couple of Culvers here, looking for help. Is Alpha around?"

"Naw, he isn't here. You can help those girls right back to the highway," the voice laughed. Joe sighed. From the corner of my eye, I saw Morgan bend over to inspect the books on the shelf.

"They got a problem, and it might be our problem too."

A pause. "Copy that, but like I said, he ain't here."

"Well, yeah, you said that. Where'd he go? He'll be back sometime."

"Canteen, for the game, took a few with him. So he won't be back until a lot later." Another pause. "But don't get any ideas, little man, you've got direct orders to stay there." Morgan and I looked at each other. I'd thought Rachel was a little rough, but her worst tone never approached what the guy on the radio just was to Joe.

"Copy that, Pack One. Over and out." Joe flipped the switch on the microphone and leaned back in the chair.

"So Canteen, what's that code for?" I asked.

"It's a bar in the little town by the hunting cabin," he said. "The Bear's Den. I can tell you how to get there, but that's the best I can do, other than offering you sandwiches for lunch."

"Hey, I get it, we're cool with the military stuff," Morgan said, coming up just behind me. I shuffled to the side a little, shoulders stiff, and hoped she wouldn't go after me for it. "Let me get the map out of the Jeep, and you can tell us how to get there."

Once she was gone, Joe looked at me. "I don't really think you two can just walk right in there and talk to Grandpa or anybody," he said. "It's not really the way things go."

"Tell it to Morgan."

He pulled a face. "Yeah, I'd rather not."

"We'll figure something out." Glancing around, I saw a giant container of vanilla protein powder on the counter, starched white curtains on the windows, a generations-old cast iron skillet on the stove.

Morgan brought back a road map of New Jersey and Pennsylvania, edges fuzzy from being folded and refolded, one corner lacquered with an old ketchup spill. Joe took it and laid it out on the glossy wooden kitchen table, knocking the place mats askew. "It's like, four hours. You take 195 to 476 to 80, and then you'll be up in the mountains. You'll see a bunch of Williamsport signs, but that's not where you're get- ting off, you go past that. The Bear's Den is right down the main drag. You'll see it, there isn't much else there. They got a new sign and everything."

"Four hours? Would they even still be there?"

Joe shrugged. "Probably, yeah. It's not unusual."

Morgan watched Joe trace the route on the map, nodded, and folded it back up. "All right. You ready?"

"Just about." I looked at Joe. "Restroom?"

"Top of the stairs," he said.

"I'll be outside," Morgan said.

I'm sorry to say that Morgan was a bad influence on me. I did have to use the restroom, but after I'd flushed, I left the sink running and pulled open the medicine cabinet. Lots of tooth brushes in a couple different cups, Arm and Hammer toothpaste. Some orange prescription bottles, a clear glass vial with clear liquid, but I didn't want to turn anything to find out what it was or who it was for and leave my scent on it. This place made me think of Kyle Dodd, and I wondered how he was healing up and then gagged and almost threw up in the sink.

I closed the cabinet and splashed some water on my face before I turned it off. There was a plaque with a little prayer in it on the wall, and I dug in my pocket for the cross I'd found in the woods and looked at it again. It wasn't my silver necklace after all; it didn't burn my skin and the chain was a lot longer, but it was close. I guessed it was a copy? Maybe Dulcie got it made for me, thinking I missed the other one. I fastened it around my neck and tucked it into my shirt collar.

Downstairs, Joe and Morgan were out on the porch. Morgan had her thumbs through the belt loops of her jeans and was tonelessly whistling, looking out over the driveway and lawn. Joe turned as I came out the door, looking relieved. "I gave Morgan the number here, if you get in any trouble."

"Well thanks, hopefully we won't."

"Yeah, you never know. I'd say to tell them I sent you, but I'd guess you know how that would go." Joe grinned ruefully. Morgan was already off the porch and swinging into the driver's seat.

I wanted to ask about the picture. I didn't ask about the picture. "Anyway, thanks a lot for your help, really. Maybe we'll see you again, in better circumstances."

"Yeah, maybe." Morgan leaned on the horn, which made all the dogs start barking again, coming out from wherever they'd gone, and I rolled my eyes and crossed the driveway to get in the Jeep.

Chapter Eleven

Morgan didn't talk much on the drive. I knew enough to recognize it as cause for worry. "So what's the plan?" I asked.

"We're assuming they know something," she said.

"Yes, assuming that."

"And that they'll share it."

"Yeah. They don't have any reason to, but they might just decide to go ahead and bury the hatchet anyway, right?" I asked hopefully. Morgan gave me a sidelong glance. "It isn't outside the realm of possibility."

"I guess not." She didn't sound convinced in any way. At least she put on music after that; it was already a tense time in the jeep.

"Joe was nice."

"Sure he was."

The Bear's Den was a low slung building with a long, narrow parking lot. I could hear the hum of the air conditioning and I could also smell the beer, booze, and smoke from the place. The parking lot was full of trucks and motorcycles, and some sports cars. Morgan jerked her thumb at a black pickup with tinted windows; the license plate read ALPHA. "He's here, anyway. Maybe we should just be glad he doesn't have truck nuts too."

"Is that...is that a thing?"

"You can't tell me you've never seen that." I just shrugged. Maybe that was what some of the boys at school had on their tow hitches. It wasn't like I ever got close, or asked.

We got to the door, which had a sign on it that said something about members, and Morgan waltzed right inside. I followed, and could hardly see once the door closed behind us. The light was dim, and there was smoke in the air. A hulking, shaven-headed guy stepped up to Morgan. "Sorry, miss, this is a membership club."

"I'm here to see Bill Ward."

"Are you a guest of his?"

"Of course. He'll be real happy to see me. Us." The big guy looked at Morgan for about a full minute, and she looked right back at him unwavering. Then he looked at me. If I had to guess, I'd say my face was what gave us away.

"I'm sorry, I need to ask you to leave." No amount of Morgan's protests, long or loud or vulgar, changed his mind, and he didn't throw us out so much as herd us back out the door, walking until we had no choice but to back up. He was bigger than both of us put together, and nothing he did was what even Morgan could consider provocation. When the door banged shut behind us, I could hear the other patrons laugh and give a cheer. I'm sure he was very proud of himself.

"Motherfucker," Morgan muttered, and stalked back to the Jeep. She pulled open the back and leaned in to rummage.

"What now?"

"What do men like that respect?" She pulled out a collapsed down microphone stand, made a face, shoved it back.

"God, now we're playing riddles? I don't know."

"Strength and balls." She finally straightened up, handed me a dented aluminum baseball bat, and inspected the hooked end of a tire iron.

"Morgan, what are you doing?" She slammed the back of the Jeep closed.

"It's either the perfect move, or it's really Goddamn stupid." It was hard to keep up with her as she strode towards ALPHA truck.

"Oh, Morgan, it's really stupid. We're going to get arrested. At least."

"They won't call the police." Morgan let loose with a long, unearthly howl, took a hop step and smashed the truck's rear windshield with the tire iron. The alarm started whooping, and Morgan whooped along with it as the horn honked, and the lights flashed. She was *so* loud, even with the alarm. She turned, dropping the tire iron on the cracked pavement with a crunchy clatter as she opened her arms to the five guys that came slamming out of the door to the Bear's Den. They moved too fast for me to see if they looked like Wards, and I guessed that was confirmation in itself.

The first one to reach her was a match for height, and Morgan did the same hop step and rode the momentum down into the guy's nose with her right fist. He yelled in surprise and grabbed his face, blood dripping through his fingers. She grinned and drew her work booted foot back to stomp on the top of the next guy's knee. I took a half-hearted swing with the baseball bat, mostly just to keep two of them away from me. I couldn't imagine hitting a person with a baseball bat, even scared in a strange parking lot. They laughed at me, and I suddenly remembered Kyle's voice, hateful and taunting: "Don't you like boys, Allie? You'll like me."

My vision went swimmy and I was terrified I was going to change there in the parking lot in broad daylight. I flung the bat at the Wards' feet and backed into the tailgate of the truck, only a few feet away from Morgan, my hands up and out.

"Enough." The voice was deep, and left no room for argument, thrumming in my ears. The men stopped. I looked over at Morgan, who was still grinning, despite a busted lip. She had her hands up too, but when she did it, it looked less like surrender and more like she was still ready to swing.

Bill Ward was middling height and barrel-chested, his brown hair thinning and graying, his brown eyes hard. He crossed the parking lot and stared first into my face, then Morgan's. "What in the actual fuck do you think you're doing?" he asked in a much lower tone, not growling, not really, but the suggestion of a growl. The skin along my spine shuddered.

"More polite channels were not effective, sir," Morgan said.

"Joe said you were civil," he said with something like disappointment.

"Joe's behavior let us just all be civil. Your guard dog here did not." Bill looked from Morgan to me again.

"What makes you think we'll help with Culver troubles? Especially after this stunt."

"Whoever took them intended for us to blame you, and for us to kill each other while the trail ran cold."

"And damaging my property is in no way further incitement?"

"Well like I said, we tried to play nice. Made you come outside, didn't I?"

Morgan was still grinning and I was still scared, in a cold sweat. Then, impossibly, Bill laughed. "You've got some balls," he said. Morgan's eyes flicked to mine a moment. "Well, come on then, let's talk about this."

I expected the five young men with him to protest, especially the ones Morgan hurt. In addition to Nose and Knee, there was a third with a black eye, holding his left elbow. But no, it seemed like Bill's word was all they needed.

The bouncer eyed me and Morgan as we came back through the door, but Bill waved him off and we passed through the main bar to another room. There were tables and chairs enough for everybody, and one of the guys closed the door behind us, shutting out the rest of the bar noise. Another still sat there nursing his beer, looking like he never even moved when the room cleared. He didn't look *happy* about it, maybe he'd been told to stay put. He was much younger than Bill, seemed rangier. He handed a wad of napkins to the one with the broken nose, who started to mop up the blood, glancing occasionally at Morgan. I got the sense that these guys weren't used to taking what they handed out.

"Luke, this is…" Bill gestured at us.

"Morgan and Allie Culver," Morgan supplied.

He didn't even say a word, just nodded and watched. I liked the look of him even less than Bill. He was one like Morgan, just barely on this side of civilized.

"All right, so lay it out for me," Bill said, and Morgan told the story. He had a way of concentrating when he listened that made everything seem very focused. When she was done, he sighed and sat back. "I don't see the point."

"The point of what?"

"Why anybody would do that. Plus, I'm surprised your Rachel didn't take at least a couple down with her. Nobody sets foot in those pines without the ladies in residence knowing."

"Honestly, it's so out of the blue that I haven't got a single answer," Morgan said. "Your truck was the best information we had."

"That truck's been gone three months. Stolen right from the Legion lot, nobody has respect anymore."

"But you followed up on it," I said, surprising even myself. It just didn't seem to me like Bill was telling the truth. Bill and Luke both looked at me. I couldn't tell if they were father and son or cousins or what, and I couldn't tell whose sons I'd say the others in the room were. "It seems impossible that you wouldn't."

"We did," Bill said after a minute.

"And what'd you find?" Morgan asked.

"Well, I guess that's above your pay grade, little lady," Luke said with a slow grin. Morgan's eyes and mouth hardened.

"Oh that's bullshit," I said, before she could curl up her fists and start in like that again. That wasn't a fight we could win, and I didn't know if that thought would cross her mind. Or stop her. Out of the corner of my eye, I could see Morgan tilt her head to look at me, but I looked at Bill. "You'd rather make her mad than help us out? What about when they come for you? There seem to be far more of you Wards than there are of Culvers."

"Exactly. There are more of us." Where Bill's voice had a low thunder, Luke's had an icy sharpness. I met his gaze, and held it for longer than I thought I could, then sniffed.

"Meaning you have a lot more to lose, all that family."

"We've got more defense. More training too, I'd say." Luke was still smiling unpleasantly, and really, I felt the Morgan impulse to hit him. He was daring me to. Daring us to.

I sighed, looked from Luke to Bill, and their faces were closed books. "Well fine. You can sit in your bar and drink your beer and when they come for you too, you won't ever expect it because you're too damn prideful to listen. You'll pay for that pride. If you get there in time, you'll watch the roof on that nice house fall in, and find your living room full of blood, just like us, your dogs run off. Your people taken." I turned to stalk off. The glitter was back in Morgan's eyes, and I was so glad. For the first time, I felt like I had access to that anger, that predatory handle on myself. It was a big, powerful feeling, and it was exhilarating and it was scary and if I had to hit anybody right now I was going to cry.

"It isn't like you're bringing anything to the table," Bill said.

He was right, but that wasn't what I was looking for. "I'd've thought a Navy man would have more sense than that, but I guess a grudge is worth more to you. It's fine, we'll just go down through the line in Rachel's connections and make sure to tell every last one of them that the Wards didn't want any part of this. That they preferred to sit at home and let everybody else do the work. We'll let the Coutards know that you knew what was going on and didn't care because it wasn't at your door." I wouldn't say that one of those strapping young men growled at me, exactly, but the sentiment was there.

"I don't know if you know what you're getting yourself into." Bill Ward was getting a little bit red in the face. Luke still sat and watched, his feet up on the chair next to him, but his smile wasn't so smug anymore.

"I'm sure there's somebody else who'll help us out and be happier for it. I guess you don't know anything anyway. You probably can't help us even if you wanted to, sorry for wasting your time." I turned on my heel, turned my back on them even as every instinct told me this would make me so vulnerable to them, and I hoped that Morgan would follow me. She did.

"You got a lot of gall coming here," Luke said as we reached the door. I paused, my hand on the handle. Nobody else but me and Morgan had moved. "With a pretty big ask."

"It isn't just for us. Like Allie said, you can't imagine they're just going to stop with the Culvers. Once one of our families is in danger, we're all in danger," Morgan said. I was glad she had, because I didn't know what else to say. I wasn't exactly prepared to call these men out on all their macho bullshit, taunt them into behaving the way it seemed like they should. "If they know about us, with the low profile we keep, they've gotta know about you. I mean, at the very least you can get your truck back, because if they have your truck, they have all kinds of stuff on you. Fingerprints, hairs, DNA. Loose change. Those are your nickels, gentlemen." I wished she'd stopped at DNA.

We looked at the gathered Wards expectantly. One of Luke's nostrils twitched, and after a moment, Bill guffawed. Maybe the nickels part was all right after all. "Is it hard work, being this Goddamn smart all the time?" Bill asked.

"It is my cross to bear, but I try to do so with dignity," Morgan said.

Bill settled back in his chair and picked up a half-burnt cigar that rested in an ashtray in front of him. "So all right then, let's say you're in the boys' club for now, and at the very least, we get our truck back. You get your kin back, we have a truce. We're getting pretty entangled here, wouldn't you say?"

"Worse deals have been made." Morgan shrugged.

"True enough. Let's get a pitcher and talk about this."

Morgan was more than all right with the pitcher of beer showing up. I took a glass to be sociable, and maybe to help calm my nerves. People said that's what alcohol did; it's clearly what Mama thought it did, when she gave me that brandy. The hair on my neck still stood up a little, between imagining Kyle's voice from that night, and the booming thunder in Bill Ward's voice. I wanted to go lock myself in the bathroom, but I doubted they had a ladies' room. Or locks. The bitterness of the beer stuck in the back of my throat, and I drank my first glass quickly to keep from having to taste it too much. Somebody refilled it.

There was some small talk, that Morgan and I mostly listened to. I could see Morgan getting impatient, fidgeting her glass on the table, shifting her feet. Luke watched us, waiting for a mistake. I drank my second beer and then just held the empty glass. Morgan was on her third or more.

"Silvernail," Bill finally said.

"What does that mean?" Morgan asked.

"That's who's been messing around. Stealing cars. Surveying properties. Another family, in Maryland, saw them and ran them off. Somebody in South Carolina lost a car, and the dog in it. They hadn't initiated engagement yet."

"So you were just going to let them keep going and not tell anybody else?"

"It's a pretty big corporation, with a private security force, and their fingers in a whole lot of pies. Medical research. Pharmaceuticals, mostly. That branch makes the most money, and has the most lobbyists."

Morgan snorted a laugh. "You're saying Big Pharma kidnapped our family? That's a little bit out there, don't you think?"

"We're genetic freaks with our own rules. You gotta figure Big Somebody was going to notice."

She glanced at me, and I could almost hear her, loud and clear, thinking: *like the military you all keep enlisting in?* "I just don't know what they'd get out of it. We're either people, or wolves, from one minute to the next."

"Hell if I know. Stem cells, cloning, gene therapy, none of it makes sense to me. They might announce tomorrow that they've figured out how to cure cancer with sloth claws." Bill finished his beer and set the mug down on the table. I watched the thin suds slide down the glass and realized I was a little tipsy and just felt dread in the pit of my stomach.

"We ought to get back," Luke said, standing.

Bill looked at him, at his watch, and then at us. "You going to come to the campground, or get a motel room?"

"Campground for now, I guess. It hasn't mattered to us yet." Morgan rattled her keys in her pocket and tilted her head at me. I nodded. "We'll follow you there."

I added, "Thank you." I stood up, and though things were kind of blurry at the edges, I was all right. It wasn't like the night of the party.

We walked out to the Jeep; Morgan picked up her baseball bat and tire iron along the way. "You're okay to drive?"

"Yeah. That was practically water." She glanced at me, smirked a little.

"Think there's any hard feelings?" I asked once we were on the road behind the ALPHA truck, another pickup behind us.

Morgan shrugged. "Maybe the one whose nose I broke. Or the kneecap, though I think that was just a bad bruising."

"That was pretty impressive, really."

"Thanks." She paused. "We need to figure out what you're going to do."

"What do you mean?"

"Well, we don't have time for the training montage; if you don't have the stomach to fight, you need to either get over yourself, or figure something else out."

"Hey, I helped back there." I was so surprised I almost burst into tears.

"Yeah, your winning smile and can do attitude will pave your way for a career as a Wal-Mart greeter. If Bill hadn't stopped them, I probably couldn't have handled all five, and then it's not just you in deep shit, it's me too. And I don't like that."

"Well sorry if my life hasn't been a regime of warrior princess training and larceny."

Morgan glanced at me. "I know it makes you feel superior or whatever to think of me as a criminal, but we're talking about survival here. It isn't safe for anybody if you're just a liability."

"Well, then why did you bring me at all, if you're so good all by yourself? You were great at winning the Wards over, that's for sure."

"Frankly, I thought you'd be more useful. Can you see what I'm getting at? At least a little?"

"I guess." Ahead, Bill made a turnoff, and Morgan followed him up a gravel road, through woods so thick and green I couldn't read the big wooden sign we passed. State forest maybe or a mountainside campground or something. "You know I'm new at this."

"I do, and it's not your fault. But it would've been useful if your mama had at least gotten you tai chi lessons or something."

"She didn't want this for me."

"No, but it's what you've got, and it seems she dropped you soon enough after she was sure of it."

I really wanted to be mad at Morgan for this; she didn't know Mama. But she was right, and I was so mad at Mama that thinking about her just made me sick. She gave me pills and kept me in the dark, and when it turned out that didn't work out, she got rid of me. Rachel would have gotten to teaching me everything soon enough, but somebody got Rachel first.

"What should I do, then?" I asked. "Ask the Wards for pointers?"

The truck ahead of us pulled into a gravel parking area and stopped in front of a sprawling two story log cabin. Morgan looked at me and laughed. "No, we don't want them knowing any more about us than we have to. I'll give you a crash course, after we know more, and when we're not surrounded by another camp. Plus, your beers could stand to wear off."

She opened her door and got out. I started to protest that I was just fine, and almost fell out of the Jeep when I missed the bar to step down. Morgan watched me, lips pressed together, not laughing out loud for once. "Yeah, we should wait," I agreed, my stomach swimmy and nervous.

Chapter Twelve

We came around the side of the cabin in the falling dark, and the Wards who hadn't gone to the Bear's Den had a fire going outside. There was more beer, and I could smell burgers and hot dogs. My clearly confused stomach muttered, and I saw Morgan's head move a little towards me. If she heard me, they heard me, and I flushed a little. I didn't want to look like a dope in front of the werewolf cool kids, and a lot rode on appearances, clearly.

Bill kind of waved us towards seats by the fire, and went inside the cabin. The guy with the broken nose didn't look to be there. Luke settled in across the fire from us, and I could see the looks that the Wards already here gave him. There seemed like a whole lot of them at first, but counting, there were really only five or six more. I took the beer that was handed to me, for something to hold. More beer was really the last thing I needed or wanted.

The Wards weren't threatening us, but they were dangerous; even I could tell that. They watched us with their dark eyes, and they all moved like killers. After a while, conversation began to crop up again, a lot of it braggy, none of it directed at us. Morgan bore it well enough for a little while, and then I could feel her getting twitchy. I had an idea that Bill did it on purpose, to keep us off balance, let us know that we weren't just one of the gang. He came back out of the cabin before Morgan acted on any of the thoughts that she might have been formulating, though. I guess he didn't want any more broken noses.

"Our people watching the Silvernail compound said that there were a lot of vans that came in and drove right into the garages. That could be your people."

"Oh, it's a compound now?" Morgan asked. "That you have people what, already surveilling?"

"Well. I'm sure they call it a campus. But it's got ten foot fences, razor wire, and as I said, a security force. That says compound to me."

"Okay, all right, it's a compound. Now what?"

Bill looked at her a moment, then me. "We're seeing about whether we can compromise their surveillance network, get a peek inside. We get confirmation it's your people, we'll go in."

"What, you've got a hacker?" I asked. I wanted to laugh; this was too ridiculous.

Bill wasn't laughing, though. "We have people involved in cybersecurity, yes."

"You've got quite the private security force of your own," Morgan said. I saw Luke shift a little, in the flicker of firelight.

"Comes with the territory, little lady, you know that."

"That I do," she said, smiling, looking relaxed. "Easier for strapping men like yourselves to throw a lot of sons and just go gather 'em up when you're ready. Next time any of you calls me little lady, we're going to get a good look at that quality versus quantity argument." She really had masterful control of her voice.

"So now we wait?" I interrupted. Luke's face was getting a little red, sure, but he deserved that.

"We wait. We drink. We eat. You want to get a motel, you can. It doesn't really matter." Meaning, you can get out of here if you want. We might help you. Or not. They already had people watching. They made us argue with them at that bar for nothing. I wasn't used to being this angry, and didn't know what I was supposed to do with it.

"How long?" Morgan asked. She very pointedly wasn't looking at me.

"No telling." Probably why they offered us the motel option earlier, but Morgan wouldn't see it like that.

"I guess we'll just wait, then, if that's okay with you, Allie." She looked at me then like she cared about my opinion, and I nodded.

"Seems like sticking around is best," I said.

As the evening wore on, we both drank more beers, had burgers and hot dogs, made idle conversation with each other, since nobody else would. Mostly she just told me rock star stories and true or not, I couldn't say. Once she got talking about music and bands, though, she'd ramble along on her own and even once in a while stop to explain something. There wasn't a whole lot of talking amongst the Wards, just a lot of eyes around the firelight. Morgan took it all in stride; she had achieved some sort of werewolf serenity. She returned stares with the ghost of a smile, utterly calm yet also radiating violent intent. She had smashed one face in this evening, and was perfectly willing to do so again; indeed, she might be disappointed if such an event did not occur. Other than Luke, nobody stared at her for long. It was clear they weren't threatened at all by me, even I could see that, but Morgan was a wild card.

I was starting to get drowsy when Bill came back outside "You ladies settling in all right?" he asked me.

"Fine, thanks. Everybody's just making us feel so welcome," I said with a smile. I saw a couple of frowns from the guys who had been ignoring us so pointedly, but Morgan smiled too, and I felt the thrill of her approval.

"Well now that's good to hear," Bill said, after a very slight pause. He knew what I meant. "Don't want you telling anybody we treated you poorly." He gestured to Luke, and headed back to the cabin.

"Behave, children," Luke said, and followed.

There were a few minutes of no conversation, silence broken by the crackling of the fire, and one of the guys got up. He was the one who'd gotten a specially crafted black eye from Morgan, and he addressed the group "I'm getting another beer, anybody else want one?"

"Yeah," Morgan said.

"Soda, if you've got it," I said, the first time I felt like I could speak up since getting here. I never wanted any beer in the first place.

I could only assume these guys were all cousins, though I guess some had to be brothers. Drinks guy game back, and handed us the wet cans. "I'm Zeb. You made quite the entrance, I'll give you that."

"It's our winning smiles and our can-do attitude," Morgan said.

"Right. You like these girls' winning smiles, Zeb?" another Ward asked as he pulled over a chair.

"I was more of a fan of the can-do attitude," he said, winking at Morgan and sitting down with the group of us.

Morgan popped the tab on her beer, sucked the foam. "I'm not sure everybody was."

"Aw, Brett broke his nose before. No big deal," Zeb shrugged. I wondered if Zeb was short for Zebediah and whose mother in good conscience named their child that in this day and age. Or maybe it was Zebulon. "And Neil here just gets prettier the more beat up he gets, he'll have a new girlfriend in a week, you mark me."

"What about the other one?"

"Ah, Mark. Since he isn't back yet, I'd guess you jacked his knee up pretty good."

"Sorry," Morgan said, sounding the least sorry of anybody I've ever heard.

"Hey at least you didn't take any of us apart with that bat," Zeb said to me, I guess trying to include me in the banter. I'd been more than happy to just watch and listen, try and soak up the postures, the subtleties that everybody knew already and took for granted.

I shrugged, smiling nervously. "Morgan handed it to me. I didn't really know what she was going to do."

"To be fair, I thought it was pretty clear what I was going to do," Morgan said.

"Well, if you'd clued me in, it would've been nice." I could hear the whine in my voice but didn't know any good way to stop it.

"Yeah, probably. Maybe you would've done something." We looked at each other for a long moment. Morgan wanted me to take a swing, and I really didn't know why. So I waited.

"I think she is more given to gentler diplomatic negotiations," Zeb observed, finishing his beer.

"Her mama gave her sort of a different upbringing," Morgan said with a sniff. After a pause, the conversation moved on. A lot of talking went on after that, none of it useful. Everybody but me had been raised with the full knowledge of their wolf nature. It seemed like if they knew I was a newcomer, it would affect the delicate situation we had formed. So I kept quiet, drank far too much soda, ate just enough hot dogs, and after a while, went to the Jeep to nap in the backseat. After that much time, I figured Morgan would be fine, and there would be no fighting. Or I was too tired to worry about keeping Morgan from fighting anymore.

I bunched my jacket up as a pillow and tried to get comfortable. For a little while, I listened to people walk around and talk, and Morgan's knife edged laugh reached me more than once, and then the dream I slipped into was both memory and a dream, and I didn't know where the lines were.

I was at a party at the school, out behind the football field, and it was getting on towards nighttime. This wasn't exactly a school sanctioned event, but nobody was going to stop the football players from having a party after a winning game; the football players had another status entirely from the rest of the school. A lot of the girls were cheerleaders. It was a small enough kind of school where everybody knew everybody, though I forgot who even invited me. I was just so stupidly grateful that they would, instead of ignoring me, or taunting me for being the homeschool Jesus freak. Somebody stepped up kind of close behind me, and I turned, poised to drop my beer can behind the fence I'd climbed up on to sit, like I wasn't already caught if it was Mama and I'd never be able to set foot on this school property again.

It was Kyle Dodd, the star quarterback, the one 'going places', already scouted, already had a scholarship to a big football school. Maybe a shot at the pros, because that was the kind of thing they always said. He took my glance as an invitation and leaned against the fence.

"I think I saw Christie over by the coolers," I said, my tone honed to drive him off, not invite him to stay. He grinned at me, though, the sunset light in his prom king, golden boy baby blues.

"Yeah, she probably is. It's too bad we couldn't get a keg for this; maybe if we have it at my place next time." He looked at me a little too long, and I finished my beer and hopped off the fence, scanning the crowd for the garbage bag we'd been throwing them in. Kyle started walking with me.

"Yeah, maybe a keg would've been good," I said, because it seemed like the only thing to say. There were a lot of cans in the garbage bag, and another bag already full and tied up in the back of somebody's pickup. I didn't even really like beer, but if you didn't have one at a party like that, people got after you. I didn't make it to parties often, Mama saw to that, and even though I didn't like beer I felt like I should drink a couple. So I could be cool too. I stopped short to avoid a thrown football, and Kyle walked into me.

"Look, Kyle, back off." Nobody really paid attention to us; most of them had been here and drinking for a while. Somebody had all the car keys collected in a plastic fishing bucket, I knew, and everybody would clear out in time to go to church with their parents tomorrow morning at ten, probably hungover but kids would be kids, right? It wasn't like I had a long way to go home, just through the woods and I was there. "I'm going home. Leave me alone." I couldn't imagine why I had drawn Kyle's attention like this, all the sudden. I wondered if he was more than drunk, though; his eyes were oddly dilated. He wore his varsity jacket, and his hair was artfully ruffled with a combination of gel and helmet head.

"Come on, Allie. You never go with anybody at school. Why don't you give me a chance?" He was wheedling me like a dog that was reluctant to be patted. I drew out of my comfortable slouch to my full height and glared down at him with anything but invitation. He hesitated a moment, surprised to be shorter than me, I thought. I stayed several steps ahead of him after that. I guess I should have been more wary, called Mama for a ride or something. But really, I was more worried about what Mama would say if she knew I was at a drinking party behind the high school. Everybody knew everybody here, so it didn't really occur to me to not just enter the woods and march home. What was going to happen? He'd give up sooner or later. Ignore him and he'll go away, right?

He didn't say anything for a little while, and I tried to gauge how far he'd follow me. The neighbor's dogs hadn't started barking yet, so we weren't quite halfway there when I heard the thumping on the path of his running steps before he slammed into me. I face-planted in the dirt, the wind knocked out of me in a painful rush, and he got a handful of my hair before I bucked up to my knees, twisted, and tried to hit him in the mouth, in the face, anywhere to make him stop. He yanked my hair, jerking my head around, and punched me. I struggled up again and he hit me again, harder, and I was dazed for a moment. He knelt over me, and I heard the jangle of his belt buckle, and then he reached down for the button on my jeans. "Don't you like boys, Allie? I know you'll like me. I'll help you out," he whispered against my ear, his breath beery and hot, and got my zipper down.

In a haze of pain, I tasted blood and dirt, and I could smell the green woods around us, and his Axe body spray, and the leather of his varsity coat. I could hear my heartbeat, and then I could hear his. My hands didn't work anymore; I wanted to ball them into fists again, or spread them out to scratch his face or jam a thumb in his eye. But I didn't have fingers anymore. And his hand wasn't in my long hair anymore, because I didn't have it. My legs tangled in my jeans, and I thrashed once, twice, to get out of them and my underwear, t-shirt clinging to my shoulders and rib cage, and head slung low, I pulled my lips back from my long gleaming canines, and I growled, deep in my chest.

Kyle's face changed, and he scrambled back from me, almost on his feet already, looking down in terror. Remembering and dreaming, I wasn't thinking at all, just acting on instinct. I ran at him and hit him with my shoulder, took his ankle in my long jaws, twisted. I heard his knee pop. He put his arm out, and I bit that too, feeling the bones creak and then crack between my big back teeth. I pulled him off of his feet, and he glanced his face off of a big gnarled tree root coming down. He lay still and I dropped his arm and backed off, scared and confused. He might get up. I was going to get in trouble. I didn't even pick a direction, I just ran.

A hand closed on my shoulder, and I jerked away so far and fast that I hit my head against one of the front seats of the Jeep. I squinted at Morgan, who was looking at me with a narrow concentration that I'd never seen on her face before. "I was dreaming," I said after a moment, when my heart had stopped jackhammering in my ears, and my mouth wasn't so dry.

"I can see that." She stepped back, leaving the door hanging open, and I sat on the edge of the backseat with my feet out on the running board, grasped at the cross around my neck, breathing short and sharp through my nose. She didn't say anything for long enough that I had to ask.

"Did you need something?"

"Just wanted to tell you that Bill heard back from his spy team, or hackers or whateverthefuck."

"Did he? Was it good news?" I rubbed my eyes. The back of my neck still felt all prickly.

"They're not in New Jersey, but they might be in Pennsylvania or Georgia."

"Georgia's kind of far, isn't it? That's a few more state lines to cross than I'd think a kidnapping team would, even if it does work for Big Pharma."

"Georgia is where the CDC headquarters are."

"That could be bad." I couldn't formulate all the reasons why, but she nodded.

"It could."

"We're hoping it's Pennsylvania then."

"Yup, that we are."

I looked past Morgan towards the campfire, where the Wards stood in groups now talking, instead of sitting in lawn chairs drinking beers. "What would anybody like that want with us, anyway? I mean, okay, we're freaks, but how do you make medicine off of that?"

"Truth is, people will pay for products that make them what they aren't. Imagine if you could choose to be a werewolf. And anyway, people pay all kinds of money for medicine that doesn't really work."

"I guess." I hadn't chosen this and I couldn't honestly say it was going so good just now. I was happy it'd stopped me from getting hurt, but that didn't mean I didn't have all kinds of complicated feelings about it. Trauma? I guess trauma.

"You okay now? Do you want to talk about it?" She surprised me, but Morgan was looking at me in all seriousness. But no, I didn't want to talk about it yet, and I was pretty sure she wanted me to say no anyway.

"Let's just go see what's going on, so they don't get started without us."

Morgan shrugged. "Okay, If you say so."

Chapter Thirteen

Inside of the cabin, we were led into what was a scarily complete war room. No way they set this up just tonight. There was a state map and then county maps on the table and walls. There was another short wave radio on a table in the corner, with big headphones and a composition book next to it. The pencil had been thoroughly chewed and the eraser was gone. The Wards were gathered around the topographical map of Pennsylvania, and a red circle had been drawn around where the Silvernail compound was. Another small miracle, they'd waited for me and Morgan to come in before starting.

"There's only so much I'm going to bore all of you with tactics. There is a chance that the targets we're looking for are here, but we aren't sure. They've got their security system on an offline, closed circuit system, so we can't hack into that from the outside. There's a security force on property, with shifts of ten on at once, five pairs, three of which are patrols, two of which are on entrances. They do not have dogs at this location, though they do at others. This is a no-visitors facility, so there's no reception area, no guest parking. Only people with passes get through the gate." Bill put his hand out, and one of the guys put some papers in his hands. He glanced at them and tossed one onto the table. "This spot is where the perimeter is the closest to the wood line. There is a hill that looks down, and there are no residences or other habitable buildings in a ten mile radius. There is a camera here as well, of course, but one well-placed person can take it out, and get enough people over the fence before the patrols scramble. We'll put people on hills with rifles here, here, and here." He pointed to the map.

Bill dropped another page on the table. "Now, this is a little outside our realm of experience just yet, but they're trying out drone patrols at this location. I don't know how quiet they are, but they're decently sized, rapidly moving targets that we need to take out quick as we're able. Now, I'm guessing the Culvers won't just go with anybody at this point, so Morgan, we're taking you in. Allie, can you handle a rifle?" All eyes were on us for a moment, calculating.

"I can," I said. Bill held my gaze for a moment and I didn't waver. I *could* handle a rifle. I'd hunted with Daddy, and done skeet shooting at the range. Done my hunter safety courses. Bill nodded.

"All right, then." The next page on the table. "These are blueprints from when Silvernail put this compound up. We think that any people they would be holding would be in these medical bays, here, probably drugged to their eyeballs. We might need to be prepared to carry out more than the three we're going in for. We leave nobody behind, dead or alive, understand? Over the fence, while we hit the building a group cuts a hole there for the return trip. In, find your people, get out, get back to the vehicles. We scramble in different directions, rendezvous at this location." He tapped another place on the map, miles away from the compound. "Nobody, and I repeat nobody, goes feral in view of that facility." Bill looked around at each of us in turn. "Questions? Concerns?"

Morgan didn't say anything, so I didn't either. I didn't know what I could ask that wouldn't make me look a fool. There was more talk, planning the route each vehicle would take to get there, satellite photos of where to park, where to meet on the perimeter. Then the guns were being handed out, to those who didn't have them. Morgan put her hand on my arm. "We got our own," she said. That's right. The duffle in back of the Jeep.

"Get some rest everybody, we're up at dawn to get a move on, and we do this tomorrow night." Bill turned to Morgan and I. "We're a full house here, but if you want to stay the night at the Motor Inn, back off the road there, we'll meet you in the parking lot before heading out."

Morgan nodded. "Sounds good, a bed would be nice." She grabbed another beer on our way out, and carried it, unopened to the Jeep. "Nightcap," she said with a grin when I quirked an eyebrow at her. That I could tell, nobody spared us a glance as we pulled away.

"I wonder if they'll actually stop by for us in the morning," I said.

"They will. If I'm one of the people going in, that's one less man Bill has to risk. If you're on a hill with a rifle, that's another one of his men he gets to keep safe. Added bonus that it isn't one of his guns either. That, and he's right; Rachel won't go with just anybody, jailbreak or not. None of them would, not even Dulcie, and she's the nicest one of us. To the perimeter of the property, maybe, but trusting people doesn't exactly get us too far."

"I thought he was just humoring us."

"Probably. But, we got them to admit they were already interested. I'm just not sure if they're invested enough to carry this past Pennsylvania, if need be."

"Let's hope they are." We turned into the Motor Inn parking lot.

Morgan shrugged. "If they're not, they're not. I'm sure there's somebody in Georgia we can win over, if need be. We'll be Goddamn werewolf ambassadors to get this done, you seem good at that." I wondered if she'd somehow forgotten the Wal-Mart greeter crack, but Morgan was already out of the Jeep, stomping her feet to straighten the legs of her jeans, and we walked into the too-bright reception area of the Motor Inn.

After hours by a campfire, and then some time in an old cabin that was lit with comfortable old yellow light bulbs, the fluorescent buzz and glare made me flinch. There was an antique Coke machine in the corner that made a regular thumping noise, and the clerk had a laptop open on the front desk with a wheezing, overworked fan. Morgan gave me a sidelong glance, but got our room booked without incident. I'm not sure the clerk even really talked, just kind of nodded and took our money and handed over the keys.

I shuddered in relief when we got back outside. Morgan threw me the hotel key and headed for the Jeep. "You having an episode, or what?"

"Everything just seemed so loud," I said. "Hey Morgan, does anybody ever change just a little bit? Like, instead of all out, just your ears or whatever?"

She pulled the clattering duffel bag out of the back of the Jeep and shoved it in my hands, then reached in and got the bundled quilt and books. "Can't say that I've heard it discussed."

"Have you ever tried it?"

"What, and end up looking like some anime wolf girl? No, I haven't tried it." She closed the Jeep up and locked it, then led the way to the room. I followed, and looked around while Morgan unlocked the door. Nobody else was around, though there was a light on far down at the end of the line, with an old Volvo station wagon parked in front of that room. It occurred to me that I'd never slept in a motel or a hotel; until a few months ago, I'd only ever slept in my bed at home.

There was only one light, suspended above the little round table that was just inside the door. I was happy to find that it was a regular yellow light, not the fluorescents that were apparently going to plague the rest of my days. I closed the door behind us, locked it, and put the chain on, though I was pretty sure anybody could kick it down should they have the notion. I guess the chain would make it two kicks instead of one, and that was enough time for Morgan to wreck somebody, I was pretty sure.

"So, can you really handle a rifle, or were you just trying to look good for the boys' club back there?" she asked, taking the bag from me, setting it on the bed, and unzipping it.

"I already told you I could shoot. It's something Daddy did at the range for fun, and we went hunting. There's an open season on boars a couple times a year, because there's so many of them."

"I didn't think you were that good a liar, but I figured I'd check." Morgan pulled a shotgun out of the bag and laid it on the bed. Then she pulled out a rifle that she handed to me. "This one good?"

I looked at the window; the shade was already drawn. I put the rifle to my shoulder and sighted down into the bathroom. "Yeah, should be fine."

"Cleaning kit's in the bag, if you're so inclined." There were two double beds in the room, and Morgan flopped on the one closer to the bathroom, boots still on, and picked up the remote. "Hey, Dog the Bounty Hunter is on."

"I don't know what that is."

"What? Well you're in for a treat. It's garbage television, but when you grow up without TV..." Morgan grinned at me, and cracked open the beer she'd brought, licking the foam off of her thumb. I just shook my head, and looked in the bag. There were boxes of rounds, a cleaning kit, a zipped up bank pouch, and two more shotguns. A couple of hunting knives in leather sheaths. A first aid kit. "You're probably going to want to get some more sleep," Morgan remarked after a little while. On the television, the bounty hunter and his cadre had just surrounded a skinny guy in track pants, screaming at him, pepper spray out. The guy, holding a sandwich, looked confused.

"Yeah, probably." I sighed, and moved the stuff off of the bed, onto the chair. I pulled off my boots and dropped them on the floor, followed by my socks. "I'm going to take a shower first."

"Go ahead."

I dropped my clothes on the counter as I took them off. I didn't look forward to putting them right back on, but that t-shirt, bra, pair of underwear, and pair of jeans were all I had at the moment. I wasn't raised being casually naked; even alone, I wouldn't have slept without clothes. I waited until my reflection steamed itself off the mirror, then got into the shower, tiny bottles of shampoo and conditioner lining the edge. I washed up with the small thin washcloth and the individually wrapped bar of soap. My fingers brushed the cross again, and I sagged against the shower wall, overcome with the wave of grief that never quite hit me when Mama abandoned me. I cried hard, covering my open mouth with my other hand, hoping Morgan wouldn't hear me over the water.

When I was done, my fingers were pruney and my eyes felt hot and itchy. I squeezed my hair out over the tub and toweled myself dry before getting back into my clothes.

"I wouldn't mind going to the store at some point for, say, some underwear."

"Tomorrow. After we either get them back, or don't."

"Makes sense." I looked at Morgan for a moment, but she didn't take her eyes off of the screen, occasionally sipping the beer. I thought about asking her to turn down the volume, but once my head hit the pillow, sleep reached up and pulled me swiftly down. At some point, minutes or hours later, I opened my eyes and lifted my head a little; Morgan was still awake, and had a book in front of her. The television was off, and the air was damp, probably from her shower. I meant to ask her what she was doing, if she was going to sleep, but fell back asleep instead.

Thin gray light came through the edges around the curtains when I woke up. Morgan was flat on her back, her mouth open a little. The books were packed away, and all of the guns but the rifle, which was on the table by itself, in a nylon carrying case. I got up and went into the bathroom, trying to be quiet. I didn't have a toothbrush, so I brushed my teeth with my finger and some of the tiny complimentary toothpaste. I wet my hair down and braided it, then studied myself in the mirror for a moment; there hadn't been one at the house in the pines. I wish I exuded the predatory self confidence that Morgan did. I tried Morgan's "go to hell" grin, and then stifled a laugh. Yeah, not quite.

Morgan was sitting up in bed when I came out of the bathroom. "You ready?" she asked. "They'll be getting here soon."

"Ready as I'll ever be. I don't have any sense of where in Pennsylvania we're going, if it's just down the road apiece or like, an eight hour drive."

"Yeah. More bonding time." We both laughed.

I heard a truck pull up outside, headlights probing at our window shade. "I guess it's time." I opened the door right as Joe was about to knock.

"Uh. Morning," he said, blinking.

"Morning," I said. I was surprised to see him, but kind of happy actually. The first and nicest Ward we knew.

"We getting this show on the road?" Morgan asked, shouldering bags. I looked past Joe; Bill was in the driver's seat of the truck in the parking lot, and that was it.

"Yeah, I guess. You need to stop at a drive through or something?"

"Would be nice," Morgan said. "You want to return the room key?" she asked me. I nodded, and she pushed past me out the door with the bags. Joe looked after Morgan, then looked at me and shrugged. I pulled the door closed and walked towards the office; he fell into step with me.

"Any plan updates?" I asked.

"Not that I know of," he said, then hesitated. "You sure you want to do this?"

"Can you honestly ask that?"

"No, I guess not." The elephant in the room; I seemed different to the other wolves, but they couldn't quite put their finger on it. Though Joe seemed different from the other Wards, in a way I couldn't put my finger on. He was just the friendliest, maybe, the least big bad wolf among them. Maybe he'd make it easier for me to be around the lot of them.

There was a different clerk in the office, a middle aged bleach blonde who looked all revved up on coffee. She looked at me, looked at Joe, and gave me what she must have thought was a knowing smile. I half smiled back at her and slid the key across the counter.

"You kids have a good day now," she chirped.

I smiled; it was just nice when people were nice. "We will, thanks."

We got back outside and Joe laughed. "Oh boy."

"What? What's funny?"

He was blushing a little, starting at the tips of his ears, maybe utterly mortified, I couldn't tell. "Uh...well, that woman thought that you and I just. Spent the night together."

"*Oh*." Now I was mortified. I had no idea that's what she was getting at. How could I not know.

"I expect she sees a lot of that." He shoved his hands in his pockets, cutting his eyes away from me. "So there's something I'm going to tell you that's best coming from me. It isn't a secret, really, but. Yeah."

"Okay." I didn't really know what to say, or what to expect. Just absolutely understanding that anything Joe told me, yeah, obviously he'd prefer I not hear it from somebody like Luke.

"I'm trans," he said, looking up at me again.

"Okay." Well I didn't know much about that. "Thank you for telling me," I said. "Like, for trusting me. I'm sorry, I don't know what the right thing to say is but I don't mean anything bad."

"No, it's okay. There isn't a good guidebook anybody hands out." We both laughed. "And you can tell your sister, so there aren't any surprises from us or whatever."

"Cousin. And I will." I'm glad he said that, because I almost told him *my* secret, and probably shouldn't. Though now it didn't feel fair.

Morgan was standing at Bill's open window, but when she saw me coming, they nodded to one another and she went and swung up into the Jeep.

"See you when we get there. I'm your, uh, partner for your rifle position."

"Are you? Good, okay. See you there, then." I gave Bill a wave and got into the Jeep as well. Morgan had the radio on already, and she backed out of the spot as I buckled in.

"McDonald's okay?" she asked. "That's what me and Bill decided on." I'd only ever had illicit McDonald's before this all started. Mama couldn't stand it, said there were so many chemicals in everything. We had home cooking or we had church cooking, and that was pretty much it. Sometimes we got treated to something from the bakery in town.

"That's fine," I said. "I need coffee."

"Isn't that the truth." She checked for traffic before turning, looked at my face, looked again harder before pulling out. "What's up?"

"You act like I'm such an open book."

"Maybe to me you are. We've got that *bond.*" She slid her sunglasses on. "Spill. What did that Ward boy say to you? I thought it was Luke we had to worry about catching shit from, not—"

"Joe told me he's trans," I said. She stopped, cocked her head a little.

"What did you say?"

"That I didn't know what to say."

She laughed. "Oh, Allie."

"*What?* I didn't! I don't! I thanked him for telling me. He'd set it up with wanting to tell me so I didn't hear it from like, Luke. And said I should tell you. Oh, and he said sister and I corrected him without thinking about it."

"Well okay, you could've done worse. Was that your first time somebody came out to you?"

"Oh, was that so obvious too?" I asked, and she laughed again, but less mean than I expected.

"God, you are too pure for this world," she said. "Let's hope we all live through this."

Chapter Fourteen.

We followed Bill after the McDonald's stop. Morgan and I pretty much got a bag of sausage and biscuit breakfast sandwiches and gnawed on them periodically as the hours went by. Our coffees were done far too quickly, and around eleven, we stopped at a gas station and convenience store. The highway waxed and waned from two lanes to six and down again, and led us through more mountains, more woods.

Morgan swiped a credit card and left me to fill the Jeep's gas tank, stretching as she stalked across the parking lot and through the automatic glass doors. Bill parked at the pump opposite mine, and Joe hopped out and followed Morgan into the convenience store, and she turned a little to talk to him as they went through the automatic doors. The thick smell of gasoline coated the inside of my nostrils, and I sneezed three times, quickly.

"Bless you. Making good time," Bill observed as the gas started running into his tank. "We're almost there."

"I guess so," I said, eyes watering. I constantly tried to gauge how well I 'passed' and where I needed improvement. At least smelling like a wolf wasn't something that I could mess up. I rubbed my nose with my free hand and sniffed. Gasoline and oily asphalt. I pinched the bridge of my nose to head off another sneeze.

"Yup," Bill said. "Heard on the radio from the others, they're about on track too."

"Well that's good." My pump thunked, startling me. I took the receipt it spit out and shoved it in my pocket. Morgan had taken the keys with her, but it seemed rude to just walk away. "See you inside, I guess."

"Sure," he said. "Let me ask you something first, though."

Already headed, I paused and turned around. "Yes, sir?"

"How was it that you've turned up? None of our intel on the Culvers includes you." Bill smiled and kind of chewed at a stub of unlit cigar in his mouth. "Just idle curiosity, mind you. It's really none of my concern."

I smiled sweetly and kept my breathing nice and even. "I guess you just need to work on your intel." Morgan, bless her, came part way out of the store and waved at me. I guess I was taking too long for her taste. Or maybe they had special edition junk food that she hadn't tried yet.

"What did he want?" she asked me in barely a whisper as soon as I was right next to her.

"He asked where I came from. Said he has 'intel' on us."

"What'd you say?"

"That I guessed he needed to work on his intel." Morgan laughed and slugged me in the shoulder.

"You're not that good a liar, but you could be worse. Maybe I should take back the open book thing."

"Oh Morgan, you do say the sweetest things." We parted ways to use the restrooms and forage. I didn't have Morgan's apparently insatiable sweet tooth, and I tried to find what could be considered close to real food. The hot dogs in the display looked like something dug out of a grave, shriveled at both ends, charred in places. I was afraid to investigate the burgers. As a last ditch attempt, I grabbed some pepperoni twists out of another display, a Coke, and a bag of trail mix. I got to the register right as Morgan reached the front of the line, and put my stuff on the counter with hers. She had burritos, a giant coffee, and about seven individually wrapped banana moon pies. We paid and passed Bill and Joe in line; I hadn't noticed Bill come in.

"See you out there," Morgan said, holding up her coffee like it was toast time at a wedding. Bill tapped his Styrofoam cup against hers.

"Won't be long," he said, and winked at me.

"This is weird," I said once we were back in the Jeep.

"Yeah, it kind of is."

"No, I mean really weird. It just occurred to me to wonder why a guy like Bill would put his head in the sand over a problem like Silvernail, when he has all of that 'intel' on them. And so much to lose. Hell, we die before fifty; imagine if Big Pharma knows that there's another line that lasts longer and has a habit of being military trained?"

"You saying Big Pharma already knows about the Wards?" Bill and Joe crossed the parking lot, and Morgan put on a big grin and waved.

"I'm saying it's something we maybe should've thought of yesterday but it also might be nothing."

"Maybe we should've." Morgan unwrapped one of her burritos and had it finished before we were even out of the parking lot. "Except that we did. He had the police report for the stolen truck."

"But didn't tell us how he knew who'd stolen it."

"Maybe we shouldn't complicate things unnecessarily."

"Maybe we should watch our backs when they have us separated on enemy lines." I was less worried for me than for her.

"I hear you on that, cuz. I just need to keep thinking this is going to be a win situation. Otherwise, I don't really know what our next step is." It probably took a lot for her to admit that to me.

"I know." I bit into a pepperoni twist; it really wasn't bad. I couldn't think of what I thought pepperoni was made of. Beef? Pork?

"So I was reading a book I got from the Wards," Morgan said.

"They gave you a book? When did that happen?"

"Give might be a generous word for the actual series of events."

"Meaning…" I looked at her and she looked at the road. "Morgan did you steal it?"

"I may have liberated it from the first Ward household we visited, yes."

"Morgan."

"You just said, we have to watch out for ourselves! And if they've got all this 'intel' that they're hoarding like weirdo spies, then we have to get information out of them somehow, don't we?"

"I don't think you're going to get me to agree with you."

"What, are you gonna turn me in?"

"No." I thought a second. "Okay, well, I guess it depends on the book."

"Relax, it isn't super personal like Joe's baby book or any-thing. Actually, it's super weird, a lot of it's in code."

"What do you mean, code? We talking werewolf super spies now?"

Morgan looked at me for longer than was comfortable, seeing as how she was driving and all. "Word replacement code. Instead of words, there are sections that are strings of numbers instead. You have to look in the book that was the key, to figure it out."

"Oh. So another dead end then, perfect."

"Well, 'til we figure out the book they used. We've got a lot to choose from. Military survival manuals. And Rachel al-ways said that everything you needed to rebuild society was in the Foxfire books, so I tried it with both of those."

So that's what she was reading in the middle of the night. "Well?"

"Part of it was the survival manual and then it switched."

"So, any earth shattering insight into our horrible situa-tion here?"

"Not really. Which doesn't mean there isn't later. Or it means I didn't grab a useful enough book. I was trying to do it without Joe noticing, poor kid already didn't know what to do about us."

"I don't really know what to do about us, can you really blame Joe?"

"I guess not."

We were quiet again, for a long enough time that I needed to talk, even if it wasn't about anything. "You know, I've had more road trips this year than I had in my entire life," I re-marked. Morgan glanced at me and smiled.

"Really?"

"Yeah, really. We stayed close to home."

"Well I guess we did too, most of the time. I mean, until I ran away to be a rock star and went on tour."

"How'd that happen, anyway? Nobody seemed very mu-sical, at the house."

Morgan laughed. "What, you want to hear my rock star origin story?"

"I guess so, if that's what you want to call it."

"Sure, I'll call it that." We drove another few miles, while she thought it over. "Hunter, who I called the other day? We'd go to their house sometimes, Rachel and Ardith having busi-ness together. So it'd be me and Hunter having to amuse our-selves. And Hunter isn't musical at all, can't carry a tune in a bucket, bless her heart." She grinned, looked at me. "You know. The Southern style of bless her heart."

"I figured that's what you meant."

"Well she kept trying. If singing didn't work, maybe she could play an instrument. Not at all. No timing, no rhythm. It's like she's got a fairy curse on her, she enjoys music so much but can't make it, other'n pressing play."

"Wait, are there fairies?"

"No Allie it's a figure of speech."

"Okay."

"So we'll be at the Coutards, and me and Hunter'll be hanging out in her room, listening to music. I'll mess around with whatever instrument she's given it up most lately, if she hasn't sold it on Craigslist or returned it to the music store or what, and I'm okay. Nothing really catches my attention though, she started with the violin or maybe that was Ardith's doing. The saxophone, pretty cool, Bruce Springsteen and the E Street Band territory but still a no. And then one day, she had an electric guitar and a little amp, just a basic setup. An *electric* guitar, not an acoustic, not an acoustic you could plug in, she just tried to go full rock star."

"And that was the one?" Wait, the Coutards? She already *called* the Coutards right in front of me but didn't say anything?

"That was the one. She just told me to take it, and I put it in the Bronco. Now tell me, quick, what's the problem with me having an electric guitar back home?"

"Well we kind of keep a low profile," I said. "Though it's really hard for me to believe that we've been wolves in New Jersey for more than a hundred years and nobody noticed."

"Allie, a tiger got lost in North Jersey in the nineties and they never even identified for sure who owned it. Like, the literal tiger lady in that neighborhood was all 'oh no that can't be one of my tigers.' Wolves that're actually people that're actually wolves? Piece of cake. So no, that's not the problem."

"No electricity," I said. I felt like slapping myself in the forehead. Wait, a tiger?

"Exactly. And if you think they'd let me plug into the generator, you've got another thing coming."

"So what'd you do?"

She grinned at me. "I talked the bowling alley into taking me on as entertainment."

"What, the one with the pay phone?"

"The very one."

"Without any kind of practice?"

"Without a lick of electrified practice."

"Were they *paying* you?"

"At first they just agreed to pay me in like, games and snacks. Which honestly, was a pretty sweet deal, and I messed around with a whole bunch of covers, just songs that I liked and knew the words to, my take on them. And that library saved my ass, I could watch technique videos on YouTube and print out tabs and stuff."

"It's hard to imagine you in the library."

"Right? But to the library I went. They had tapes and stuff too, that I could listen to in the car, or CDs that I could listen to in somebody else's car. I was playing at that shitty bowling alley but it just grabbed me like nothing else had. Well nothing else but being a wolf."

"And then what, a record label exec stumbled in one day, lost in the Pine Barrens and needing directions, and they discovered you?"

"No, and then I started writing my own songs, but because I was just playing at the bowling alley nobody really noticed. I had a tips bucket, though, and nowhere to spend the money since I was getting paid in snacks. So I saved it all, and then after yet another fight with Rachel, I ran away up to Asbury Park. It worked for Bruce Springsteen, and there's still a lot of music there, and I got into the clubs and bars, and I listened, and I watched bulletin boards and online for local talent, and eventually Howling came together."

"Just like that?"

"It took a few months. Maybe six? We got together, were all still figuring out what we were good at and what we wanted to sound like, and little by little it all just fell into place."

"Just like a real rock legend," I said, trying not to sound like I was sick to death with jealousy.

"Just like," she said, seeing right through me and very pleased with herself.

"How old were you?"

"Oh I guess...let's see, I'd just turned seventeen." When she was my age. Wait, it couldn't have been all that long ago, then.

"So Rachel must've been furious. And worried."

"Equal parts both, I think. It's not like I didn't call her, I just didn't tell her where I was. I didn't want to just go back and sit at home in the pines plinking away at my non electrified electric guitar and waiting for dinner. Waiting for my turn at the loom. Waiting for one of the chickens to lay an egg. It's a good life for some people, but it's not my life, it just can't be."

"I can see that." I thought it over for a while. Would I have been happy to stay in the pines quietly, if I was born and brought up there? Or would I have been more like Morgan? I had no way to know. "Well okay, so if you always stayed pretty close to home, where do the Coutards live and why didn't you say anything to Hunter when you called?"

"Because Hunter was already in trouble on account of the mailbox baseball and like I already said, if it's just a Ward-Culver dispute, the Coutards can't be seen picking sides."

"If you're sure," I said, because what else could I say. If Morgan's good enough friends with a Coutard that they got arrested together, but is still worried about neutrality, it's serious. Maybe I'd spent only about a day with Morgan so far but it didn't seem like she was serious about much.

"What's there to be sure about?" she asked. "Mostly, I'm hoping we get them back and don't get fucked on this deal."

"Me too."

Chapter Fifteen

We drove through the mountains and passed a bunch of bear crossing signs, and then Bill turned onto a road that, after a quarter mile, had peeling yellow saw horses across the road like it was supposed to be closed, but no signs to that effect, and no visible disaster around. Joe got out of the passenger side and moved one of the saw horses enough for both vehicles to pass, waited, then put it back and ran to get back into Bill's truck.

The road curved back and forth, blacktop bleached gray, crumbling at the edges with some cracks reaching further and further across the road surface, and we could glimpse rusted out equipment through the treetops. We came to a clearing, and a "Welcome to" sign that had the rest of it so graffitied that it was almost black. There were round blank spots on the big sign that used to hold insignia for things like the Lion's Club, or the Elk's, or maybe the local union.

There were a couple of seventies-era cars still parked on the main drag, tires rotted out, lights and windows broken, lacy with rust at the edges. The storefronts were boarded up, the awnings tattered and skeletal. The occasional skinny, mistrustful cat stared at us from the sidewalk, or under one of the cars, or a half collapsed porch. "Well this is depressing," I said as we followed Bill through his turns, until he stopped at a large garage bay with only half of the doors still hung. He pulled into it and cut the engine; Morgan pulled into the next open one.

"Yeah, it is. It's what happens, I guess. Mine leaks fumes, plays out, company goes bankrupt, whatever. Then the town dries up and people go on to the next mine town, or factory town. Or Wal-Mart. There's at least one town around here that's got a big old fire under it, that's been burning for like, fifty years."

"What, really?"

"Yeah, the Silent Hill stuff is based on it. Wait no, not the games. I don't *think* it's this town, anyway." I looked at her blankly and she rolled her eyes. We got out and stretched. The sun was setting, and as Morgan locked the Jeep, I got stuck for a moment watching the golden light catch the dust in the air. "Hey, you ready?" She tossed the rifle case to me and I had to juggle it a second to keep from dropping it. Guns were always heavier than I expected them to be, somehow.

"Yeah, ready."

Bill and Joe stood behind their truck, just outside the garage. Joe looked back the way we came; Bill had an eye in a different direction. I thought of the maps from back at the campground and figured we were a twenty minute hike from the grassy knoll that Joe and I were supposed to camp out on. It was probably a little further to where Bill and Morgan would be meeting up with the 'insertion team' I think they were calling it.

"I just want to make sure that we're clear on the rules of engagement here," Bill started. Morgan held up her hand.

"Joe and Allie wait until shit starts to hit the fan down in the compound, take out the drones, make sure they aren't noticed or followed. I go with you and the rest of the boys' club, we get in, get my people, get out. No changing, as little blood-shed as possible, split up once we're out, hunker down for an hour after avoiding pursuit, meet up back here."

Bill sniffed and cleared his throat. "Well, young lady, I guess you sure told me."

"It's a gift."

"Joey, you're clear?" Even now that we weren't yelling at each other, I couldn't really get a read on Bill. Maybe that's just what the problem was, I had such a hard time reading people who were wolves. I had a hard time being around peo-ple, a little, after my dream. After remembering. That had to be what it was, a memory.

"Yes, sir."

"Okay then, time starts now. We'll meet back here in a few hours." Bill checked his watch and started walking. Mor-gan surprised me by giving me a rough one-armed hug around the shoulders before falling into step with Bill. I watched them go, then oriented myself and looked at Joe.

"I guess we should get to our post, huh?" He nodded.

We kept a comfortable pace with one another, pausing at times to take note of landmarks for the way back, a big rock, a really old tree, passing through the woods surefooted and qui-et. The sun sank beneath the horizon as we reached the crest of the hill, and looked down on the Silvernail compound. The lawn was tremendous, country club sized, with lines mowed into it and everything, the kind of plush emerald green that looked like it should be in a movie. The kind of big lawn that hardly anybody ever looked at, or used, at a place like that. What a waste. The fence around it was easily twelve feet, with razor wire on the top, like they said. I wondered if at least one line was electrified. There were some bushes here, and the dry rotted stump of a long fallen tree.

The sky was light blue, and then darker, and finally black and star spangled. The lights at the compound snapped on in increments. I wondered if there was an airstrip or helipad on the far side of the buildings. I wondered what part of the building the security drones came from, and if they were the kind I've read about in the paper, that can shoot people, or if they only had cameras.

For a very long time, we didn't see any movement on the property. No cars, no people. We waited on our stomachs, arms and legs close but not touching. I closed my eyes and bit my lip, trying to put the Kyle thoughts out of my head, when those thoughts came crawling back. He didn't hurt me. I hurt him. My stomach rolled and I realized I was panting, trying to stay calm. But Joe didn't reek of drunk football boy at least. Joe smelled like clean sweat, and wolf, and the mossy side of a tree. Maybe a little like lemons. And Joe had to know that I was silently freaking out, and wasn't trying to bother me about it, and for that I was thankful. There really just wasn't anything to be done.

Then the first patrol crossed the lawn. Two men, in so much tactical gear it was almost funny. One of them carried a big remote control with long antennas on it, and I looked for the drone. I didn't see it. Would it have lights on it? Would I hear it? I could smell the gun oil, and the aftershave one of the men wore, and hot plastic. The patrol passed out of sight, and we waited a little more.

Some more time passed, and very slowly, I moved the rifle into position and sighted down its length. There was a half moon overhead, but there was enough electric light inside the fence to make it as bright as a stage. A different patrol came past, no big weird remote this time.

The clear air was a little bit chilled, just enough to keep things sharp. I could feel a rock digging into my knee, but at this point, I didn't want to move. I heard a click from Joe's pocket, and I turned my head in his direction just slightly. He'd tensed up immediately, and I could tell that he meant to stand, and stopped himself. He gave me a sidelong glance and grinned in embarrassment. That must have been the signal. I stayed on my belly, propped on my elbows, rifle heavy in my hands.

I sniffed the wind, pretending that I'd be able to tell Morgan from here, when the group moved. I sniffed again, right as the wind blew, and then I stiffened, because I *could* smell Morgan. I thought I saw a shadow swiftly cross the lawn, and then another one. I could see the two patrols, at opposite corners of the property, looking away towards the perimeter. I strained my ears, expecting to hear an alarm immediately, and squinted, expecting more lights, something. It remained quiet. I glanced at Joe again, and he at me. A slight tilt of the head from me, a nod from him; he'd seen them too. He looked at me, and then at each patrol, and back at me. I gave the barest nod. Yes, I could see them. We waited.

Then, I heard an alarm, deep inside the compound. More followed like dominos falling, getting louder. Was that gunfire? I couldn't tell. Lights came on, every light in the place.

Then I did hear the low whirr of rotors, almost like white noise but tonally deeper. I scanned for the drone, considered, aimed for the main body of the thing, led with the barrel, led with the barrel, took a smooth breath and squeezed the trigger like a firm small hug. I rode the kick against my shoulder and there was an explosion of sparks when the round tore through it and it dropped like a rock. The nearest patrol, the one with the remote, stood over it, staring around, and one crouched while the other talked on a radio.

I waited, trying to picture the blueprints of the compound. How long would it take people to run out, with wounded? Carrying people who were drugged? I saw another patrol, another drone lifting off from them, cross the lawn to the first. They stood and tried to clear vectors, but seemed confused, searchlight raking the lawn, tiny rotors thumping. I dropped the second drone as it paused to hover over the building, scanned wildly for a third. I strained my eyes, and saw a group break free of the building. I recognized Morgan's stride, and turned to Joe, making eye contact.

We both rolled back down our hill, and at the bottom stopped and froze in the underbrush. Another drone looped around, passing our hilltop without pause. We waited, breathing at the same time, arms pressed against each other. I could hear Joe's heartbeat, and my vision went swimmy at the edges. God please, don't change. Waiting, I heard another drone, and watched them through the leaves overhead as they crisscrossed without stopping, then faded. I didn't hear any more gunshots, and no barking. I was so glad they had drones and not dogs, I wasn't sure if I could've just shot two dogs. Time passed, so much time, and then I heard Joe's radio click again. All clear. I was so relieved I could cry, but instead, I slowly looked around, eyes wide, ears open. Nobody around. I slowly slipped the rifle back into the nylon case, and we ran, crouched at first, towards the rendezvous.

Chapter Sixteen

Bill was already in the driver's seat of the truck. I didn't see Morgan, and my heart stopped for a minute. Then Bill tossed me the keys to the Jeep and said, "They're okay, they're in the back seat. Just follow me out of here."

I could hear helicopters still, and wondered why he was ready to move out so soon. He didn't turn on the lights of his truck, so I left my lights off as well. As I started the Jeep, the passenger door opened and Joe climbed in, a sawed off in hand. "Grandpa says I should keep you company."

"Well, all right." There wasn't really time to argue. And I didn't want to be alone. "Thank you." Bill backed out and drove off, and I followed. We took a different road out of town, this one overgrown and parked up in places with big trucks. It was like a coal rig graveyard. When Bill turned onto a dirt road, he stopped short, and I had to jam on the brakes to keep from rear ending him, the Jeep stalling out with a fitful buck like an angry horse. Bill got out and unhooked a chain that hung across the road. Morgan took the wheel for long enough to roll the truck through, and I followed, before he hooked the chain back up and took a pine bough to scuff away the immediate tire tracks.

We drove for about forever on that dirt road and others, unmarked, branches scraping the sides of the vehicle and the roof. I saw deer run off occasionally, white tails flashing silver in the moonlight. I saw what might have been a fox. I saw no lights, and after a while, realized I hadn't heard a drone since we were in the abandoned town, hadn't heard any sirens, nothing. Joe remained silent for the duration, shotgun resting across his knees. Morgan would probably have kept up the banter, I thought. Or tried to pump him for information. But I was just so overloaded, I couldn't think of any one good thing to ask him, and everything, my thoughts, even my skin, were buzzing so bad.

When Bill's brake lights flashed for the final time, we were probably three miles from the middle of nowhere. Joe and I got out of the Jeep, and as we did, other Wards appeared from the trees, opening the rear doors of Bill's extended cab. Morgan hopped out and turned around, and she got Sela out of the truck, wearing a white tank top and scrub pants, no shoes. Doors slammed shut, and we walked another fifty feet to a mossed over pavilion with a state park garbage can bolted to it. A camp cot was already set up, and Morgan guided Sela to that. She moved slowly, looking around, and she tried to smile reassuringly when she saw me, but her eyes were reddened and droopy and the smile didn't reach them.

Everybody settled on the picnic tables and in folding camp chairs that they pulled from vehicles. I stood by Morgan and watched as Luke and one of the other Wards crouched with a first aid kit open between them, feeling Sela's pulse, looking into her eyes with a little pen flashlight, and taking her temperature. Her left wrist was splinted, and there were needle marks up the insides of both her arms, smears of dried blood. She was so very pale, and I could smell hospital smells on her, rubbing alcohol and latex and blood.

"Okay for now," the other guy finally said, closing the kit. "We'll do an IV when we stop for the night."

"We aren't done yet?" I asked.

"This is just the nose count and short debrief," Bill said slowly. He covered this already, probably, and it just flew out of my head. "From here, we'll go to Camp Bravo. We have communications and supplies there, and will plan the next step."

I looked around at the gathered Wards, and Morgan. Other than Sela, nobody looked hurt. A lot of the guys were grinning, full of themselves. Nothing was this easy, I thought. Silvernail really wasn't expecting anybody to just walk in and take somebody. Well, neither had we. "All right, people," Luke said. "The short story, for those of you who were outside covering our asses, thank you for that, is we got down in there quick, meeting little resistance. We were able to use nonlethal means on the guards that we met at the doors and checkpoints. They didn't even hit the alarm until we were already on our way out again. Our rifle people, thanks again, kept the drones off of us, or they would have been a serious problem, and nobody seemed to track us to the vehicles. Culver was the only person we saw or detected in the lab that was not Silvernail personnel. The other two were not present, nor did they seem to have been brought to this particular facility. We pulled the hard drive on the lab computer adjacent to her bed, and brought her chart. We hope to learn more from these things at Camp Bravo. Most of you know how to get there, girls we'll give you directions in just a second. We expect everybody to leave from here and make it there inside of three hours. If you are late, radio in. If you are late and don't radio, we will assume that you've run into trouble and need our immediate help. Do not waste resources, people. Questions?" There were none. Wards started to break off already and head back to vehicles.

"Will Sela come with us?" I asked Morgan. We didn't have a radio. I should've asked about that. Probably Morgan already knew, already had phone numbers, exchanged burners, something.

"Of course."

I saw Joe suck his bottom lip in and look at Bill and Luke like they were going to argue, but Bill just nodded. "All right, ladies, your driving directions. Worlds End State Park is what you'll be looking for on the mile markers. Pass it. Five miles after, you'll see a dirt turnoff, no trespassing signs. Head on up two miles, make the left where the tree is blazed orange. The cabin you come to is Camp Bravo. There are more medical supplies there, and maybe even supper if we're lucky. We've sure earned it." He turned and stepped off to confer with Luke, Joe following after a moment of hesitation, casting another look back at us.

Morgan and I went to either side of Sela and got her on her feet, head lolling. She tried to make it easy on us, but she was so doped up she couldn't hardly keep her eyes open. We laid her in the back seat of the Jeep, buckled her in, and covered her with the quilt from the cabin. She sniffed it audibly, and seemed to relax, if only a little. Morgan looked at her a moment, eyes dark, and then closed the door with a sigh.

She didn't turn the headlights on until we were back on the highway. "Want to stop at a Wal-Mart or something if we see one, get some essentials?"

"Yeah. I mean, if you think she'll be okay in here"

"Windows are tinted, and anyway, Wal-Mart parking lots are always dripping with security cameras. Just need ten-fifteen minutes of civilization that isn't a weirdo antiseptic facility, and some clean clothes besides."

"I hear you." I didn't even see the inside of the weirdo antiseptic facility and got a chill at the base of my spine. An IV, they said. For what? How much blood of Sela's did they take? I got a map out of the center console, and looked at where we were headed. Three hours was plenty of time. "What was it like in there?"

"They had lots of white rabbits with red eyes. All in little cages against the walls." Morgan wrinkled her nose. "And everything was scrubbed down with some kind of industrial cleaner. Other than Sela's chart, no paper in the whole place."

"Should it really have been that easy?"

"Probably not. I wonder if they're just comfortable. Who's going to raid an anonymous looking facility like that, in the middle of the night in the middle of nowhere? Georgia will be harder."

"Georgia?"

"That's where Rachel and Dulcie are," Sela said woozily from the back, words all running together, but slowly. "That's where they sent them. They were hurt worse than me when we got taken. Both of 'em were shot, and I think Dulcie has a broken leg. She fell on the stairs, after she was hit. She screamed, she was screaming. The dogs?"

I was speechless; Morgan, somehow, didn't miss a beat. "Most ran off, they're smart enough to clear out when there's a fire. Ed'll mind them for us. How'd they get up so close without you knowing?"

"It was the truck. Bill's truck. Rachel knew him, we all met him once or twice, just didn't know why he'd come calling. The dogs started barking, and we smelled all the guns, and it was too late."

I turned to Morgan. "Wait, yeah, Bill's truck. It wasn't there?"

"Not that we saw. And there were so many computers, and so much lab equipment. If we had more time, I would've burned that place to the ground. Though I wouldn't have been able to take all those rabbits, screaming. Critters like that wouldn't survive in the wild. What do you do with hundreds of white rabbits?"

"I don't know," I said when I realized Morgan was waiting for an answer. "Eat them? Start a magic act? You're the one with the stage presence."

"Yeah, right, I need to pick up a top hat." Morgan glanced over her shoulder. "You want anything, Sela?"

"Clothes. Um." We waited long enough that I wondered if she'd drifted unconscious again. "Meal shakes. Vanilla."

"You got it."

The Wal-Mart parking lot was all but empty, and we parked right at the front, next to the handicapped spot and put the top up on the Jeep. Sela snored gently in the back, and

Morgan locked the doors. Walking into Wal-Mart after what went on the past few hours was surreal; it was late enough at night that there was no greeter, just a cashier and a manager hanging out at the one register that sold cigarettes. They nodded to us as we got a cart.

Morgan knew Sela's sizes, so we got jeans for her, and us. Socks. Underwear. Bras. A few packs of t-shirts. Some hoodies, and a cheap coat for Sela. Boots for Sela, and a belt. Tank tops, pajama pants. We got the vanilla meal shakes, another bag of trail mix, and some jerky. Morgan disappeared for a minute when I was looking at magazines, wondering at the whole big world that I didn't know. She came back and tossed a box of black hair dye in the cart. The cashier rang out our stuff while keeping up chatter about nothing we cared about.

Back in the Jeep, Morgan shook up one of the shakes and handed it back to Sela, who held it for a while without doing anything, then started to sip it slowly. She moved like she was swimming through glue. "They drew a lot of blood," she said after a while. "And gave me a lot of drugs, I guess sedatives? They didn't know, at first, how strong we were. Rachel took down two in the transport van and then they tased her." Morgan didn't say anything, but I could see her nostrils flare. Did took down mean killed? Incapacitated? They tased Rachel?

"Just get some rest, Sela. That stuff'll work out of your system soon enough." I tried to sound calm, and like I had any idea. I wondered if I was ever going to stop being overwhelmed and on the edge of panic. I took the half full bottle from her as it started to tip and put the lid back on.

Driving country highways in the night is like driving on your own private planet. You hardly saw another soul. When you saw animals, they don't look the same as they did in the daytime, and you found yourself second guessing all the time. Coyote? Dog? Wolf? I never used to guess wolf. Even deer were something else, eyes glinting green in the headlights, frozen on the shoulder, jaws mid chew. Winged things dipped down from the sky, but not low enough to tell what they were. By the time we turned at the orange blazed tree, I was about ready to crawl under the dashboard, I felt so dazed. One of the Wards stood just off the road, and waved as we went past, and when I looked in the rear view mirror, he followed us down the road at a long legged jog.

Chapter Seventeen

There was significant tree cover at Camp Bravo, and the roof of the cabin itself was covered in netting with branches woven into it. The lights were unreliable, and so were my eyes all the sudden. Military failsafes or something, I'd ask in the morning, or I wouldn't. Zeb came out to meet us, and after watching us slide Sela, boneless, out of the Jeep, he said "Scuse me," and scooped her up in his arms and carried her, cradled, into the cabin. I looked at Morgan, who shrugged, and we gathered up our Wal-Mart bags and went inside. She was tired too, but damned if she was going to let it slow her down.

Everybody was being quietly loud, talking about what they'd seen, what they'd just done. Guns were being cleaned, beers opened, maps examined. The cabin was almost identical to the first one we visited, but had a moose over the fireplace, which probably wasn't shot here, but maybe there were moose in Pennsylvania. I sure didn't know. I could smell it as soon as I walked into the door, dust and fur and tannin. Another guy was bent over a computer in one of the corners. Zeb carried Sela upstairs to a bedroom, and Morgan followed with a set of pajamas. I parked it in a musty armchair to wait. "You want to use the shower, you're welcome to," Joe said, suddenly at my elbow. "Hoyt turned the hot water on and everything."

"That's great, actually." I'd spent part of the car ride picking twigs and leaves out of my hair, and I absolutely didn't want to get in the way of Morgan helping Sela uninvited. Joe pointed me out the door, and there were a bunch of plywood shower stalls rigged up under another netted roof. I ran the water as hot as I could stand it, and lathered my hair until it squeaked. The shower next to me started after a while.

"Just me, Allie," Morgan said.

"I know." Even though I'd occupied myself by letting hot water run on my face, I could tell it was her. At least I wasn't crying again.

"Wait for me when you're done?"

"Yeah, of course." I didn't feel inclined to wander too far from her anyway, even though I wasn't sure that we'd exactly bonded. I turned off the water and stepped to the bench that was in the stall, just outside the spray, toweled off, and put clean clothes on. Morgan came out a few minutes later, wearing new jeans but her old shirt.

"You done this before?" She held out the cardboard box of black dye.

"Dyed hair? No, but I figure it isn't too hard, considering some of the girls in my school that managed it."

"Harsh."

"Seriously?"

"Hey, I could almost envy you your public schooling. All of those teachers to rebel against and upset. So many other young minds to influence." Morgan put the plastic capelet around her shoulders and handed me the gloves.

"God, I can just imagine you at my school." I scrutinized the instructions on the side of the box, then started in with the dye. There wasn't really any need to tell her how little time I'd spent in an actual school. I didn't need to tell everybody everything about myself, and somehow, it was a comforting feeling to have. She kept things from me awful easy.

Morgan snickered. "Yeah, I don't do well with the norms in extended contact."

"I don't really know how well you do with anybody in extended contact," I said before I could stop myself, but she just laughed again, louder and harder. I didn't need to say that it was apparent why she never met any of the Wards before now.

We let the dye sit for twenty minutes, and then Morgan got back in the shower. I finger combed my hair while I waited again for her, then bundled it all into a braid.

When Morgan was done, she still kind of smelled like hair dye, but it wasn't too bad. "Somebody mentioned dinner, didn't they?" she asked as she stuffed the empty packaging in the outside garbage.

"I think they did." Now that she mentioned it, I was unbelievably hungry. This was getting to be a regular thing. We went back inside, and in the kitchen, there was a giant pot of spaghetti and meatballs, and trays of garlic bread. There were ten or fifteen Wards in the cabin, and it felt like so many people. So many men. Mostly, they were all wrapped up in conversation with one another, but this time it didn't feel as though they were hedging us out. Morgan and I ate, though she kept glancing at the stairs. "You think Sela's okay?" I asked.

"I don't know. They started a saline IV for her, anyway. Maybe that and a good night's sleep are all she needs. We brought her chart with us, and I looked at it, but the drug names didn't mean anything to me."

Bill came through the room, then saw us and sauntered over. "You heard the news?"

"News? What news?" We both sat up straighter.

"I got on the horn with one of my state police buddies, and it turns out they found my truck. Up on blocks by the highway down near Philadelphia."

"Well that's good," I said, surreptitiously wiping spaghetti sauce from the corner of my mouth. "I mean, you'll need to replace the wheels, but it could be worse." Morgan looked thoughtful.

"Seems like weird timing. Called your wife lately?" she asked.

Bill's eyes narrowed, just a little. "What's your line of thought?"

"They took a lot of Sela's blood. They left your truck, but you can bet that they vacuumed it clean. They've got the DNA of everybody that's slid across your seats. You're in the crosshairs too, and you might want to get your wife out of that house and your dogs someplace else, right?" Morgan mopped the last of the sauce out of her bowl with a crust of bread and popped it in her mouth. "Though I guess you probably already thought of all that, what with your experience and all."

"Something like that," he said in a dry tone. "Mrs. Ward is on her way, yes."

"That's good. I don't want to see this happening to any other families, if we can help it."

Bill shook his head. "One raid does not a ruined company make."

I wasn't thinking about that. I didn't even know how to think that far ahead. Did we need to ruin the company? How did somebody ruin a company? We just wanted our aunts back. Well. Aunts and Morgan's mama.

"You're right. Plus they're gonna be worried now. They thought they were untouchable."

"Which is what will make Georgia harder."

"From what we've seen, it seems like Georgia is the main facility for this black ops shit, which'll have more security anyway. Speaking of, you're committed to Georgia?" Somewhere along the line, the joking dropped out of Morgan's voice, and she'd become deadly serious. I watched the change happen and it still surprised me.

"I can't commit everybody that's here tonight, but I'm going to send Luke and Joe down to muster the family there, and have a team ready for you."

Morgan nodded. "Good enough."

"Excuse me now, ladies." Bill nodded, looked at me a moment, and went to the map room. Every time him or any other Ward called us 'ladies', or 'girls', something in my throat tightened, and my shoulder blades prickled. Something about the tone just made it uncomfortable. Nobody was saying it to be nice or anything, they were saying it to point out that we were different. Outnumbered.

"You know, I'm not sure that he got you were still pissed about his sitting on all the *intel* they had," I remarked.

"Me neither. Men can be dense sometimes. You figure he already called his wife, or is he doing it now? That's where the radio is." Morgan sat back in the couch and wiggled her shoulder blades against the cushion.

"I'd be surprised if he didn't radio her from the truck once they were on the highway."

"You're probably right." She yawned, and stretched. "I could fall asleep right here."

"It's better than the Jeep, anyway." I finished my last piece of bread and took my bowl and Morgan's to the kitchen. Most of the cleanup was done already, Hoyt standing at the sink, elbow deep in suds.

"Thanks, just set 'em right there," he said, pointing with his chin.

I put the bowls there gingerly; he was one of the bigger Wards they had, towering over me. "Thanks for dinner," I said.

"Nobody leaves hungry," he said, and went back to scrubbing.

I returned to the living room, where Morgan had her head leaned all the way back and put her feet up. Her eyes were only half closed, though, and she moved her head a little to look at me when I flopped down on the other couch. "Sounds like the decryption will be done in the morning," she said quietly.

"That's good. Wonder what they'll find."

"Anybody's guess. Super soldier serum. Anti-aging lotion. Muscle enhancers. That's one they might be able to get out of us, anyway."

"It's a lot of trouble for a new kind of steroids."

"Under the radar steroids. New Olympic athlete steroids. Completely organic." Morgan yawned again. It was weird to see Morgan without her white rock star hair. "Nice work tonight, by the way."

"Really?" I smiled.

"Yeah, really. Taking out those drones was important."

"Never thought I'd be doing anything like that, when I was practicing on the range." This time I was the one who yawned; it snuck up on me, and practically cracked my jaw. Things in the cabin had settled down some; Hoyt was done in the kitchen, and a lot of the other guys weren't circulating any more. Did Luke and Joe leave already? I couldn't tell, my nose was a normal people nose again.

"Should I check on Sela before we fall asleep where we sit?" I asked.

"Yeah. Try not to wake her, if she's out. I'm assuming she's out."

"Me too, but I want to check." With effort, I got to my feet and headed up the stairs. I glanced in the map room as I went past, and Bill and Luke were both leaned on the table, pointing. Zeb sat by the radio, nursing a beer and nodding every once in a while. He saw me go past and raised his beer, just a little.

Sela was asleep, and it seemed to be peaceful, even. We'd brought the quilt in for her, and there was another blanket on top of that. I looked at the IV bag and it was half empty, and I didn't know if that was good or bad, really. I leaned in just a little, and she didn't seem feverish, and I didn't know what I was smelling for. Would I be able to tell if she wasn't well in some other way? Probably not. I closed the door softly behind me and returned to my couch. There was a blanket on the back that I pulled off and wrapped around me. I thought about going to change into pajamas after all, and didn't feel like moving again once I lay down. It was funny, most of the day was spent driving, but that was still exhausting. "Goodnight," I said, and Morgan kind of grunted back at me.

Chapter Eighteen

T he first thing in the morning, I heard an unfamiliar female voice saying "William, you know I need to be there when that baby comes."

"Yes, ma'am, I know."

"I don't fancy playing Navy boys with the rest of you. At least there's an indoor bathroom here." The screen door shut, and there were rapid steps through the main room, pausing briefly to scrutinize Morgan and I before continuing to the kitchen. I could only assume it was Mrs. Ward. I yawned and cracked my eyes open; it was just dawn. I stretched and sat up. On the other couch, Morgan opened her eyes and looked at me, and I wondered how long she'd been awake. From the kitchen, the refrigerator opened and slammed a few times, and pans clattered onto the stove. Morgan raised her eyebrows and looked in that direction and back at me. I shrugged. Maybe Mrs. Ward cooked when angry. Morgan grinned.

The screen door slammed and Bill came through, chewing the end of a new cigar. He looked at me and I pointed at the kitchen. He sniffed and squared his shoulders slightly. The sizzle and smell of bacon wafted through the cabin, bringing Morgan to her feet. "We ought to check Sela, and see if Mrs. Ward wants help with breakfast," she said. I nodded and headed for the kitchen, Bill falling in step with me.

"She'll either appreciate it or chase you out," he muttered.

"That's what I'd expect, really."

Mrs. Ward was a short woman, though I would hesitate to call her little. She was younger than her husband, I thought, or at least looked younger. She wore cropped khakis and a white t-shirt, silvered blonde hair pulled back in a flat barrette. She gave me a cursory glance and put me on scrambled egg duty with a gesture. She turned to Bill and said "William, is there more orange juice?"

"The fridge in the shed. I'll get it," he muttered and made his escape.

When I'd helped with church breakfasts, eggs were my station. The memory made me smile a little, and it faded when I wondered what Mama was doing right then. My whole life, she was up at dawn. Mrs. Ward finished whisking a massive bowl of pancake batter and started pouring those out. We worked well together, without jostling or bumping elbows.

Morgan came and sat at the kitchen table while we finished up cooking. It bothered me when she was quiet. When I glanced at her the third time, Mrs. Ward took the spatula out of my hand and shooed me away. "Go take care of your business," she said brusquely.

"What's up?" I asked once we were out the front door.

"We need to get Sela someplace safe before we head anywhere else. We can't just drop her off next to the smoking pile that used to be the house and figure she'll be okay. It's possible that we can never go back there, but it's extra stupid to go back there the day after jailbreaking a recent resident. So I don't want to drop her off at the neighbor's either."

"Well, where? Not like we can take her to Ivy's people."

"No, we can't. Seems the only answer is Sidney."

"Will Sidney go for that?"

"She will by the time I'm done talking to her."

"Let's call her, then. There's probably a payphone at that gas station that we passed."

"We'll just use one of the burners."

"I thought you didn't..." she stared at me until I stopped talking.

We walked further from the cabin, to where its private road met the mountain road. Morgan stood still and scanned the area, then closed her eyes a moment. I did the same thing, to test myself. If she didn't sense anybody, I didn't have a chance in hell, but it was worth a shot. At the very least, that I could tell, nobody had followed us from the cabin.

Morgan dialed, then paced on the soft shoulder and counted the rings on her free hand. When she got to five, she pulled a dubious face and was taking the phone from her ear when she jerked it back and said "Hi, Aaron? It's Morgan. Can I talk to Sidney?" She listened for a moment. "Yeah, I know it's early, but it's kind of important. You know us country girls, up and at 'em!" She rolled her eyes at me, then waited some more, rolling a rock around in the dirt with the toe of her boot. "Hey Sid. We've got your mama. Seems she was in a car accident, and just needs a place to stay for a little while where people are going to be around to help her out. Nothing too major. They gave her painkillers for whiplash and a broken wrist, so she's all spaced out." I couldn't hear what Sidney said, but she didn't sound happy. Morgan closed her eyes as she listened, jutting her chin out. "Well, we've got to help

Rachel with the other car. No, I can't put her on the phone, I'm outside so I don't disturb her. She needs rest." I wondered what we would do if Sidney said no. Then Morgan straightened up again. "Thanks, Sid. You know you'll be happy to see her. It'll be good for you to spend time together. No, not today, either tomorrow or the day after." Sidney hung up first.

"I'm kind of surprised she put up that much of an argument."

Morgan slid the phone into her pocket. "Like I said, she's doing the live a normal life thing. It's fucking selfish, but it's what she's doing. Rachel would ream her. I'm not sure Sela will have the heart. Besides, between all this and the baby too, she was probably going to be coming back pretty soon anyway."

"You said that we always do."

She kind of shrugged and nodded at the same time. "Anyways, hear anything interesting this morning from our hosts?"

I shook my head. "Other than William getting dressed down by the missus? No. How was Sela this morning?"

"Still sleeping. Probably better, really, there's no telling what she'll be feeling after everything wears off."

I had a hard time thinking of 'after' anything right then. I wasn't sure how any of the pieces were supposed to fit back together again. "We'd better get some breakfast before the menfolk eat it all," I said instead.

"Crap, I didn't think of that."

Up at the cabin, Joe and Luke were throwing bags in a truck. "There you are," Luke said with a sly smile. "Joey here was wondering where you'd run off to. Wants to say goodbye, I guess."

The tips of Joe's ears got red, but he kept his head down as he put the bags he carried into the back of the truck. "I just wanted to make sure you were as involved with the planning as you needed to be," he said, voice hardly more than a mutter.

"I figure we can move Sela tomorrow and then meet you in Georgia. That's as much plan as I've got right this second," Morgan said, ignoring the tension. "It depends on her."

Luke nodded. "About what I thought. That gives us time to team up, straighten our intel, and form a plan." He clapped Joe on the back, hard enough that it looked like it hurt. "But, ladies, we've gotta hit the road. *Somebody* saved you some breakfast inside. I'm surprised you'd walk away from food on the table."

"Sometimes things need to get done," Morgan said.

"Yeah, I guess. Here, let's make sure we have each other's numbers." We stood around with our phones out, me and Morgan clicking buttons on our burners, Luke and Joe with smartphones.

"He seemed cheerful," I said to Morgan once they'd pulled away.

"He likes having somebody to rag on."

"Yeah, what was that all about?"

"I'd guess maybe Joe has a crush on one of us. Or Luke thinks he does."

"God, really?"

"It makes sense. You were just in high school, you know all about this." She nudged me with an elbow.

I flinched without meaning to, saw her take note, and then shook my head. "I don't like thinking about it." Dropping it was the last thing I expected her to do but she just held up her hands and did just that.

Inside, there were two covered plates on the kitchen table, a pot of coffee and what was left of the carafe of orange juice. Hoyt was washing dishes again, his shoulders rigid, with Mrs. Ward drying. She turned and gave us a stern look as we sat down. I froze, fork partway to my mouth, but Morgan was already shoveling food. I couldn't imagine what we'd done wrong in the twenty minutes we were outside. Morgan, she just didn't care. "I hope you ladies appreciate what we're doing for you," she said. Ladies again, Heaven preserve us. Morgan looked up at her, finished chewing, and set her fork down with precise deliberation.

"We certainly do, Mrs. Ward," she said, folding her hands. "Really, I'm unsure as how to properly express my gratitude for your time and efforts with regards to the matter at hand. We understand the risk your men are taking and can't thank them enough." I waited for Mama Ward to detect Morgan's stinking bullshit with her disapproving matriarch powers and start something bigger, but instead, she smiled.

"Well thank you dear. You're Morgan?"

"Yes'm." Morgan started eating again.

"So that means you're Allie. What is that short for, dear? Allison?"

"Alleluia." Crisis averted, I started eating as well.

"Well isn't that pretty? Hoyt, isn't Allie's name pretty?" Mrs. Ward smiled more. I wondered if Hoyt was her grandson, or her nephew.

"Yes, ma'am." Hoyt's voice was a resigned sigh.

"Now Margaret, don't be hounding the young people." Bill came in from the back yard, screen door banging. I hadn't known he was out there, and wondered how long he was listening. Morgan didn't seem surprised. He was so quiet for a man his size.

"We were just making conversation," she said in a sweeter tone, drying another dish.

"I know what kind of conversation you make," he said, taking the dishcloth from her and setting it on the counter. "And I think it's best to leave well enough alone."

"Now William," she said, and he steered her out of the kitchen and out to the rockers on the front porch.

Hoyt turned off the water, wiped his hands on his jeans and turned around, almost looking like he was making sure the coast was clear. When that checked out, he came and sat at the table with me and Morgan, pouring himself a cup of coffee.

"You jealous that it's just Luke and Joe going to Georgia?" Morgan asked him.

"Me? No. I'm re-deploying next week. I wish I could help out with family stuff, but there's plenty of action to be had."

"That's the truth." Ever the surprise, Morgan got up and took our plates to the sink.

"You aren't worried about going over there?" I asked. I didn't know where there was, but he'd fill in his own blanks, I was certain. "Getting shot? IEDs?"

"Well, my squad has K9 bomb detectors, so I'm pretty confident about how good they are at their job. That, and I'm pretty good at sensing that kind of thing myself, once I'm in country long enough to get acclimated. IEDs, ambush, that kind of thing. It comes with the territory."

"I guess it must," I said.

Morgan finished up with the dishes and came back to the table. "What do you want to do with the rest of the day?" she asked me.

"I really don't know. Any more shopping we need to get done? We just kinda threw a band aid on things last night, in more ways than one."

"Not a bad idea, but I kind of feel like going for a run first. Stretch my legs, get some of this good mountain air. We've been on the road an awful lot."

"Sounds good." I could always use more practice. I could also use time away from all these Wards.

"You mind company?" I wondered if Hoyt was our designated handler. I shrugged and looked at Morgan. She considered for a moment.

"All right, but I'm sure your rules are like our rules. No peeking."

"Scout's honor." He solemnly held up two fingers. "We can even change in the showers, if you want to, for extra privacy."

Chapter Nineteen

We went out the back door, and each of us got into a shower stall and started shucking boots and clothes. I felt like giggling. I think it was honestly the first time I was excited to change. We were safe for five minutes, we had a plan, and Morgan was the only one here that knew I was kind of a freak. I had the easiest time changing that I had yet experienced.

It was easy to crouch a little and slink out of the shower stall; Morgan and Hoyt already waited there for me. Hoyt was bigger than either of us, mostly brown, with a lot of fur in the ruff around his neck and shoulders. His tail was black tipped. Morgan huffed and started off up the mountain. I followed her, and Hoyt bounded ahead of both of us. Showing off, probably, but I wondered if he was going to overheat quicker because of how big he was. He was familiar with this place, though, and he led us a merry chase up the mountain and through the trees, splashing down into a creek at one point, water spraying everywhere. Wet dog smell didn't begin to approach wet wolf smell, though I guessed it would bother me more if I wasn't a wolf myself.

I was still getting used to just how different things felt. Little things, like the way my toes flexed, or the fact that I could move my ears independently of one another. The existence of a tail. I put on the speed just because I could, and passed Morgan. She flicked an ear towards me when we were shoulder to shoulder, and let me go briefly. Then she gunned it as well, and put her shoulder to mine when we were even again, sending us both tumbling. She gained her feet again first, prancing, tail held high. I rolled on my stomach and stayed crouched there for a second, tail still and level. I heard Hoyt come thundering through, and when he piled into Morgan, I let them roll for a second before jumping into the fray as well.

I'd never seen wolves play, but I'd seen dogs play, and I'd guess I could say it was a little like that. Open mouths, snarling that wasn't actually mean or angry, shoulder checks, rolling in the dirt, jumping around. I wouldn't say any of us won, that wasn't what it was about. There came a point where we sat, or lay, in the clearing, panting and looking at each other. Morgan seemed pleased with herself, so maybe there was some kind of underlying struggle that I was totally ignorant of. Once we caught our breath, Hoyt got to his feet and led us back through the river, and then down the mountain back to the cabin. It was a good trick, changing in the shower; a quick shampoo was not out of place after what we'd just done.

"Combs. Put combs on the list," Morgan said when I dressed and came out of the stall.

"Yes, definitely."

"You ladies have fun shopping. Drive safe, and make sure you aren't followed."

"Aye aye." Morgan snapped a salute. "I'll see if Sela wants anything."

"Okay, I'll wait out front."

Bill and the missus weren't on the front porch anymore, though his truck was still parked there. Wards in general were kind of sparse on the ground today, but I guessed most of them had scattered back home to do whatever it was they normally did. Morgan stepped out onto the porch and closed the screen door quietly, then all but crept down the stairs next to me.

"What are you doing?"

"Bill and the missus are knocking boots upstairs."

"Oh. Uh. Goodness."

"I couldn't bear the burden all on my own." We both grimaced, and walked to the Jeep.

"Sela's okay? Did she want anything?"

"She's sore as hell, and still really woozy. I think that Ward medic offered her some Valium or something, and she took him up on the offer. Can't say as I blame her."

"No, not at all." I tried to think of what it would have been like, if I was at the cabin when the Silvernail people stormed it. All I could imagine was the fire, and the smell of the blood, and I shuddered a little. "So, there was an outlet mall back by the main highway."

"Yeah, I remember that. It had a Home Depot and probably someplace we could buy combs. Maybe a computer store where I could do some illicit Googling. Oh yeah I forgot, look at this." She rummaged for the book, flipped it open towards the back and shoved it at me.

"I didn't know they sold phones that didn't do that anymore, honestly." I looked at the pages, a rough sketch of the United States, with red dots in various places.

"Even if you never take any other advice I give you, please always remember this: web browsing on a flip phone is fucking garbage." Morgan popped her sunglasses on and cranked the radio.

"I'll remember it forever. But what is this map? The dots aren't state capitals, there's more than one per state. And they've got dates next to all of them."

"Is the house one of them?"

"Maybe? No. There's one near the Lakehurst house, though." I looked at it for a little while longer. Little red dots, across the country, none too close to another, though of course I wasn't sure of the exact scale.

"Bill's truck," Morgan said, after I'd turned the page and found another series of numbers.

"I don't follow." Or I didn't want to.

"Silvernail stole Bill's truck near their house. The American Legion." I turned back to the map.

"And Bill said that they had been screwing around with other minor things."

"That's a lot of screwing around."

"But if it's little things, all spread out like this, and everybody's isolated from each other...well, nobody'd know until they were already being paid a visit."

"The Wards are the most isolated of the families that didn't really join the club. The Coutards kind of keep tabs, but it makes me wonder when Rachel would've seen Bill recently enough to know his truck, unless she stopped by once in a while to yell at him or something." I stared at the dots; a couple were down in Alabama. But by their own admission, the Wards didn't know about me. They hadn't seen me before we turned up the other day. Bill would never have acted like he didn't know something if he didn't have to.

"And you said those numbers are dates? I'll write down a couple, see what's in the news. Any houses burning down or whatever."

"Maybe the Wards figured nothing else would happen so soon, with their truck being stolen?"

"Or maybe just that nothing would happen to *them*, and that's what mattered."

The outlet mall was the usual strip of ugly concrete boxes. Mama used to like shopping at places like this for church clothes, or for if the church was doing a clothes drive to send somewhere, like for people displaced by horrible hurricane seasons. There were big hearty flowers in the landscaping, and lots of mothers towing unhappy children. I'd forgotten it was a Saturday as soon as Morgan got off the phone earlier, but there were too many people here for it to be any other day. I tried to think of the last time I saw quite so many people; it had been months, to be sure, maybe even the last time I was at school. Everybody was on cell phones, or talking too loudly to each other. Kids were screaming, parents were impatient, tempers were short.

The computer store was quiet as a library. We circulated until one of the employees went on break, and I corralled the other asking about iPads and iPods and Kindles and just in general being the wide eyed tech yokel that I am until he was stuck talking to me about megapixels and touch screen inputs and smartphones, while Morgan latched onto a computer in a corner display and pecked away at the keyboard for a few minutes. I knew she was done when she pulled out a pen and scribbled down her forearm. She left the laptop a few minutes later, wandered over to look at headphones, then left without a backward glance. I disentangled myself from the employee after that with his business card in hand, and followed my nose for the pretzel stand.

Morgan was already there, and handed me a pretzel as I walked up. "I wish I could say I felt enlightened, but I don't. It was mostly a bunch of nothing."

"Well if they were all backwoods recluses like us, I guess it isn't much of a surprise? Even our fire might've just gone reported as a forest fire, nothing to do with a house." The pretzel was warm, buttery and salty. I closed my eyes for a second and just enjoyed it. "Sela might know something, if we show her the map."

"Maybe, maybe not. Rachel would almost definitely know." We both just kind of stood there thinking that over, not really looking at each other, not really moving.

"Well we're going down to Georgia to get her. So long as the Wards don't recover their 'intel', and if you put it with our books and bury it with the other stuff in the back of your Jeep, we'll be able to show her." I didn't know if I was trying to make her feel better or trying to make me feel better. Maybe Rachel wasn't my favorite, but it didn't mean her being gone didn't have me in a kind of low-grade panic that I didn't know how to address.

Morgan gave me a crooked smile. "Hey, you're right. And maybe we'll have time for that training montage after all."

"Really? Just like the movies?" I finished my pretzel and balled up the paper, tossing it into the nearby garbage can.

"Just like. Let's get combs and some other stuff, so they don't get all weird about us. We'll never shake them again if we get their suspicions aroused. Though I guess we'd rather their suspicions than something else. Depending."

I wrinkled my nose. "I'm not really..."

"You can't honestly tell me you're immune. Some of them are some fine specimens."

"I'm not really, um, looking right now." I couldn't think of when exactly I would be ready to even try and talk about it. I could still feel Kyle's breath on my face, the back of my neck, while he fumbled with my jeans.

"It's your choice. I'm not picking one to mark for my territory or anything, just admiring the scenery. Besides, can you imagine Rachel's reaction if I shacked up with one of the Wards?"

"I'd think imagining Rachel being mad about it would only encourage you."

"You're not far off." She stood up and stretched. "Oh yeah, let's go into Home Depot."

"Uh. Sure." I also forgot that it was October until we walked inside and saw the giant skeletons. I followed Morgan around with an orange plastic hand basket and she dropped in cans of spray paint, rolls of duct tape, steel carabiners, copper wire, a bunch of very long nails, and a ten pound sledge with a rubberized grip on the handle. I knew better than to ask. At the end, though, after we'd carried the bags out to the parking lot and headed to the Jeep, I worked up the courage to say, "I don't know what any of what we just got is for."

Morgan shrugged like she didn't know either. "Just some stuff I anticipate being useful in Georgia."

"I don't know how to begin anticipating what will be useful in Georgia." I shook my head.

"What do you mean?"

"Me, as a for-instance. The place they've got pictures of in Georgia is practically in a city, not like we can put snipers on rooftops there." Not like I thought I could shoot a person. Not like I could trust myself to not freak out and change in a creepy medical research facility that was run by people who kidnapped our family. But the Wards didn't know that.

"I'm sure we'll figure something out," she said, and we drove back to Camp Bravo.

Bill was on the porch smoking a cigar, a bloodhound at his feet. I didn't remember seeing any dogs around the night before, and wondered if somebody else had gone to the Ward place and gotten them all. "Your aunt seems to be doing all right, medic says. Looks like you'd be on schedule to head out tomorrow, if that's what you're of a mind to do."

"That was the plan, yeah," Morgan said. She sat on the edge of the porch and began working the comb through her hair. The bloodhound watched her with interest, moving his head so that his nose was nearly on her knee. She gave him a pat every once in a while.

"It seems like a no-brainer, but the place you're leaving her is safe?"

"Should be. Smack in civilianville, anyway. If we can't keep her in a compound of our very own, at least lots of eyes make things a lot harder."

"That's the truth. The hard drive we took isn't decrypted yet, but we'll forward the information on to Camp Foxtrot if we get it before you head in."

"Definitely appreciated. Do we have blueprints for the Georgia facility?" Morgan set the comb down and shook her hair over her shoulders. The dog reached out and delicately took the comb in his teeth, bringing it closer to set between his paws and snuffle at it. When he opened his mouth to start gnawing on it, Morgan reached over and took it back, wiping it off on her jeans before tossing it back in the shopping bag.

"At Camp Foxtrot already. They're getting a sense of the schedule at the place, guard rotation, that kind of thing. You'll be debriefed there."

"Makes sense. Don't need stuff crowding in our minds when we're out in the world." Morgan looked at me. "I'll be right back." She got up and banged into the cabin. I wondered why she kept leaving me with Bill, but I guess she probably didn't think much of it. It wasn't like she was a master strategist, chaotic Morgan. Maybe it was just because she was having a struggle to keep from laughing every time 'Camp Foxtrot' was mentioned. I sure was.

The bloodhound got up and shuffled over to me, sniffing my head intently, his ears swinging against my cheeks. I let him because really, what the heck. He slumped back down on the porch and put his head on my knee, looking up at me. "I don't have any food," I said. "I ate it." He sighed and closed his eyes. Bill laughed.

"That dog hasn't been hungry a day in his life, but he's always mooching."

"That's just kind of how dogs are." It's how the aunts' dogs were, anyway. They didn't come to the table, but when I came back with the egg basket, there was a whole lot of begging involved.

"True." Bill rocked in his chair for a few moments, looking out into the woods. "This must be a pretty hard time for you girls, but you're taking it well."

"We weren't exactly going to sit around wringing our hands," I said. "Or waiting to get picked up ourselves. Morgan is a woman of action." Or wolf of action. Rock star of action.

"It's hard to judge a person without meeting them," Bill said, relighting his cigar, and it took me that long to realize he was apologizing to me. Kind of.

"I think that went both ways," I said. I stood up and dusted off my jeans, done with requisite uncomfortable conversation for the day. It was starting to feel about like lunch time, and I was both hungry and didn't want to get roped into kitchen duty again. When I got inside, though, that's exactly what had happened to Morgan. She was just outside the kitchen door, balefully turning hot dogs and hamburgers on the grill. It was a wonder where all of this food was stored. The fridge in the shed I guessed. Probably there was a freezer out there.

"I don't want to hear it," Morgan grumbled when I came outside.

"Hey, I wasn't going to say anything. Maybe thank you. You'd better watch out that nobody wants to kiss the cook."

"You mean they better watch out." Morgan curled her lip briefly.

"I'm sure they know better. You're the one who was talking about shopping, though."

"Because everybody loves having their words thrown back at them, Allie. Take some water to Sela, will you?"

I went back into the kitchen and opened a couple of cabinets before I found a pitcher to fill. I climbed the stairs and knocked softly on Sela's door.

"Come in," she said, sounding more or less normal.

The curtains were closed, but diffuse yellow light filled the room. Sela sat propped up on a pillow. She smiled when she saw me; her eyes were a little droopy, and dilated. "We thought you'd be thirsty," I said, holding up the pitcher.

"Positively cotton mouthed," she said. I sat on the edge of the bed and poured a glass and she took it in a bandaged hand, carefully, and drank it down in small sips.

"We're thinking that we'll get out of here tomorrow," I said.

"Where to?"

"We're taking you to...well we've been calling it surburbia. Civilianville. For safety's sake." Sela drank some more water.

"I wouldn't have expected Sidney to agree to that."

"Morgan is extremely persuasive."

Sela laughed. "That Morgan. She always has been." I took the empty glass.

"More?"

"Not right now." We sat there for a moment. "And what are you doing after suburbia?"

"The other compound, in Georgia."

She frowned. "That isn't going to be a walk in the park."

"No, but we have to."

She looked at me for a long moment, still frowning at first, and then smiling instead. "You're a good kid," she said, then lowered her voice until I could just barely hear. "It's almost like we raised you."

I laughed. "It's nice to hear you say that."

She reached out and took my hand with her good one, gave a little squeeze. "We'll have more time," she said. "Now get out of here, let me sleep."

"Yes'm" I set the pitcher and glass on the bedside table.

Chapter Twenty

For all her appearance as a punk slackoff, Morgan was strict and on the ball with some things. Come dawn the next morning, the Jeep was packed and we were getting Sela settled in the back. She'd felt well enough to take her own shower, but had a few Valium rattling around in a prescription bottle in the event things got bad again. In addition to her wrist, some of her ribs were cracked, or broken, from what the chart said. The x-rays weren't included.

"Call this number when you're about an hour out from Camp Foxtrot," Bill said. "Somebody will intercept and bring you in, then bring you up to speed."

"Roger that, thanks. We'll see you again, after things settle down," Morgan said.

"It might be nice to maintain speaking terms," he said. Mrs. Ward, standing with her arm through his, nodded in agreement.

"Right, we'll get a Coutard and have a Potsdam or whatever once Rachel is able." Morgan got in the Jeep and started it up. She raised her hand to the Wards one last time, and then backed out onto the road down the mountain. "You watch, he'll be talking intermarrying first chance he gets."

"I don't know, but I'm not sure it'll work the way he thinks it would."

"I don't really know what'd happen," Sela said from the back, then gave a slight, off-kilter laugh. "But isn't it funny, how much we all look alike, and how different they all are?"

"They do a lot more breeding than we do," Morgan said. She gave me kind of a look, maybe daring me to say anything about window shopping, but I kept my mouth shut.

"Anyway, it's hard to stay with a man indefinitely. When you're there with him in the first place, it's true love, and you're smitten. When I lived with Sidney's father, I couldn't imagine going back to live with my sisters. But then one day, Sidney was only four or five, that was it. We started fighting all the time, I pushed him away at somebody else, packed us up, and went back to the pines. The timeline kinda varies, but it's like that with all of us, even Rachel."

I shook my head. "No offense, but it's hard to imagine Rachel in love."

"She was, once."

"Then what happened?"

Morgan spoke up. "He didn't believe her that all babies are born with blue eyes. He did a pharmacy paternity test on Fran and me, and when it showed we weren't his, kicked us out."

"That sucks." So that's how they knew about what paternity tests looked like.

"It is what it is," Sela murmured, and fell asleep. Morgan shrugged and kept her eyes on the road, occasionally bobbing her head to a song only she could hear. Maybe she'd spent this entire time writing a new album in her head. I couldn't imagine it was ever quiet in there.

"You know, Rachel was probably only as hard on you as she was so that you'd learn," Morgan said after about half an hour.

"That's one excuse," I muttered. "How do you know how hard Rachel was on me?"

She gave me a sidelong glance. "Where was hand holding going to get you?"

"There's hand holding and there's being decent. Well, decent isn't what I mean; I guess she just rubbed me the wrong way. The way she talks is one part bossy three parts confidence and experience, and it's hard not to want to argue with."

"I've felt the same way."

"You're a lot like her, you know," I said after a moment's hesitation.

"What, you still mad at me for the Wal-Mart greeter comment?"

"Well. Yeah."

"Look, the clock is ticking for all of us here. If that got you to focus a little, straighten up, it was worth the cost of whether we were going to be besties."

"Yeah, speaking of that, since it wasn't covered in class. What's the deal with—"

"Our expiration dates?" Morgan asked.

"It's kind of scary." Terrifying. It's terrifying.

"James Culver was forty six when he died and Mary cut the wolf strap. We think it's because of that."

"So everybody's going to be different? Is that why Bill's so old?"

"The first Ward was almost seventy," Sela said from the back seat, startling me. I didn't know she'd woken up. "I do know that story, even if I am kind of high. Or I know the story they tell." She paused for a really long time. "The Wards came from somewhere in Eastern Europe, I don't remember where. One of those places that's kind of an in between country, that Russia took, and then Germany, but the people there really didn't identify themselves as Russian, or German, or whatever else. I don't even remember what their original family name was; I probably couldn't pronounce it anyway. After some war or border war, some mercenaries came through, put the Ward homestead to fire, killed the dogs, killed the sheep, stole the women and horses. The first Ward, whose first name I also can't pronounce, was left for dead. They'd wounded him pretty badly in the fighting, and killed his sons too, but he crawled to the altar in the woods. He prayed to whatever dark god they worshipped there, or gods, and there was plenty of blood around for sacrifice. They say that he turned wolf right there, went and killed the mercenaries, got the women and horses back, and then all of them that survived fled to America before whoever it was hired the mercenaries could come retaliate."

"So you're saying that the Wards are werewolves now because of black magic?"

Sela sighed. "We turn into wolves, kiddo, it ain't exactly science."

Morgan snickered, but didn't comment.

The drive from Pennsylvania back down to Sidney was a pretty one. The leaves were changing, the weather was clear, the sun was out, and even though Sela slept for most of the trip, she didn't mind having the soft top down on the Jeep. We stopped for gas once when we were still in Pennsylvania, me pumping and Morgan going inside for snacks and things.

Then I ran inside to the restroom while Morgan sat with Sela. I could tell, could smell that Sela was in pain. She also had no intention of complaining about it. If anything, she seemed a little embarrassed at the state she was in. I didn't have the right words to try and comfort her, so I just let her be.

When we pulled up in front of Sidney's, she came out to meet us almost immediately, followed by a man wearing wire rimmed glasses, skinny and a shade taller than her. When she saw Sela, the bandages, and the splint on her wrist, Sidney looked like she wanted to cry. "Mama, how do you feel?"

"Tired, mostly. I'm not so bad." Sela accepted help getting out of the Jeep, taking the quilt with her.

"Morgan said there was a car accident? Was the other driver injured?" The man asked. I looked at Morgan, whose face didn't change.

"Not a scratch on him. Drunk drivers!" Sela gave a dismissive laugh. "God looks out for children and fools, and drunks are certainly fools. It wasn't his first offense, so he's already cooling his heels in a cell for parole violation."

"Serves him right," the man said. He looked at Morgan and I and smiled. "This is the most of Sidney's family I've seen in one place. I'm Aaron."

"Aaron, this is Morgan and Allie," Sidney said, putting her hand on his arm.

"Nice to meet you," he said. "You all look so much alike, it's such a surprise."

"Some families are like that," Morgan said. If she had a watch, I was sure she'd be looking at it. She yawned and stretched. "Well, we've still got some road to drag under the bumper before we're done for the day. Don't like to drop and run like this, but Sela you call if you need anything, you've got the new cell number, right?"

"In my pocket," Sela said. Aaron put his arm out, and Sela took it and walked up to the house with him. At the door, she glanced back at us, and I raised my hand in goodbye.

"What the hell happened?" Sidney asked in a low whisper.

"What, did you think they were just going to play checkers? She got hurt when they took them from the cabin, and then they drew a lot of her blood. Did x-rays."

Sidney pinched the bridge of her nose and then rubbed her face. "Okay, I'm sorry. I just was trying not to think about it. Thank you for bringing her here. What are you doing now?"

"Going to Georgia for Dulcie and Rachel."

"Georgia?" Sidney looked at Morgan and looked at me. "You're okay with this?"

"Of course," I said. "What else am I supposed to do?" From the expression on Morgan's face, it was the right answer.

"You've got less of a commitment here than the rest of us."

I shook my head. "No, I don't. You're my family. This is my life now." Morgan smiled.

"We gotta go, Sid," she said. "Take care of your mama, she's got the numbers of the prepaids we have. Things change, I'll call you with other contact info."

"Morgan," Sidney said, and sighed. "I know I all but ran you off last time, and I'm sorry. If things were different, I'd come with you."

"What changed your mind?"

"Family's family, right?"

"Ain't that the truth." Morgan gave her cousin a quick hug and walked off to the Jeep, boot heels clomping on the sidewalk.

"Is Aaron going to think it's weird we're just leaving like this?" I asked.

"Yeah, maybe." Sidney shrugged and smiled. "It won't matter." There it was, that detachment. It must've been an emotional survival thing, a defense mechanism that developed. What mattered was the wolves, and the men could only matter for so long.

"All right then. Bye." Morgan started the engine, and I went and got in. We left that calm New Jersey suburb and got back on the highway, top down, radio playing. It was the kind of day that made you feel like nothing in the world could be wrong.

Chapter Twenty One

An hour away from Sidney's house, we stopped at a Dairy Queen and Morgan shoved her hand in her jeans pocket and came out with some crumpled bills. "I'm going to get a milkshake."

I waited, and laughed a little to myself as I watched a group of teenage boys watch Morgan walk inside. They were probably my age; I spent more time avoiding looking at people's faces than not, even in high school. Maybe especially in high school. I wondered how popular her band was, if we were going to run into groupies. No way to guess how Morgan would act for that, either standoffish or happy for the attention. One of them looked over at me, and elbowed his friend. I looked back at them, wishing for a pair of sunglasses. Wishing I didn't care they were looking at me.

Morgan came out, cheeks sucked in as she drank her milkshake, holding another one. She glanced at the boys, and then came over and handed me her spare. "What's wrong with you?" she asked, looking me up and down. "You didn't want to talk about it the other night, but now that we've got a minute to breathe, do you?"

I took a deep breath, my stomach flip flopping. I didn't know how to talk about it. Morgan was the last person I wanted to talk about this with. Morgan was the only person I had to talk about this with. "I don't know how," I said carefully. Breathing carefully. She watched me peel the paper off my straw, poke it into the milkshake. I could smell the boys from here, their deodorant, their sunscreen. One had new flip flops. One was chewing gum. We'd just spent so much time surrounded by boys and men and it wasn't until I got a breath of fresh air and then smelled them again that I got all knotted up about it. "And I guess...I guess I don't want to bother you? I don't know how allowed to be upset about it I am. It's a thing that happened but that didn't happen. The night before Mama brought me to the aunts. It's why."

Morgan stared at me for longer than was comfortable, but for once, there wasn't a challenge in her face. "Feel what you're gonna feel. It's bullshit to think you're not allowed."

"Thanks," I said. Rachel was Rachel, but she didn't know my mama. I drank some of the milkshake; vanilla. Was it a surprise that Morgan got vanilla milkshakes, or did Morgan only get *me* a vanilla milkshake? I couldn't tell and my ears were ringing with the boys' laughter. I took a breath to talk, then closed my mouth again. I almost couldn't do it. Morgan waited, which was unbelievable. "The night that I turned into a wolf for the first time, I was walking home from a party at school, after a game. One of the football players was pestering me, is why I left, and I kept brushing him off, telling him to leave me alone. He knocked me down, was on top of me, and he had his pants open. I couldn't fight him off, and then I changed. I went after him just enough to hurt him and scare him, and then I got scared and ran into the woods. I didn't remember any of this until that night I was sleeping in the Jeep at the Ward camp; before, I only remembered leaving the school, and then I was puking in the woods with no shoes or jeans. I had to find my way home." I stared straight ahead as I talked, my fingers getting cold on the milkshake, my face getting hot. When I finished, Morgan was quiet, and after a moment I looked at her. I was waiting for the smirk, or the laugh.

"Are you glad you didn't kill him?" she asked finally.

"Yeah, I am. But I don't want him to attack anybody else. I can't imagine I was the first one."

"And you never heard anything about this guy?"

"No. I never heard any rumors or anything about him. There wasn't any graffiti in the bathrooms, nothing." Morgan listened, nodding a little.

"Did Rachel know? And the others?"

"They knew something like that happened. They knew there was a boy. I knew I wasn't raped. But everything was so horrible and confusing when I got here, I guess they just figured they'd handle the wolf issues, and maybe I'd forget the rest. Or because nothing really happened, it wouldn't be such a big deal."

"So I'm the lucky one," she said, then as my stomach dropped, she held up a hand. "No, stop it, that wasn't fair."

I took a deep breath, surprised at how steady I felt. "It's okay. You didn't sign up for this. I didn't sign up for this."

She thought about it for a second and then she did laugh, and I bristled. "What?"

"The look he must have had on his face," she said, shaking her head. I licked my lips and thought about it. Through the fear, the nausea and the shakes, thinking about how I thought Morgan's perspective probably worked, I pictured Kyle's face in that moment, when he realized that for once, something had gone horribly wrong for him. I couldn't manage to laugh, but I kind of half smiled. I didn't realize I was crying until Morgan shoved a bandana in my hand. "There, see, I helped already."

"I guess maybe you did." We climbed into the Jeep, put our milkshakes in the drink holders, and I mopped at my face. Then I sat forward, my elbows on my knees, and cried some more. I hoped I wouldn't throw up in Morgan's Jeep. I didn't think she could be so big-hearted about that. Maybe I was wrong. She let me cry, didn't tell me not to, didn't tell me it was going to be all right, and after a while she put her hand on my back.

"Can you do this?" she asked, in the softest tone I'd ever heard from her, which was still pretty rough.

I didn't hesitate. "Yes." Everything we did was crazy but I didn't have time to think about it, which made me sure. Yeah, I could do it. And if I said I couldn't, she'd leave me somewhere, and I didn't know where that would be. It'd waste too much time to turn around and go back to Sidney's.

"You're sure." She was looking at me seriously, no jokes, no judgment. Well. Not a lot of judgment.

I took a shaky last breath, wiped my face again. "Yes, I'm sure." We sat in the Jeep for a minute, drinking our milkshakes. The boys weren't there anymore.

Chapter Twenty Two

Morgan did the driving, stopped for gas and to pee and to get food and cigarettes on her own mental timeline, and the drive to Georgia was and wasn't like my drive north with Mama. Me and Morgan didn't talk a whole lot, but not because she was mad at me for being a genetic freak, but because I felt too awkward with myself and upset to even try to say much. So she did me a kindness by turning up the music and singing along, and when she couldn't find what she wanted on the radio, we listened to a procession of unmarked tapes that I guess were bands she'd done shows with, or met on tour, or whatever. And we listened to the fuzzy guitar, bluesy hard rock that was Howling. Maybe it was metal? I didn't know enough. There was something about it that I liked, really liked. It was like scratching an itch in my brain that I didn't know I had.

I didn't want to just be with my own thoughts. I didn't really want to be thinking much at all, though it was a weird relief that Morgan told me I was allowed to feel what I wanted. Like I knew it already but just needed somebody else to think so too. I looked at the books or looked out the window, or read the song names, hand-scrawled on the cardboard liners of the Howling tapes. I couldn't say I was learning all the words, it was like I had to train my ear to listen to this kind of music, so I could figure out what the words were, but I was learning the basic tune anyway. The texture of what I thought were the guitar and bass; it was hard to tell sometimes, with whatever techniques they were using, the feedback or effects or whatever. I needed music school and werewolf school all in one. I wondered if Morgan smoked on stage. I wondered what the other people in the band were like. Fake ID Al was the bass player, and he was real quiet. Did the rest of the band know Morgan was a wolf?

"Well, depending on how things go in Georgia, maybe none of us will have to worry about Silvernail for a long time," she said somewhere in South Carolina, squinting in the afternoon sun and sniffing the air to decide on a fast food drive thru; there were a few to pick from, all clustered together.

"Yes, depending." I couldn't make it real, though. Thinking about whatever we were going to do in Georgia, even after Pennsylvania, was far too imaginary to me. Maybe if I'd been inside, instead of on a hill with a rifle. All I could think of was red eyed rabbits in cages, medical tables. All I could think was what Bill said, a company like that, they just had more people, more money, more plans. "This is still so weird, like we're planning a raid on evil Johnson & Johnson's."

Morgan laughed. "It is weird, and I guess we kind of are."

We crossed the border into Georgia around sundown, and then Morgan got off the highway. I was reading the moonshine chapter in the Foxfire book, and it took me a minute to realize she deviated from the script. I sat up and looked around; there were signs for a reservoir, and it looked like we were in an area heavy on the trees and light on the people. She pulled off at a parking area sign and got out. For once, she waited for me.

Morgan stretched, and reached in the Jeep to toss her sunglasses on the dashboard. "We've got the time to throw some punches and get a couple of things in mind. Stretch our legs, get ourselves settled."

"All right." Stomach tight and nervous, I followed Morgan into the tree line. She tilted her head at sounds I wasn't aware of, and sniffed a couple of times. We weren't following a path. After a while, we came into a clearing, and she stopped, and we faced each other. "Now what?"

"Crash course. First off, if you're facing somebody with a weapon, get the weapon out of their hands. On the ground, kick it away, throw it away, something. If you're lucky, they don't know anything about hand to hand, and they'll concentrate on getting that knife or gun back, or keeping you from it, and it'll be a horrible distraction. Don't rely too heavily on anything. You have feet, you have hands. Cultivate a good head butt. Accept that hitting somebody will hurt you as well. We're women, we're built to handle pain."

I wondered if all her not-talking time just now was spent trying to figure out how to tell me things like this, that she somehow already knew. "Is this where the stronger and faster comes in?"

"It helps. We haven't had an Unbreakable 'how much weight can you lift?' session, or at least I haven't. And actually that's kind of a pity. But I'd bet Luke Ward has, or any Ward you can name. I can tear the bumper off a car, but that's not too hard when you think about it. I can run a six minute mile even in jeans and steel toed boots."

"All that and mailbox baseball." I wished I was more like Morgan. I'd bet Morgan never had a Kyle Dodd catch her vulnerable. Morgan wasn't vulnerable. She was relentless and strong and wild.

Morgan smirked. "Smartass," she said. Then she picked up a branch. "Okay. This is a rifle. If they're dumb enough to poke you with the barrel, that's great for you, because it means you know exactly where the gun is even if the guy is standing behind you. If he's in front of you, push it up, knock the butt down, hit 'em in the face with the barrel. Make sense?"

"I think so?"

"Do it." Morgan shouldered the stick and pointed it at me like we were playing soldiers. I stood there, flexed my hands a second, and breathed. I tried to think of how I would feel if I was really looking down a rifle barrel, and decided if that ever happened to me, I was going to try to remember Morgan with a stick instead. I took a breath, let it out, and moved. Pushed the barrel up, slapped the butt down, and if Morgan wasn't faster than me, I would hit her in the face with the stick. She laughed. "Good."

"Have you ever actually done that?"

"No, but I like watching tactical videos on YouTube."

"Great. Yes, of course." Well, we had that military survival book in the back, I could flip through that instead of reading about moonshine. Did it have combat stuff in it? Maybe it was just about animal traps and edible plants. "Now what?"

"It sucks for everybody to get kicked or kneed in the groin. Knees too, knees are real vulnerable. Don't try to figure out what somebody is doing by watching their eyes; stare at them in the chest, center mass. That way you can see which way they're going to move. If they have a gun, get in close. If they have a knife, make them come to you. If you have a jacket, try and get their knife arm trapped up in it. Hit that elbow, then their wrist, make them drop it."

This was a lot, and I was getting all nerved up again. "How much of this have you had to do?" Then I remembered her stomping that Ward's knee in the Bear's Den parking lot.

"I've had my scraps. Not typically with knives or guns. But like I said, YouTube is a goldmine." She dropped the stick, and when my eyes flicked down at it, she punched me right in the jaw. I tensed at the last moment, kept my teeth from clacking together, and I gave an involuntary step back. It hurt an unbelievable amount.

"Morgan, what the fuck." That was three. The more I said fuck, the easier it happened.

She swung again, and this time I stepped into the arc of the swing and put my shoulder against hers, knocking her back a step and trying to trip her. That backed her up another step and we stood apart again. I was breathing hard; she wasn't. My heart thump-thumping in my ears. "All right. Now hit me."

I wound up and stepped in, and she didn't move. Punching her in the jaw hurt almost as much as getting punched in the jaw. "Now with your left hand." I did, clumsily and with far less power. When Morgan brought up her hands again, I dodged in time. We went back and forth like this for what seemed like a long time. Never in my life had I been in a fight, other than the pushing and hair pulling that siblings get into.

And that one instance of pushing and hair pulling from Kyle Dodd. I gritted my teeth and buckled down.

We got back to the Jeep after dark and slightly worse for the wear, a fresh rip in the knee of Morgan's new jeans, a split on the inside of my lip that I kept poking at with my tongue. I was far from comfortable and confident with the idea of fighting, but I was closer. I wondered how Morgan had learned, other than YouTube. I imagined Rachel as the lesson master; it was a shame she and I hadn't gotten that far. Or maybe not. I wished I'd just known all of Mama's family all along.

"Just gotta make a phone call," Morgan said, taking out her burner.

"Doesn't bother me any," I said, mystified.

She dialed, let the phone ring twice, then snapped it closed. She opened it and dialed again. "Hunter? Yeah hey, it's me. Look, off the record, what do I have to worry about from Luke Ward?" She listened for a minute and shook her head. "Other than testosterone bullshit." I kind of nudged her, and she looked up at me and rolled her eyes. I got in the Jeep and waited, watching Morgan pace back and forth, chew on her lip some, laugh, then smile and end the call. I half expected her to break it in half and drop the pieces in the oil drum garbage can by the trail head, but she didn't this time.

"I thought we weren't getting the Coutards involved?" I asked. Though really, I wanted everybody involved. Anybody we could get to help, who was actually helping and not with some kind of weird shadow over it like dealing with the Wards.

"I needed some friendly advice, and Hunter's where I can get that from. Nothing official."

"If you say so. What was her advice?"

"To watch our backs."

"That isn't new."

"Guess not." The way Morgan smiled, they talked about more than that. They had to've been friends for a long time. "Nice to have the reminder, anyway. Especially with how welcoming they've been."

"Oh yes, they're princes, every one." I didn't have the courage to ask more about Hunter, the only non-family, non-Ward person she'd talked about since I'd known her. I didn't even know the names of the people in her band. Other than Al.

An hour or so down the road, Morgan dug another burner out of the center console and said "Okay, dial that and put it on speaker."

A few rings, and somebody that sounded like Joe picked up in a house that was surprisingly noisy, for how late it was. "Ward residence."

"Hey, uh, Foxtrot." She rolled her eyes. "We're on approach."

"Roger that, Foxtrot hears you, we are on the lookout."

"Okay, see you soon." Morgan said and I poked the end call button. "I don't imagine we'll hit Silvernail tonight, probably tomorrow earliest."

"That makes sense."

"From how they talk about it, they've obviously been watching them already. I wonder if you and I ought to have our own contingency plan, or fallback point, or whatever. We don't know the area, though, so it's pretty much impossible to plan."

"Well okay. I know Hunter just warned you, but you're still having trouble trusting them? Even after Sela?"

"It's hard to shake. It's not like we can do this alone, but if something goes bad, I need you to just back me up, I guess. Just trust me."

"Back you up how? Trust you to do what?" I kind of already trusted you more than anybody else, I thought, but I didn't say. I was going to tell Dulcie first, I thought. I was going to talk about it with Dulcie, who was so welcoming, so warm, so fast to mother me. We would get them back and then we wouldn't have to make all the decisions anymore.

"Well if I knew that, I wouldn't have to ask. Can you just do that? Follow my lead? Trust me?" Morgan took her eyes off the road and stared at me.

"I trust you," I said. "I've been following your lead since I got you out of jail."

She looked ahead again, nodded. "Good. Good. Let's just hope this goes as smooth as getting Sela did."

"Hoping and praying."

Chapter Twenty Three

A hummer pulled up next to us on the highway, we exchanged some meaningful glances, and they led us in. It came as a surprise when Camp Foxtrot was in fact a yellow, vinyl-sided house in a cul-de-sac, suburb to Atlanta. Another hummer and some SUVs parked up the wide driveway and the street in front. Groomed lawn and shrubs that were sure to be emerald green in the daylight, magnolia tree, laundry on the lines out back, the whole nine. The smell of food grilling hit us strong when Morgan and I got out and closed the Jeep doors, assessing the situation. It was the picture of a Modern South idyll, right out of one of the glossy magazines the church ladies sometimes looked at, even as they disapproved of the decadence of some of it. The yellow house had a satellite dish on the side, and an array of antenna clustered around the chimney.

We clomped up the front walk, behind the two Wards from the highway, and I flinched when the automatic sprinklers kicked on. The front door swung open before we reached the stoop, and three dogs ran out to dance around us, two black labs and a German Shepherd. There was much panting, sniffing, and some hand licking, and then they let us go forward.

"You ladies run into trouble?" Of course it was Luke in the doorway, holding a beer and looking us over. My lip had swollen a little, and I noticed now that one of Morgan's knuckles was split.

"Nah, just blowing off a little steam," Morgan grinned, looking him dead in the eyes.

"Fair enough. Come on in." He turned and walked into the house, leaving the door open for us to follow. I glanced around the neighborhood once before closing the door behind us. Still quiet. Somebody hosing their car off down the street. Kids running around in one of the yards. I could hear news on the TV in the house next door. The dogs clicked down the tile hallway and I closed out the world.

The house was full of people. Wolves. There were kids playing a video game on a big TV. There were women in the kitchen, cooking and chattering and drinking wine. I couldn't tell what the people upstairs were doing, but I could hear ping pong balls in the basement, and keyboards rattling. Then I shook my head because the ringing in my ears overtook everything else, and when I was done Morgan had a beer and was staring at me in her 'are you fucking kidding me?' way and Luke was holding out a soda. "Thanks," I said. Why was Luke handing me a soda anyway?

"No problem." He looked at me again for a long moment, glanced at Morgan, and sauntered off. We followed him through the crowd of strangers, into the kitchen and through the open door that led to the basement stairs.

"Hey, when did you get here?" Joe appeared at my elbow, smiling.

"Just now." I hoped I didn't look as dazed as I felt.

"Good timing, we only just finished parsing the intel, and dinner will be ready soon."

"Late dinner isn't it? What intel, from the hard drive you got?" I thought if I never heard the word intel again, I could live a happy life. Was it so hard to say information? Info?

"No, from Silvernail Atlanta," Luke said shortly, looking like he could deal with Joe going somewhere else. We passed the kids playing ping pong and in the next room was a row of three computers, Wards busy on them, and a big wooden table with maps and files and coffee cups spread over it. "In a way, it's almost the same compound. Setting is different, though. It's in its own office park that abuts a residential neighborhood. Oh and they have dogs instead of drones." Luke motioned us over to one end of the table, where there were computer printouts, pictures of a tall fence with barbed wire, security cameras, a gate, a handler with German Shepherds.

"What are we going to do if the dogs are out?" I asked, because everybody else seemed to know. I was having a hard time concentrating on any one thing, with all the smells, and people, and noise. I really hoped the answer was not that we were going to be shooting the dogs.

"Bear repellant," said the Ward in the room who looked next oldest. He came and shook my hand, and Morgan's. "Tyler," he said, looking at me a little too long. Maybe I was just tense because Morgan's faceless friend Hunter told us to watch our backs. Hunter who couldn't carry a tune in a bucket. Hunter who always answered when Morgan called, and who Morgan said *sorry* to. Oh, Hunter was—

"Bear repellant, and barring that, you catch them on your left arm, and kill them with your right. Or vice versa. You've seen a demonstration of a trained dog attacking somebody?" I nodded automatically when I heard the question, then my brain caught up. I forgot why I'd seen it, maybe a military video in history class? It didn't matter. "Depending on how it hits you, the dog will take you down. If you roll with it, it'll be easier, and then sink a hunting knife in the neck just behind the jaw, where the artery is." I nodded again, as my stomach did a slow roll. I was never going to remember that. I never imagined I'd be surrounded by people who gave out killing advice so casually.

"What's the plan?" Morgan asked, glancing at me with a little frown. I popped the tab on my soda and drank some, bubbles almost making me sneeze.

"Tomorrow night, right around midnight. It seems like the shift change, so a patrol won't be on the grounds right then. We make it through the fence in three groups, and enter in these locations." Tyler pulled over a map of the compound, and Luke pointed at the entrances. "Kennels are here, so only this group should have to deal with the dogs. Inside, they probably don't use them. Dog hair and equipment, we're familiar with that, right?" There was laughter around the room.

Next was a photocopied blueprint. "Group two is here for the computer lab. We want to take or damage everything that we have, do our best to break the back of whatever data storage and processing they have on site. The medical bay is in the sublevel, with some research labs along the way. The third is there for extraction. There's no telling how much time we'll have before they scramble backup. We've managed to finagle access to a lot of material, but that wasn't included; they haven't had to deal with this before, and because of the op in Pennsylvania, they're more ready for us than they would've been otherwise. They know now that somebody's keyed to them."

Morgan took it all in, nodding. She hadn't opened her soda yet. "Have you heard any chatter about Pennsylvania?" she asked.

"Surprisingly little. They've got internal networks that we haven't gained access to yet, and they've been careful all along with communications. An additional target is their main server; employees can dial in from home, and we plan on jacking in a virus that fucks those computers on contact."

"How do you plan on fucking the computers on site?"

"That's not something you need to worry about."

I tensed, because there was no way Morgan would be happy with that answer, but she just nodded. "So what, you get into the server room, get the virus on there using a thumb drive or whatever?" Morgan looked at Luke, one of the papers in her hand. I tilted my head just enough to see; it looked like the medical sublevel. "What kind of a virus?" Luke tapped the nearest computer guy on the shoulder. He'd stopped typing when we started talking, and spun his chair around.

"This is Everett, he did the virus work."

"It collects information based on a search of certain keywords and stores it on a secure server we own that's hosted in Europe. Then it deletes the hard drives and overwrites them three times with garbage." Everett was the computer tech model of Ward, rather than the military model. He looked really young, though, like he was fresh out of college. I wondered if it was a Ward objective to go forth and sow the wild oats. I guessed everybody in the whole house was in the know. I took another drink of my soda, resisted the urge to press the cool can against my neck and forehead. The carbonation burned in my throat.

An honest to goodness dinner bell sounded upstairs, making me jump nearly out of my skin. It rang in my head for too long, and the Wards started to mosey upstairs for their meal. Morgan caught my elbow and we hung back. "What the fuck is wrong with you?" she asked in a barely audible whisper.

I cleared my throat. Morgan learned a lot about me today, and here was her chance to learn more. She was sure to be real excited. "This happened sometimes, early on. I feel all achy and feverish. Dulcie said it was because I didn't have the luxury of doing things gradually."

"Shit." She noticed Luke looking at us and flashed him a tight, steely smile, and put the printout she still held back on the table, nodding at me to move. "What, you need to sleep it off? Run around the block?"

"I don't know. I just need to ride it out I guess."

"Let's just be glad the beer's already flowing and probably nobody's gonna notice."

"Maybe I can pass it off from being in the car all this time over the past couple of days?"

"Look, just don't explain anything to anybody, it's not their business."

"I'm sorry, it's not on purpose." She just shook her head. The stairwell had cleared of Wards, and we climbed up. Plates got shoved in our hands and we joined the buffet line. More burgers, and ribs, and potato salad.

Joe fell in line behind me with a fresh plate. "Gotta move faster than that to get food around here," he said with a grin. Kids were running around, and a baby cried out in the living room, piercing my skull.

"There sure are a lot of you," I said. Just like the most crowded church picnic, day in and day out.

"Can hardly hear myself think sometimes at get-togethers." Morgan moved to the other counter to where the different salads were, and I started putting burgers on buns. There were plates of cheese and bacon, and jars of pickles. I tried to concentrate on doing that, and quickly; my hands were going to start shaking soon, I was sure. Joe stepped in a little closer and lowered his voice. "Morgan should be more careful about how she talks to Luke."

"Why's that?"

"Her attitude rubs him wrong."

"He's a big boy, he'll manage," I said. "And I think it's on purpose anyway."

"Just thought it would be fair to give a warning." Joe shrugged and started loading his own burgers. "It'll probably be less crowded out on the patio," he said when he saw me flinching at another high-pitched kid-scream.

"Thanks," I said. The potato salad did look really good. My nose cut out on me, but it looked like there might be mustard involved. Mama always put celery in her potato salad, and I never knew why. There were baked beans, thick and dark with molasses, and the knives and forks were in a basket.

I got those, another can of soda, and looked for Morgan; she was already at the sliding door to the patio. "Surprised you waited for me," I said.

"Somebody's got to look out for you." There were tiki torches lit around the perimeter of the patio, and some littler kids playing freeze tag. A slate path led to a gazebo further back in the property, and I could see the glowing ends of cigarettes as the people out there, people and wolves, smoked and talked. We had the patio to ourselves, until Joe came out too, balancing his food and utensils and a couple of drinks. "What, you're our shadow now?"

Joe paused in the act of lowering himself into a seat, looking kind of hurt. "I just figured you'd like having somebody around that you kind of knew. Instead of just complete strangers."

Morgan shrugged. "It's a nice thought, I guess." She started in on her plate. I gave Joe what I hoped was a sympathetic smile. If I told Morgan to be nice, she'd just be worse instead. It wasn't Joe's fault, he had to know that. He smiled a little, and shrugged. Bill probably did have him spying on us, but I wasn't sure that was the case. Maybe he just wanted to be away from Luke, I could relate to that. That's probably why he gave a warning about Luke; he knew what it was like if Luke didn't like you. I concentrated on my plate, and on trying to keep myself together.

People passed in and out of the back yard, and the kids were eventually all rounded up either to bed or to be carried off home by their parents. Morgan and I drew some looks, but much like the first night at the campfire, nobody was much interested in mingling. At least we hadn't just been in a fist-fight with them. Morgan, not really we. Actually, I was kind of glad that Joe had decided to sit out there with us. Then Everett came to the sliding door and leaned out to us. "Rest of the debriefing down cellar."

"Thanks," Joe said. Everett gave a wave, and slid the door closed against the bugs. I heard him whistle for one of the dogs, then the hiss of a bottle being opened, before feet thumped on the cellar steps again.

"Ready?" Morgan asked me. I nodded, and we got up. Joe reached for our paper plates, and we handed them over.

"Hey Joe," I said, when Morgan was already to the door and we were still making our way.

"Yeah?"

"I appreciate you trying to make us feel welcome. Thank you."

"You're welcome," he said, looking surprised but pleased. "It doesn't look like a lot of fun, being in your situation. It's the least I could do." He paused, kind of glanced around, maybe to make sure Luke wasn't around to go after him. "It's the only decent thing to do."

Morgan turned around, frowning, and we hurried up.

Downstairs, some of the printouts had made their way onto walls, and there were more. It was beginning to look more like what I'd come to see as a War Room in the eyes of the Wards. The table now had a much larger map of the compound and its environs pieced together on its surface. Tyler and Luke stood at the head of the table and waited as we filed in. They looked close enough to be brothers, I thought, not cousins. I was surprised at the number of wolves here, twenty or more. I didn't spend too much time fidgeting and looking around to get numbers; I didn't need to draw any more attention. Morgan caught my eye and nodded very slightly. Good, I was doing good.

"Rest up tonight, people. Tomorrow after sunset we'll find safe parking and waiting spots, and around midnight we'll move in." Luke's voice cut through the other conversations, and everybody straightened up and listened. He counted people off, breaking everybody into groups of three or four. There were just the three teams going into the property, but there was more work to be done, driving and surveillance and even just cars to be on the road and confuse traffic for our retreat. Of course Morgan and I were in the group that went to the medical bay for Rachel and Dulcie, and they put Joe and Everett with us.

"We realize that there is no way for us to destroy all of the data that Silvernail has gained and gathered," Tyler said. "But we can do a lot of damage, and get a firm grasp of what they think they know. Understanding their activity and how far they've gotten is of the utmost importance, in addition to getting family back for these girls. We're in a unique position here, where we don't think that Silvernail will be calling the police. If they're holding private citizens for scientific experimentation, they will not want the general public knowing this, and that includes law enforcement. Of course, this also means that we're playing for keeps."

Morgan tilted her head towards me slightly, and I took a deep breath to get myself in hand; of course they would try to kill us. Of course we might have to hurt badly, or kill, some of them. Even after Pennsylvania, it wasn't real until Tyler said it. In Pennsylvania, I'd only shot drones. I didn't even ask what the others had done. None of them had come out with a scratch on them, other than Sela. I thought of Sidney's sleepy neighborhood for a moment, with the smell of so much new coming off everything.

Tyler continued. "The first team will get in and cut out the security cameras as quickly as possible, and make sure all the keycard doors are disabled. We will stagger the groups, second team in five minutes after the first, and so on. Keep your ears open for the signal to abort, or the signal to come on early. Each team will be apprised of fallback positions, should anybody become separated. We will not leave anybody behind." He looked to me and Morgan. "Ladies, your team comes in last, and you should be cleared to come straight up the middle. Due to intel, we don't anticipate any security on the medical level; your people are sure to be in both physical and chemical restraints. We'll give you adrenaline shots to administer at your discretion. Of course, you won't know their condition until you're at their position. Your people, your call." I glanced at Morgan, who nodded, stone faced.

"We'll apprise you of your parking and fallback locations individually," Luke said. "Due to the nature of the mission, compartmentalizing information is the way to go. I really hope I don't need to say this, but I will anyway, regardless of what the security camera situation is or seems to be, do not go feral on Silvernail property or in view of the compound. We never know when there are eyes and ears. If anybody has a problem with this, we will pull you now and replace you with another member of the family." Nobody said anything, just watched and waited.

"All right, we'll give you the locations then. Any other questions you want to address privately, now or tomorrow morning is the time." Luke picked up a stack of plain folders and motioned the first group forward.

Chapter Twenty Four

They put me and Morgan in a second floor guest room with two twin beds and not a whole lot else. The house, the whole *neighborhood*, was quiet after the Ward party broke up, quiet and so very bright, with street lights and other house lights, and a growing half moon. I laid on my back and listened to cars on the nearby highway, and listened to Morgan's even sleep-breathing. The rest of the house went to sleep in stages after we did, the last person to bed doing some of the washing up in the kitchen before they climbed the stairs. I couldn't fall asleep.

The chills and aches set in, just like I was worried they would, and I tried to just stretch out on my back, then rolled onto my stomach. There was a blanket on the bed, but I still couldn't get warm. I tossed a little longer, and then Morgan rolled over and snorted in her sleep, so I got up and crept out of the room and down the stairs, flinching at every creak in the floor. I stood in the kitchen for a few minutes, shivering, listening to the fridge run, and listening to the clock tick. It was 2 a.m.

I was at a loss. In this house, on uneasy ground, I didn't really feel like I could do anything. I was still in all right territory to lie that I was looking for a bathroom should I be caught out. Sleepwalking was pushing the boundaries too far. I paced around the kitchen once, and stopped to look out the sliding glass door.

A cold nose pressed into my hand and I almost screamed, but kept it to a gulping inhale of breath instead. It was one of the black labs, looking up at me with soft brown eyes, her head cocked. I crouched down and took her head in both hands, scratch-rubbing her ears as the dogs in the pines had taught me was the best way. She groaned a little, happily, leaning into my hands. I smiled and pressed my forehead against the top of her head, inhaling. There was something calming about the clean grassy smell of dog, and some of my chills stilled.

The lab swiped my cheek with her tongue and padded away again. None of the other dogs came to investigate. I straightened and went to the sink, filled a plastic cup with water. As I drank it, the hairs on the back of my neck stood up, and I turned to face Luke, too close. Morgan would've known he was coming before he was even in the room. "Not spying on us, are you?" he asked, joking but with a knife edge of danger.

"Not unless spying on leftovers counts," I said.

"Find any?"

"It occurred to me that it would be weird to go through somebody else's refrigerator. I was just going to settle for a drink of water and go back to bed." I started to step away from the sink, but Luke didn't move.

"Good thing I came down, then. You want a sandwich? You can have a sandwich." He smelled like shampoo, and beer, and gun oil. He held my gaze for too long, and I thought only about my breathing, keeping my breathing slow and even, and going back to bed. I thought of Morgan upstairs, and turned my head to yawn.

"I was just going to go back to bed after all," I repeated. I needed him to get away from me.

"Bullshit. Sit down." He sniffed once, then turned and went to the refrigerator. There was an entire roast turkey in there, and big stacks of sliced cheese. Bread was on the table; maybe midnight sandwiches were a Ward tradition. He set out plates, and some knives for the mayonnaise and mustard. He went back to the fridge and took out two beers, opening one and setting it down in front of me. I shut up and concentrated on making my sandwich. The turkey smelled good, though I wasn't the slightest bit hungry.

Luke sat down across from me and cracked his beer open before slapping his sandwich together. "The two of you are kind of a mystery to me. Your cousin, she's kind of like one of the guys, but you, you've hardly said anything since we got started. You just watch and listen."

"Can't always have a lot to say." I kept my head down, and cut the sandwich in half in triangles, the way Kevin and Jason liked it. I wasn't sweating anymore, but my heart still pounded in my ears. I didn't doubt that Luke could hear it. Werewolves, the ultimate lie detector.

He drank some of his beer. "Most people run at the mouth too much. Maybe we need some kind of get-togethers, so we're all accustomed to one another. Our families have the potential to get pretty friendly."

"Might not be a bad idea. That way we could avoid some of the posturing when paths cross," I said dryly. He hadn't started to eat yet, was just watching me across the table. "And property damage."

"Morgan's idea, I assume."

"Most things are." If Morgan was at the table here, she'd be getting information out of him. I couldn't do that.

"That level of confrontation doesn't seem to be your style."

I shrugged and ate my sandwich, trying not to look like I was rushing. The turkey was as good as it smelled. I drank the beer, slowly; maybe it would help me sleep. We sat in silence, in the dark, chewing. I finished and started to get up; he grabbed my wrist.

Don't change, I thought through my adrenaline rush, my immediate impulse to just panic as hard and as long as I could, until he stopped whatever he was doing. "Let go of me," I said through gritted teeth, breathing rapidly. I didn't look at him, I looked away and down. There was no way I was going to win a stare down with Luke. I thought for a second that he wouldn't let go, and I would just lose it. I didn't know what would happen after that. He let go, though, sat back and sipped at his beer.

"Interesting," he said. I couldn't begin to wonder what he was even talking about, process it; I just needed to get away from him, unable to stop my lip from curling. "Sleep tight."

I backed down the hall, and climbed the stairs slowly. Nobody else in the house stirred; I could hear Luke in the kitchen, opening another beer, getting up to put my dish in the sink. I made it back into the guest room, closed the door softly, and lowered myself onto the bed. "Who did you talk to?" Morgan asked abruptly, her voice clear and awake.

"Oh Jesus Christ," I jerked upright, my heart in my throat.

"What, like right there in the kitchen?"

"Morgan, you scared the hell out of me." I realized I was holding my hand to my chest.

"You think I wasn't worried, with you creeping about alone in the night?"

"I didn't expect you to be, no." I took a deep breath and let it out, laid back down again. "I went and got a drink of water. Luke came down into the kitchen to make a sandwich and make sure I wasn't spying."

"What did you say?"

"That I was getting a drink of water."

"That was it?"

"Then he made me sit down with him and make a sandwich. He said you were like one of the guys."

Morgan propped herself up on an elbow. "Made you make a sandwich? That's kind of weird."

"It was kind of weird." After the encounter with Luke, and Morgan almost scaring me to death, I felt almost normal again. Maybe a scare would've been the cure for my werewolf growing pains all along, like startling a person with hiccups.

"He was just intimidating you for the sake of it. That kind of guy just wants to feel like he's in control. What else did you say?" She lay down again.

"Nothing, really. I was concentrating on keeping calm. I blamed you for Bill's truck, at the bar."

"Good job."

"Thanks. It didn't surprise him one little bit." Morgan's breathing evened out again into sleep. I stared at the ceiling for a while, trying to relax enough to sleep. Then I slept like a rock until dawn.

Judging from the mom-yells emanating from the first floor, there were several children in this Ward household that needed to be packed up to get on the school bus. I imagined a sandwich assembly line in the kitchen; maybe that's what the turkey was for? I rolled over and looked at Morgan; she had one of the family diaries open, a pad of paper on her knee. It was funny to see her using paper instead of her skin.

"Find anything new?"

"I was looking at some of the older stuff, actually. Tried to get a sense of the history of this Ward bullshit. Or if Silvernail did anything before. Or other families working together, and how long it lasted."

"Well that's a good idea, I guess." Two kids thundered past our door, fighting over a video game system or fake gun or something. I watched her chew on the end of a pencil and waited for her to go on. "Well?"

"Well what?"

"What did you find??"

"Well, Rachel wrote down some notes on it in another book, so that was useful. It looks like somebody married into somebody else's family once. Not us and not Wards, so I guess that's why it always got skipped in the werewolf history lessons. There was a train wreck before the marriage was consummated. Man, what're the chances?"

"An actual train wreck? That's terrible, Morgan."

"I'm surprised it's been done at all. We're sort of territori-al."

"Oh, you think? I'm half expecting people to be peeing on things."

Morgan laughed. "The Wards probably do." She closed the books, stuck them in a plastic bag and tucked them into the duffle with the guns. I hadn't noticed her bring that in, maybe she went out for it after I fell asleep. "We should probably go throw elbows for some breakfast."

"I'm sure it won't be that bad."

"No, but tell me you wouldn't want to take a shot at Luke." She looked at me and I shrugged. I was afraid of Luke. I wanted to be far away from Luke, which was unfortunately not a current option.

We got dressed and went downstairs just as the last of the kids trickled out the front door towards the bus. The dogs danced about the front door, watching them go, and came to Morgan and I for a cursory sniff when we reached the bottom of the stairs. The lab girl put her nose to my knee and I patted her. In the kitchen, there were fewer Wards than the night before. Tyler was doing something to the garbage disposal, head and shoulders under the sink, and Luke supervised, leaned against the counter.

"Where is everybody?" Morgan asked.

"Got on the road. No sense hanging around here all day when there's ground to be covered." Morgan looked at me; that hadn't been the plan as I understood it.

"Well okay then. I guess give us our orders and we'll head out as well."

"There's no rush. It's just best to let some people stretch their legs." Luke smiled, relaxed and smug.

"Oh, I'm not rushing. I do aim to have breakfast and a shower first." Morgan smiled and helped herself to the cereal bar.

Luke looked at me. "How about you, how'd you sleep?"

"Slept like a baby, knowing we were safe and sound in a houseful of menfolk like you," I said, trying Morgan's grin on for size. It fit a little better this time. Morgan snickered into her Cheerios.

Luke laughed a little, and shook his head. "Well that's good." Tyler sat up and wiped his hands, got to his feet.

"Try it now," Tyler said, and Luke turned the sink on, then flicked the disposal switch. It gave a throaty growl. "Sounds right."

As Morgan and I sat and ate cereal, Joe appeared, and then Everett, Joe's hair sleep mussed. Or come to think of it, that was just how Joe's hair always looked. "Where is everybody?" Joe asked, and Luke stared at him until he put his hands up in surrender and rooted around in the fridge. The girl lab came and sat next to me, resting her head on my knee. I finished my cereal and stroked her head absently. I wanted to ask what the dogs' names were, but didn't want to talk to Luke any more than I had to.

"Bathroom with showers is upstairs," Tyler said when I brought our dishes to the sink. "There's guest towels for both of you in there."

Once Morgan and I were upstairs, she leaned over close. "I'm really getting the feeling that Luke needs an attitude adjustment," she said in my ear.

"I can get behind that," I said. The bathroom was huge, and there were multiple shower stalls. "Maybe you've just got a high opinion of yourself, though. I wouldn't tangle with him, even after our practice."

"Never stopped me before," Morgan said, and I thought about her opening her arms at the Wards as they came out of the Bear's Den.

"Does anything stop you?"

She laughed. "Not much."

I'd never seen a bathroom in a house with more than one shower in it, just at the high school. Of course, everybody else in the world, or at least in the werewolf world, seemed way more comfortable with their bodies than me. "This is weird."

"Hope nobody downstairs flushes the toilet while we're in here," Morgan said from her shower, and I laughed.

"Wouldn't put it past them."

"How long before you figure they'll let us leave?" she asked.

"Lunch, if I had to guess."

"They keep laying out meals the way they are, I might be inclined to feel good towards the Ward pheromones."

"Morgan! Really?"

"Depends on who it is, I guess. I'm not sure how that would work out, but I'm not in the baby making market just yet anyway. If ever."

"I guess once you have your ever burning love, we'll find out." I still got wavery and ill when I thought about Kyle's hands on me. But Morgan was joking and I didn't want to ruin the mood.

"Can't argue with fate. Though how do you know I haven't already met my ever burning love?" I could hear the grin in her voice.

"Actually I have a guess at that, but I've been keeping it to myself."

"Oh, I'm dying to hear this." So was every Ward who could hear us talking in this tiled echo chamber, I thought.

"Hunter?" I asked quietly, pitching my voice so maybe only Morgan could hear it and nobody else. If I was wrong, she was going to laugh and laugh. She didn't laugh.

"Well look at you," she said, really just sounding very pleased. "I mean, I probably dropped more than enough hints but—"

"But I am entirely oblivious," I said, and we both laughed.

We finished showering and dressed in silence. I toweled my hair in front of the mirror and then brushed my teeth with my finger. I kept forgetting to get a toothbrush. Morgan did the same thing the next sink over, and then rummaged in the drawers under the vanity, coming up with dental floss. "Do you think Ward/Culver babies would have brown eyes or blue eyes?" she asked, mumbling around the floss and fingers in her mouth.

"Seriously?" She cocked an eyebrow at me. I sighed. "Blue eyes are recessive, so probably brown. And oh yeah, normal people don't turn into wolves. So I can't even begin to guess.

Maybe we need some more scientists, but the kind that aren't creepy kidnappers."

She dropped the used floss in the wastebasket, rinsed her mouth, and spit in the sink. "Geeze, I was just asking. You're awful goddamn touchy."

"I think I've got reason to—"

"You sure do, but nobody outside this room needs to know that." She pulled on a lock of my hair and walked out.

Chapter Twenty Five

We mooned around the house and the basement command center, snacking and asking questions and making pleasantries until Luke all but ran us off with a shotgun. We got in the Jeep, Morgan and I in the front seat, the Wards in the back, and she grinned at me as she settled her sunglasses on her nose. "What kind of music you boys like?" she asked, and turned on the radio. "Not that it matters, but for my own edification."

"Lots of stuff," Joe said dubiously. I could sense the hesitation borne of the fear that the wrong answer would just get him made fun of.

"Metal." Everett said, not looking up from the tablet he was working on, an earbud in one ear. They'd added their own duffle of gear to the already pretty crowded cargo area of the Jeep, and Luke had given us a pair of radios to use on site. "Some rock. Depends on the band."

"When are they leaving?" I asked. Luke and his team were still lounging about the living room as we pulled out of the cul-de-sac.

"Luke does things in his own time," Joe said.

I smirked. "I know what that's like." Morgan swatted me without looking.

Joe and Everett were quiet in the backseat for the drive to Atlanta. When we were getting close, Everett sat forward and started to give Morgan directions, but she waved him off. "I got it."

"You know where we're supposed to park?" I couldn't blame Everett for sounding confused; that I could tell, Luke had never given Morgan the position we were supposed to maintain.

"I was here on tour, so I know where we're supposed to end up. I'll choose my own parking, if you don't mind."

"I don't see why that would be a problem," Joe said, desperate to keep the peace. I glanced back. Everett shrugged, frowning.

"On tour?" he asked.

Morgan glanced at me, grinning, so I did the honors. "Morgan's the lead singer of Howling."

Everett stared back at me. "Wait, what?"

"And lead guitar," Morgan said. "I guess I'm the bandleader? The frontwoman? That sounds less like I should be spinning a baton. Anyway yeah, Howling is my deal."

"Why didn't you say something sooner?"

"Oh, do you think it would've smoothed things along? Heya Mr. Ward I've got this band, see, and these people just kidnapped my mom and my aunts so if you could help I'll throw a free concert for you or something, does that sound good?" I couldn't help but laugh; somehow she delivered it straight, though.

"Well, no, it's not like Grandpa likes Howling. I'm just...I was just..."

"He's star struck," Morgan said to me. "This is good for our teambuilding, wouldn't you say?"

"Probably? We'll see once we get to trust falls." That surprised her, she really laughed at that.

"What's it like?" Joe asked, as Everett shook off his daze.

"What's what like?" Morgan asked.

"Touring, I guess. Being in a band like that."

"It's interesting, anyway. I get to travel around sometimes. I get royalty checks, also sometimes. Interviews are a pain in the ass, but I avoid it when I can. Otherwise, messing with interviewers is fun. And I love being on stage."

"I never would've guessed that," I muttered, and she reached over and gave me a shove.

"You'd like it too, I bet," she said, out of the blue.

"I don't know." I was surprised, and more than a little pleased, especially because Morgan didn't just say things to be nice. I'd known her all of three-four days and I knew that about her.

We drove through a gas station McDonald's and found a parking lot next to a river path. If we kept up with all this junk food, I was just going to turn into an oil slick.

"You should get what you want from the duffle now, so we're not trying to shuffle through things after dark."

"Okay," I said. Morgan had a messenger bag that I didn't remember seeing, and I could only imagine that it contained the things from our Home Depot shopping trip. What could I possibly want from the duffle? Should I bring a gun? Just a hunting knife? The bear repellant that Luke gave us, definitely. The can was huge, and I wondered how much continuous spray time it had. I turned it over in my hands, reading the label, but I heard Morgan sigh, and I leaned over and pushed through the duffle. Would I be less afraid to shoot somebody or stab them with a hunting knife? I didn't want either. I took the sawed-off; I knew how to shoot, at least. I'd only ever used a knife in the kitchen. Morgan handed me another messenger bag like hers.

"Now what?" Everett asked as they checked the radios, and the straps on their gear.

"Now we hike to our waiting place. Silvernail isn't too far that way, and judging from the way the neighborhood looks, there's enough vacant to find a good hiding place until we get our signal." Morgan locked the Jeep and caught my eyes, and then moved her eyes down to the bumper of the Jeep. I crouched to fix my laces, and looked; there was a small box on the underside of the bumper, A spare key? I stood up and glanced at her briefly, hoping she got that I got it.

Everett took the lead, and Morgan let him. He was on obvious alert, trying to have his eyes everywhere at once. To a normal person, we were maybe just some kids taking a walk. It was funny what a few months in a different life does for your outlook. Not many cars passed, and nobody else on foot. I wondered what used to be upriver.

It got dark as Everett stopped us in a place to hunker down and wait for our signal. I'd only seen the map for a little while, but it seemed to me that the fence line I could just barely see, about a block away, was probably the one. I couldn't say what this abandoned pole barn structure had once been, but the door wasn't locked, and there was nothing inside but some broken glass and big spools with telephone cable on them. Morgan dropped her bag next to one and hopped up on it to sit and wait.

"Close enough," Everett muttered.

"Really, Luke'll never know unless you tell him," Morgan offered helpfully. She looked at me and patted the spool next to her. I went and sat, legs dangling.

Everett sighed. "If you had such a problem with Luke, why'd you come along at all?"

"What, you think he'd put his neck out just because we said pretty please? We couldn't do this alone, or we never would've darkened your doorstep. Don't worry, we'll be out of your hair soon as we have our people back."

"That isn't what I'm saying."

"Then be more clear." Morgan still had her iced coffee from McDonald's and sucked at the straw, looking off into the middle distance.

Everett's jaw tightened, and Joe looked to me. I just shrugged. Our time with the Wards had been an uneasy back and forth, and my time with Morgan had been a constant scramble to follow her twists and decisions. I had no idea why she'd pick a fight with Everett just then. Everett and Joe sat on a different spool, each with a tablet, and they played some game together with the sound off. As the time passed, I tried to go over in my head the various things I might have to do. Bear repellant. Cut a dog's throat. Shoot a man. I took a breath; really, I just needed to stay calm. I couldn't just send my mind away to another place and rely on instinct. My instinct and I had only recently gotten on talking terms. I had no idea what my instinct would tell me to do in a situation.

I really wondered what it was Morgan did when she stared off in space like that. Was she planning? Meditating? Writing more songs? Revisiting ancestral memories? It's one of those things I couldn't ask, because what if it was something I should already know about?

The time passed, streetlights coming on, sending shadows crawling across the floor, Joe and Everett tapping their touch screens, Morgan rocking just slightly, breathing calm. I watched and listened to everybody in turn, since nobody was paying attention to me. I closed my eyes and tried to catalog everybody's smells in my mind. Everett's hair gel. Joe's persistent lemons. Morgan's boot laces. Toothpaste. The blue goo shampoo in the Ward showers. The plastic casing of the tablets, the slight acrid chemical warmth of the batteries. The salt and grease from McDonald's, wiped into blue jeans. The detergent the Wards used. The new clothes smell from Morgan and I. The blue gray evening closed in around us and thin pale moonlight came through the broken windows. The sounds of distant traffic faded even more, becoming an occasional single car on a faraway street. I could hear the high-pitched wanderings of bats as they left their roosts for the night. The radio set next to Everett clicked once.

We stiffened up and looked at each other, awake and alert. We waited. About five minutes later, there was another click. Five minutes, another. "Showtime," Morgan said, hopping off the spool and grabbing her bag.

"Are we clear on—" Everett started.

"Yeah, we got it," Morgan said.

"Hey, we plan for what we can control. It's for our protection."

"I'm not sure you and I share the same notion of control," Morgan said.

"If this is going to be a problem," Everett tried again.

"Then you can just give me a radio and stay right there, or loop around to the flank with your boys." Morgan stared him down, flinty eyed. He shook his head, looking away. "Good. Now let's get to our assigned position and do this thing."

We went, single file and quiet as we could. There was a hole cut in the fence, edges of the aluminum raw in the moonlight. I could see the hot wire at the top of the fence, between the barbed wire, but didn't hear it hum. There wasn't a camera on that section of the fence. We crossed the lawn no problem, and reached our designated door; Morgan pulled a can of spray paint and coated the lens of the camera that looked down on us, little light on the side of it still on. The can sputtered a bit at being sprayed without shaken, but did the job. Then Morgan tried the door. It was still locked, the keycard light red. Morgan wheeled and grabbed Joe around the back of the neck and shook him. "Are your people trying to fuck us?"

"What? No." His voice cracked.

"This door is supposed to be open."

Everett stepped back, calm, but with a wary eye on both me and Morgan. He keyed his radio. "Alpha, we need entry. I repeat, we need entry." No reply.

"Too bad, the door wouldn't open, we have to abort, right? Maybe we'll try again, maybe not."

"Why would we do that?" Joe protested, and Morgan let go, shoving him away from her.

"Fuck you." She stood a moment, her chin raised, her eyes mostly closed. Joe looked at me, and I shook my head. "Stay here," she said, pointing at the Wards. She looked at me. I followed as she took off around the corner of the building.

There was a security guard on approach. He seemed relaxed, so I could only assume that the Wards had taken out other security without alerting anybody. He was surprised and only just starting to raise his weapon when Morgan and I came into view. Morgan poured on more speed than I'd ever seen from her, and hit him in the sternum with her shoulder before the gun was fully aimed; I heard the bone pop, and a single muffled shot rang out. She reached across and pulled a serrated combat knife off of his hip and drew it through the three point webbing straps that slung his gun; now that I looked at it, I realized he had an honest to God machine gun. She didn't knock the barrel up like she taught me, I thought wildly.

Morgan struck him across the wrists and the gun clattered to the ground. I took my final three steps and scooped it up, backing up out of range again. I couldn't tell if the safety was on, and in the moonlight saw the three settings: single, burst, and full auto.

No rifle, no knife, the security guard reached again, for his radio or his sidearm, I couldn't tell and never had to guess, because in her next motion Morgan opened his throat and dropped him. He pawed at his throat and his breathing made a ragged wet wheeze. His blood smelled like a handful of pennies. Morgan rummaged at his belt and came up with a keycard, and yanked the radio off of its clip on his collar. She turned to me and took the gun out of my nerveless hands. "Morgan, oh God Morgan, you just..."

"Yes, I did. Go back to the Wards, I'm going to get him out of the open." She didn't have to tell me twice.

They still stood where we left them, and when I came back alone, they stared at me in shocked silence. Then Morgan came up behind me, breathing hard, reeking of pennies and cordite. She stared at them as she wiped the keycard off on her jeans and ran it through the slot on the door. The light turned green, the door buzzed, and she pulled it open. She reached in her pocket and pulled out one of the carabiners, snapped it through the protruding latch plate, and stalked inside, guard's rifle at ready. We followed her through, and the door banged against the carabiner, propped for swift exit.

The hallway was blinding white. Slick shiny white floor, matte eggshell walls, white drop ceiling. The fluorescent lights buzzed overhead, and I heard the AC kick on with a soft whoosh. Morgan opened the next door and repeated the carabiner trick. Every time there was a camera along the hall, she ran to it and sprayed it, maybe even before she was on film, I didn't know. I hoped. Everett and Joe had the good sense to follow along and keep their mouths shut, and I could smell their nervous sweat.

The next door let us into a hallway that had glass windows on either side looking into labs, the walls lined with cages, each containing a white rabbit with blood red eyes. The rabbits all looked at us through the bars, little noses working, and the hair on the back of my neck stood up. I looked back down the hallway behind us, and jerked almost out of my skin when I heard glass breaking. Morgan, of course, putting that sledgehammer to use. "Let the bunnies out," she said.

"They'll just be trapped in the hallway, and trip us up." I didn't want to go in the rabbit rooms, I didn't want to go any further down this hall.

"If they're still in the hallway when we come back up, we'll deal with it then. If they're not, we'll know somebody else is waiting for us." We climbed through windows and started opening cages. The rabbits didn't struggle when we touched them, and when they were set on the linoleum in the hallway, they just sat there. "It's part of the plan," Morgan said, touching my shoulder briefly. I could still smell the blood on her hands; I wondered what she'd done with the knife. Dropped it on the body, maybe.

"They smell weird," Joe said.

"Just don't eat 'em," Everett answered. Joe made a face, and I laughed, short and off-pitched.

"Everett, show me how to get the hard drives out of these computers," Morgan said. There were two desktops in one of the labs.

"That's not our assignment," he said.

"Are you going to fight me on everything?" she asked. "Because we're already off assignment, through no fault of mine, or yours. We had to make our own entrance, and from where I stand, that means we can play by our rules. So. Please. Pull the fucking hard drives." Everett went and helped with the computers. Morgan put the hard drives in a padded envelope and stuck them in her messenger bag. "Good, thank you." Joe and I kept our heads down and finished putting the rabbits in the hallway. They didn't move when we picked them up, just hung in our hands, warm and soft. Once we set them down, some of them took some lolloping steps towards the slightly ajar door. Others just hunkered down, noses constantly working. I nudged one out of the way with my foot once we were done, and went to the next door. Morgan had already spray painted the camera lens.

I kept waiting for some kind of alarm to sound, or the lights to go out, or for a SWAT team to descend upon us, but none of those things happened. It was eerily quiet and very bright, and there was no chatter on the radio that Morgan had taken off the guard outside, nor on the Ward radio. She swiped the keycard on the next door, and it opened to a waiting area and an elevator door. "No stairs," I pointed out.

"We'll just have to hope they don't cut the power while we're down there," Everett said, in a tone like he couldn't decide between making a brave joke or just sounding grim.

"If they do, we'll figure something else out," I said, looking at Morgan. She'd pressed the down button and waited, foot tapping, watching the numbers above the door light up.

Morgan stepped back and covered with the rifle, but the doors slid open to reveal the empty elevator. We all stepped in, and the doors slid closed again. I stood close to Morgan, listening to my heart pound, and maybe hers too. Joe checked his watch and Everett fiddled with the radio. It clicked as he changed channels, but there was nothing but smooth static. He noticed me watching and shrugged as he shoved it in his pocket. The elevator was slow as molasses.

Morgan pinched me, and I remembered I had the sawed off shotgun, brought it up, and she braced. The elevator doors opened, and we faced another long white hallway. There was a security guard here, partway down the hall and turning to see who had just arrived on his floor. Morgan was out of the elevator before I could move, though Everett and then Joe were hot on her heels. I looked at the elevator panel, and flipped the 'door open' switch. The guard brought up his hand to his collar, for the radio, and Morgan drove the heel of her hand up into his nose. His head jerked back, and she rode him to the ground, grabbed a handful of his hair, and slammed his head on the floor. It was concrete here, not linoleum, with metal drains at intervals, and the guard jerked once and was still. I could still hear his breathing, though, under everybody else's.

Morgan pulled the guard's keycard off its lanyard and stood up again. A muscle in her jaw twitched, and I noticed the sheen of sweat on her face and neck. "Cover him, will you? If I remember right, this room is the lab, and should be Rachel and Dulcie. We can handle it on our own, quickly as possible."

"Yeah, sure. Just let us know if you need help," Joe said, looking down at the security guard. He looked as green around the gills as I felt. Everett's shoulders were stiff, and he checked the radio again. I was ninety percent sure that the Wards wouldn't leave their boys. Was Everett less sure? They said nobody got left behind, nobody. They didn't unlock the door for us.

Morgan ran the key card, and the light went green. She handed me a handful of carabiners without looking and went on; I slapped one on the door before following, and jammed the ones I didn't drop into my pocket. The smell of disinfectant was overwhelming, and there was a hand sanitizer dispenser on the wall just inside the room. The door thunked against the carabiner behind me, and I could smell Rachel, and blood, and more electronics. Morgan's spray paint. Chemicals. Blood. Not Dulcie. Why couldn't I smell Dulcie?

There were movable hospital dividers set up throughout the room, and the layers made my eyes go funny for a moment. I closed them, and followed my nose instead, bumping into Morgan when she came back to see where I was. I opened my eyes and expected her to yell at me, but she just grabbed my arm with her bloody hands and dragged me to where Rachel was.

Chapter Twenty Six

I don't know what I'd expected. Our endless road trip had only been what, four days? Five? It was hard to gauge how much scientific testing, or torture, would have taken place between then and now. I could see the burn on her neck from the Taser, and her hair was shaved right down to the skin, just the blue-black shadow of some stubble. There were lots of bandages, too many. On her shoulder, arms, her temple. Wide leather cuffs secured her wrists to the metal railings of her hospital bed, and there was an IV line into the back of her left hand, and another in the vein of her right elbow. Morgan shoved the rifle at me and started to unbuckle the restraints; I found the safety and engaged it, then set the rifle on a wheeled metal tray that stood nearby.

Rachel's eyes drifted open at the noise, the movement, and she looked at Morgan and I hazily, her lip curling. Then she gave a hard blink and looked at us again, struggling to lift her head. "How?" she asked, voice barely a whisper. Her lips were dry and cracked.

"Long story, dumb story," Morgan said. "Where's Dulcie?"

Rachel closed her eyes again and I hoped she hadn't drifted off into drugland again. I didn't want to have to make the call about the adrenaline shot. "She's dead."

My vision swam, and I clutched the railing of her bed. Maybe I hadn't heard her right. I looked at Morgan's face, the set of her jaw. That was why I couldn't smell Dulcie. "What did they do?" I asked, to keep from drifting off myself. Morgan would cheerfully murder me if I passed out on the floor. Or changed.

"Cremated. Box is over there, or they say it is when they show it to me. Measure stress levels." Rachel bared her teeth.

"Motherfuckers," Morgan said, and looked at me. Her eyes were so dilated I almost couldn't see the blue. "Go get her?"

"Of course."

I left the barrier around Rachel's bed and looked around at the tables. Lots of sterile medical equipment, a clipboard thick with charts that I took and stuck in my bag. A square metal box. The contents of it shifted and rattled slightly when I picked it up, and I closed my eyes, clutching it against my stomach for a moment. "Allie, come *on*," Morgan said, her voice tight, a little too high. I carefully settled the box into my messenger bag.

"No computers," I said when I came back to them.

"Microchip," Rachel said. Morgan had helped her sit up, and she hunched on the edge of the bed as Morgan pulled a change of clothes out of her bag.

"What?" Morgan was practically spitting.

"They microchipped me. Right shoulder blade." She nodded her head backwards a little. "Gotta take it out."

"We'll do it after we get you out of here," Morgan said, holding out a shirt. Rachel looked at her from beneath a lowered brow.

"No. Now. Tracking." She might have been drugged out of her mind, but Rachel still somehow had her shit together. I had no question as to where Morgan got it.

Morgan bit her lip. "Mama, I can't," she said, her voice breaking. Rachel turned her gaze on me.

"Get a knife."

"Jesus, Rachel, really?" I said. Morgan was the hardass, the superhero, how was I supposed to do it if she couldn't? Rachel didn't look away. I reached over and took the knife off of Morgan's belt and walked to one of the disinfecting stations to kill some time. There was an autoclave that I had no idea to use, but also a huge bottle of rubbing alcohol, and I dumped a bunch of that over the blade, wiping it off with gauze. There was a tray of instruments there, and I grabbed a pair of tweezers, squared my shoulders and went back, taking deep breaths. I had to do this. I could do this. "Morgan?"

"Mama, squeeze when it hurts," Morgan said, taking Rachel's hands in hers. I opened the back of Rachel's gown and ran my hand over her right shoulder blade. I could feel the microchip there, a little bump the size of a grain of rice. Rachel leaned her forehead against Morgan's and breathed deeply.

"All right," I said, and ran the tip of the knife along the rice grain bump. Rachel tensed, and I heard Morgan breathe in sharply through her nose, but they didn't move. Blood welled up, and I squeezed, like I was coaxing out a splinter, and eased the tweezers in gently as I could. I felt the chip, closed the tweezers on it and drew it out slowly. I was holding my breath, and Rachel was holding her breath, until I held the bloody thing up to the light. "Let me get something for that," I said, and went back to the sink for gauze, and tape. I kept my thoughts on what I was doing right that second, no more, no less.

I wiped off Rachel's bloody back and taped some gauze over the newest cut. We could do better for her after we were safe. "Go check out if there's something I missed, Morgan," I said, picking up the shirt from the bed. I got Rachel dressed, and she tried to help me, or at least tried not to get in the way. I thought about my breathing, and her breathing, and getting one arm in the shirt, then the other. One leg in the pants, then the other. Socks. Boots. "Is there anything else we need to know while we're here, Rachel?"

She shook her head like she was underwater. "Clipboard?"

"I got the clipboard."

"They don't keep the samples here," she said.

"Samples?"

"Blood. Tissue. Upstairs, other side of the building."

"That's where the Wards are. I think they've got a notion to mess up the business." She looked at me, and then reached out and brushed the chain around my neck with her fingers.

"You found the cross?" she asked, smiling a little.

"I did." I'd thought Dulcie got it but—

"I hoped you would like it."

"Allie, come see this," Morgan said from the far side of the room. I made sure Rachel wasn't going to fall off the bed, and went to her. There was a small cubicle that I hadn't noticed for all the screens, and a cage. It had a timber wolf in it, or maybe it was a wolf dog. He was lying flat on his side and stared at us with yellow eyes. He looked and smelled as drugged as Rachel.

"See if there's a muzzle, he'll probably walk out." I said, moving to the cage door.

"Wait, what? That's what you think we should be doing?"

"It's not like we're going to leave him," I said, looking back at her. Turnabout is fair play, Morgan. "Rabbits are one thing."

"Rachel comes first."

"Obviously. But there are four of us. I can handle the dog." Especially after digging a microchip out of her mother's shoulder blade.

"Wolf."

"We're all wolves." I held Morgan's gaze, and for once, I wasn't the one who looked away first.

"Fine. Hurry it up." She went back to Rachel, electric with energy, short sharp movements.

I looked around a little, trying to rush, trying not to miss anything, and there was a metal mesh basket muzzle on a nearby table, along with a leash, collar, and harness that fastened together. I approached the cage, which wasn't locked, just latched from the outside. I'd heard wolves were escape artists, but I guess that only mattered if you had a problem with drugging them. "All right, buddy, I'm just going to help you out of here," I said as I opened the cage. He saw the muzzle and a deep growl started in his chest, and though he twitched, he couldn't lift his head fast enough. "I'm sorry, I don't think we know each other well enough to get along without this," I said, slipping the muzzle over his head and fastening it behind his ears. I reached under and gripped him high on the forelegs, pulling him out of the cage. Getting the collar on him wasn't all that hard; the harness was another issue, but I managed. Increased werewolf strength and all that; it's maybe one of the first times I noticed. I used one of the carabiners to clip the leash to my belt. The wolf struggled to his feet and stood there with his feet too far apart, head down, hackles half raised, looking at me. "Look, I'll get you a burger or something," I said to him, careful to avoid his gaze.

"Come on, Allie," Morgan said.

"Coming." I motioned with my head and started walking. To my utmost relief, the wolf followed along with me. Rachel was still sitting on the bed.

"Give me your adrenaline shot," Morgan said.

"Where's yours?" But Rachel looked at me and nodded, and we didn't have *time* and I handed it over. Morgan pulled the cap off the needle with her teeth and used one of the ports on the IV still in Rachel's arm. They waited a minute and then pulled both of the tubes out of Rachel's arms, dribbling a little bit of bloody fluid onto the floor. Rachel shook her head, her eyes starting to clear already.

"Well, let's get going. I'd rather be moving when we find out if the drug interactions are going to kill me," she said. She paused a moment, looking down the leash at the wolf, and then shook her head again.

In the hallway, the guard was still on the floor, but had been rolled onto his side. I couldn't hear him breathing anymore. Everett was fiddling with the radio again, and Joe stood at the elevator. He frowned when he saw us. "Just one?" he called. He knew something was wrong, more wrong than we'd imagined, but still had to make sure, just to wrap his brain around it.

"Yes," Morgan said shortly. Rachel looked down at the security guard as we passed.

Everett waited for me to catch up. "What's the deal?

"They killed Dulcie," I said shortly. "And I wasn't going to leave him." I gestured at the wolf. He sniffed and nodded slowly.

"Come on, I'll just carry him," he said, bending to scoop the wolf up like a kitten. The leash was still attached to me, but in tandem, we got on the elevator. Joe flipped the door switch, and hit the up button. We had a tense ride upwards, the elevator reeking of nerves, and blood, and sweat. We got to the first floor and a sea of white rabbits greeted us, noses twitching, red eyes catching the light.

"What the fuck's up with Watership Down?" Rachel asked, and laughed in a high-pitched, off-kilter way.

"Do you want one? We can add it to Allie's zoo, until that wolf gets hungry," Morgan said through gritted teeth. "Saddest kid's book ever."

"I'll pass." Rachel seemed to be counting the rabbits as we passed. They moved out of our way just enough at first, and then faster as the AC kicked on again, spreading the wolf smell more quickly. Morgan paused a moment at one of the doors, her nostrils flaring.

"Motherfuckers," she said wearily, casting a baleful glance at Joe and Everett.

"What, what's wrong?" I asked. I couldn't smell it.

"Fire," she said, and picked up the pace.

I looked at Everett. "Thermite. The plan is to destroy the servers with thermite," he said, looking a little pale.

"Oh, of course," I said dazedly. Morgan asked and Luke wouldn't tell her. Compartmentalization, or he was being an asshole. I guessed it could've been both.

We were outside when the radio clicked. "Omega we are on retreat, do you read?"

Everett shifted the wolf in his arms to get to the radio. "Roger that, Alpha, we are also en route to primary fallback. Objective complete." He cleared his throat and glanced at me. "Mostly."

There was a long, long pause, or maybe it just seemed like that to me. "Roger, Omega. Alpha Out."

"They didn't fucking expect us to get in," Morgan said, teeth and whites of her eyes flashing. "I told you."

"Not the time, Morgan," Rachel said calmly. She was almost walking on her own, but Morgan was all but vibrating in place. Strobe lights started flashing in the hallway, and an alarm blared, paused, blared. The pain in my head was blinding.

"Fire, or security?" I shouted.

"Both," Everett and Joe said at once. We got outside, and I could hear barking. No more conversation; we ran.

Chapter Twenty Seven

The dogs didn't leave the fence line. I waited for Morgan to helpfully point out that there shouldn't have been any dogs, but she didn't. We got to the Jeep, and she leaned Rachel against it. "We won't all fit like this. I'll be right back." I freed the carabiner from my belt, shoved the leash into Joe's startled hands. It took me a minute to catch up with her and grab her arm.

"Morgan, what are you doing?"

"Finding a car for you to drive with your new pet. You can follow us." She brushed me out of the way, and I felt damp and looked down. My arm was wet with blood.

"Jesus Christ, Morgan."

She gave me a tired grin, face slick with sweat. "Keep praying if you think it'll help."

"What happened?"

"We don't have time, Allie." She shook me off and ran.

I dug a bandanna out of my pocket and wiped my arm off before going back to the group. I reached under the bumper and got the spare key out of the magnet box. "Morgan will be right back. Everett, you'll drive." I watched Joe help Rachel into the back seat, and she reached out and grabbed my wrist before I stepped away.

"I'm proud of you girls," she said.

I couldn't help but laugh, almost hysterical. I somehow got myself stopped though. "I sure hope so," I said, and before I could continue, headlights swung across us. Rachel let go, and I turned, trying to reach for the strap of the sawed off where it rested on my shoulder. It was Morgan, though, in an old VW Bug. She got out, leaving the driver's door open and the car running.

"You know how to get where we're going?" she asked, a little breathless.

"I do." Everett had set the wolf down, and I grabbed the leash. "Be careful for once, all right?"

"Yeah, maybe." Morgan grinned. "But you'll be right behind me to keep me honest."

"Yes, I will. Everett's driving, so you should be fine."

"The hell he is." Morgan stalked back to the Jeep. She didn't even say anything, just glared; Everett went around to the passenger seat. Joe shoved the spare radio in my hand and ran to hop in the back with Rachel. I coaxed the wolf into the back seat of the bug, and tied the leash around the seat belt.

We took a serpentine route through sleeping neighborhoods, the area slowly becoming more modern, more built up, more populated. I kept watching for the Jeep to waver, for Everett to have to take over. I didn't know how badly Morgan was hurt; I wondered if that single shot from the first security guard was what got her. The Wards would be able to help her. If it was the last thing they did for us, they would do that. They had to.

We whipped towards Atlanta on empty late-night highway, the city lit on the horizon. Then we were sitting at a red light in the right turn lane, no other cars around, and I glanced at the blue Interstate signs, then looked more closely. Interstate 20, I remembered from when Mama brought me to the aunts. A left, 20 West, would take me back to Alabama. Morgan was taking 20 East. The light turned green, and she turned. I didn't; I sat and looked at the signs for a minute. I thought of my room at home, my brothers, my mama and daddy. I saw the brake lights flash on the Jeep, and Morgan honked once, impatiently, a short blast like she'd punched the steering wheel. I bit my lip and looked to the left, then hit the gas and turned right before the light changed again. Morgan waited until I was almost on her bumper and then kept going.

The radio on the passenger seat crackled. "Morgan, ah, wants me to ask you what the fuck?"

"The wolf knocked the car out of gear," I said. Lying came more easy when nobody could see my face, or smell me.

"Roger that," Joe said, and I heard Morgan cursing in the background.

The wolf lifted his head and looked around occasionally; I saw the tips of his ears in my rearview mirror. He didn't growl, or make any other noise. At one point, he leaned forward and gently nudged my elbow with the cold metal muzzle and I yelled in surprise. I looked over my shoulder at the wolf. "Sorry," I said. He put his head down and sighed through his nose.

Half an hour later, we were off of 20 and at the edge of some nature preserve. The radio came on again. "Turn your lights off."

"Okay. I mean, uh, roger that."

We drove in the darkness for another five minutes, on a road I was sure the public wasn't supposed to access, until we pulled onto an even smaller road, and stopped. Figures came out of the woods, and I half expected them to be Silvernail security forces until I recognized Luke, and others from the Ward's house, by sight and smell.

Rachel got out of the Jeep on her own power, leaned on it as she came around and opened the driver door. Morgan half fell out, and despite everything, Rachel started to hoist her under the arms. Luke stepped in, said something to Rachel, who hesitated, nodded and let him pick Morgan up. I could hear her muttering, but she wasn't truly forming words anymore, and she twisted and tried to throw a punch as he carried her off. There was some yelling, a lot of yelling, but it was all white noise, I couldn't make out what anybody was saying. I climbed out of the bug and Joe came over. "Do you want any help with him?" he asked, peering into the backseat. The wolf looked back at him.

"It's okay. I think we came to an understanding." I really wasn't sure what I was saying anymore either. I was just exhausted, physically, emotionally, mentally. I opened the door and reached in carefully, untying what I'd done with the leash and the seat belt. I backed up a step, and the wolf stood up on the seat and stretched, then slowly climbed out. "It's weird to use a leash."

Joe shook his head. "Don't worry about it. Do what you have to do."

"Morgan's going to be okay, right?"

"Tyler was a medic in Iraq," he said, like it was an answer. I could hear more yelling ahead; Luke's voice really stood out, and Tyler's. Rachel's cut through the night. Not Morgan's, but she had to be okay. She couldn't not be okay. Not after every-thing. Oh god, Dulcie.

The tent the Wards had set up was smaller than a cabin, but barely. There was a lot of commotion, a lot of people com-ing in and out of it, and I got the sense that some people had been hurt this time, other than Morgan. Rachel sat in a camp chair out front, wearing a jacket I didn't recognize and cradling a cup of coffee in her hands. Luke stood next to her in his shirt sleeves, his back to us, looking through the tent flap. He turned when he heard the clink of the leash on the wolf's harness. Morgan's blood was smeared on his front.

"What the fuck is that?" he said tiredly.

"Nothing you need to worry about," I said.

"You've got a wolf on a leash, and it's nothing for me to worry about? Where'd you grow balls between last night and tonight?"

"The miracles of science." I looked at Rachel. "How's Morgan?"

"They said the bullet lodged against her hipbone, so we didn't need to go digging around in her guts. They drugged her up good, so we'll have peace until morning." The wolf stood stiffly next to me, turning his head this way and that, his ears swiveling around. "She said you got a bunch of the hard drives?"

"We did. She couldn't see leaving them." Luke grunted and glared at Joe, who slunk off towards the food setup. "I guess the others got burned," I said, looking at Luke.

"They did," he said. "Along with any scientific samples that we found. It was too much for us to carry out."

Rachel looked between me and Luke. "It is what it is," she said. She was still slurring a little bit, and seemed very, very tired. I wondered how long the shot would last for her. The wolf took a step towards her, ears forward. "Think he needs the muzzle?"

"I don't really know." I thought of Dulcie's ashes, hanging next to my hip. "Rachel, what are we going to do?"

"We'll discuss when Morgan is able." she said. She put her hand out, and the wolf investigated Rachel's scent with short, sniffy bursts. He didn't stiffen, or bristle, or growl. Somebody called Luke's name, and he walked off.

I sat in the chair next to Rachel. "What about you?"

"I'll be all right. They didn't use silver on me, and they treated my wounds. They wanted me in good condition for the experiments." Her voice was dull, but her knuckles whitened on the coffee cup.

"We don't need to talk about it now," I said cautiously.

"No. We don't." The wolf settled down at my feet with a sigh, his head on his paws. I looked at him a moment, and then reached down and unfastened the muzzle. He drew his nose out of it, and then nudged it out of the way and put his head down again, already more relaxed. I leaned my head against the back of the chair and let my eyes drift shut.

I jerked into motion and slapped Everett's hand away as he reached to touch my shoulder before I was fully awake. The wolf moved his head enough to look up at me, as if to say 're-ally?'

"Sorry," Everett said. "I hate to wake you, but I don't know what time we got and it's important that you know."

I looked around. Rachel wasn't in the chair next to me anymore, and the coat she'd been in was draped over me. Luke's coat. Nobody was yelling anymore; camp was pretty calm. In the darkness, I could smell gun oil, and assumed that the Wards had posted guards. "What is it?" I asked finally.

"I looked at the data we recovered," he said.

"What, your virus thingie worked already?"

"No. Well maybe it did, it's not my job to check on that. No, I put each of the hard drives into a machine they brought to the site here, and did a quick ghost and run-through of the stuff that was on them." He pressed a rubber jacketed usb drive in my hand.

"We don't have anything to use this with," I said, and jammed it in my jeans pocket. "You should probably be telling Rachel about this."

"She's sleeping, and probably needs it more than you."

"Thanks." He was right, though.

"Do you want to know or not? I'll give the short version, what I thought seemed real important. Especially when everybody's distracted."

"Thank you, I do want to know, yes. I should probably also feed the wolf." I stood up and stretched, tossed the jacket onto an empty chair.

"Feed him what?"

"I promised him a burger," I said, like it made sense, but Everett just led me to the food setup. Maybe I was in some kind of shock, and he'd seen it before. The plates of hotdogs and hamburgers were covered with plastic wrap. How many burgers does one feed a full grown wolf? I started with three. Everett looked around, and stepped a little closer.

"All right, some of the basic data that they got was just vitals and stuff. Heart rate, brainwaves, stressed brain waves, that kind of thing. Pain tolerance. Perception tests."

"And this was on Rachel?"

Everett cleared his throat. "On both of them. They didn't use silver when they shot Rachel. They did with Dulcie."

I took a minute to just breathe. "All right, what else?"

"It only gets worse."

"They killed her, I didn't figure it would get better." I sounded harder than I felt. I sounded like Morgan and I felt like the world was spinning away from underneath me. Dulcie didn't even get the short years we were allotted.

"Dulcie died because of sepsis from a silver bullet in the initial raid. Only one of the operatives was loaded with silver rounds. They didn't realize the profound effect that it would have when left in her leg as long as it was. Rachel had a normal round graze her arm, no trace of infection." Everett stopped as somebody came out of the tent.

"Everything all right?" Luke asked.

"I woke up hungry," I said. "Your jacket's on the chair."

"Use it if you need it. You're all right, only Morgan hurt in your group?" It was the nicest tone I'd ever heard him use, and I was sorry to say it just made me feel defensive.

"Yeah, Morgan was the only one. Other than how we found Rachel." Luke still lingered. "I hope nobody else got hurt too bad."

"No casualties on our side," he said with a short nod.

"Good, I'm really glad," I said, and he sauntered off. "Keep going," I said once I couldn't smell Luke nearby anymore.

Everett hesitated. "Before Dulcie was cremated, they harvested her eggs."

"They what? Why? For what?" My ears were ringing.

"Shh, keep your voice down. When they took all that blood from Sela, they had a number of men that they had tested prior to the experiment going forward. They did something to it, I'm not even sure what to call it, and injected three of the men. Then they got sperm samples." He paused and listened for a minute. I tilted my head. I couldn't hear anything. "Then they separated the male sperm from the female sperm, and put them in a petri dish. Two dishes for each man, with the aim of forming one female offspring and one male offspring."

"Culvers don't really make male offspring. We're like calico cats"

"Not normally, no. With Sela's blood therapy, they got one. Grew it long enough in a dish that they were sure, and then implanted it in a surrogate's womb. She was at another site, and the whole scientific team flew out there for it yesterday."

I knew he had to go fast but I just couldn't wrap my head around it. "Doesn't all of this stuff normally take more time? It hasn't even been a *week*, much less months, how would they—"

"I have no idea. I know it used to take forever to sequence DNA and now they can do it overnight."

"Was that the whole point? That seems like the hard way to get their own werewolf super soldiers."

"I don't know if super soldiers is the point, necessarily, but they're trying to get a handle on the genetic strangeness. There was certainly more, but we've taken their two living test subjects away. And the wolf. Which is a wolf by the way, not like us."

"It hadn't occurred to me to wonder that."

"I wondered if he might be one of us, but all drugged up and stuck. Or he was a wolf when they caught him, and he wouldn't change back. They both have microchips."

"We took Rachel's out."

"Fuck." Everett scratched his head. "You probably didn't need to do that. I think normal ones can only be scanned within like, forty feet. I guess all bets are off here."

"Look, if Rachel tells you to do something, it gets done." I kept thinking of Morgan, in that moment. *Mama, I can't.*

"I hear you. Anyway, I put the information on that thumb drive for you, just in case something happens to the drives we carried out of there."

"Any idea where this other site is? That they're keeping the surrogate?" Dulcie's baby, I thought.

"Not from this data. I expect that'll come out in the stuff we gather using the virus."

Luke walked past again, stopped and frowned. "Everett, can't you see she isn't in any state for conversation? Come on, Allie, I'm sure I can find a tent and sleeping bag for you."

It was Luke so I hesitated, but also I could just lay down on the ground and go to sleep right there. "Thanks," I finally said, following him. I felt like I should ask where Rachel was, or maybe Joe, but I'd already been asleep once, and I could only think about sleep again now, even with everything Everett just tried to tell me. All of the awful everything.

Chapter Twenty Eight

I woke to Morgan yelling, and I thrashed in the unfamiliar covers, scattering the wolf away from me and coming fully awake at the zipped up tent door. I fumbled for the zipper, and realized I heard Rachel too. She wasn't yelling, but I recognized the firm tone she'd taken. I'd heard it often enough. I got myself disentangled and out of the tent before I realized I hadn't picked up the wolf's leash. He looked at me from the tent door. "You coming?" I asked, and he stretched and followed along.

"There was no signal, stop lying and saying there was. The door was locked, and you said it would be open. You got in there just fine, you cut the hole in the fence and turned off the hot wire. But didn't open the doors for us, any of them." At the main tent, Morgan was death half-warmed over, chalky pale and wobbly from painkillers, but was as close in Luke's face as the Wards and Rachel would let her.

"If that's true, how do you expect me to believe you broke into a place like that yourself?" Luke asked smugly. The other Wards hanging around mostly seemed to think Morgan was a crazy bitch; I didn't know any of their names, didn't remember many of their faces. Just Zeb, but he'd positioned himself to hold Luke back, if necessary.

"Morgan's right, the doors were locked," I said. "She got a keycard off of an outside guard, that's when she got shot." Morgan turned when she heard me. "Joe and Everett can vouch that we had to open the doors ourselves. The cameras were still on, too."

"That's a long time to operate with a bullet in you," Luke said. I didn't know how she's up *now*, but nobody was saying anything about that.

Morgan looked back to him, and Rachel had to steady her when she overbalanced. "It wasn't silver. And adrenaline dulls the pain reaction, that's not new information. That was the point, wasn't it? Anyway, I think that you didn't care about Rachel and Dulcie at all, you just wanted to see what Silvernail had on you."

"If that was the case, why let you come at all? Why risk members of the family?"

"They're green and would listen to you. And you knew you couldn't get rid of us, you already tried."

Luke shook his head and looked at Rachel. "Hey, we got you out, right? She's just high on pain meds. We had a snafu, only got part of security down. We gave them the signal to abort."

"*They* got me out," Rachel said slowly.

Joe cleared his throat. He was as afraid as I'd ever smelled him. "There...there was no signal."

Luke turned on him. "What did you fucking say?"

Joe flinched, but stayed put. "I said there was no signal to abort. After the go signals, it was radio silence, even after Everett requested entry when we were at the door."

"This was your first mission, you probably just missed it. When we're in the shit we can't take the time to hold everybody's hand. We brought you along because we thought you'd do all right, Joey, we thought all this would be good first mission material for you. Was that a mistake?"

"No sir, no mistake. But there was no signal." Joe licked his lips and looked at Everett, who nodded.

"It wasn't my first mission, and there was no signal," Everett said abruptly.

"I knew it was a mistake, sending you with the girls," Luke said to nobody in particular. I couldn't read the look on Joe's face, but the smile that crossed Luke's face was downright cruel. "We should've only sent veterans to that end of things. Then we wouldn't be having this conversation."

Everybody just stood there staring at each other, not giving an inch. Rachel pulled Morgan away. "Come on, daughter mine. If you feel good enough to pick fights, you feel good enough to travel." She looked at me. "How soon can you be ready?"

"I'm ready now."

"Where are you going to go? Don't forget, you owe us now."

"Nobody gave you a blank check, Luke Ward; we'll return your help in kind."

"And what does that mean, Rachel Culver?"

"You've always been a smart boy, you'll figure it out." She motioned for me to wait and went inside the big tent briefly, coming out with the messenger bag Morgan had carried into the compound last night. "We know where to find you. Say hello to your father."

We walked out to the Jeep; nobody came after us, or tried to stop us. I'm sure that as far as many of them were concerned, we'd only brought trouble when we came. They were happy to see us leave, ready to settle back into their wargames, their macho world. I looked back over my shoulder and caught Joe's eye for a minute. If nobody else, Joe was sorry to see us go. Rachel opened the doors of the Jeep, got Morgan into the passenger's seat; she really wasn't good enough to pick fights *or* travel, but there we were. I loaded the bags and patted the back seat for the wolf to jump up. He stood on the seat and craned his neck to smell Morgan's hair as her head lolled back on the seat rest, but he settled down when the Jeep began to move.

"You got a prepaid?" Rachel asked, looking at me in the rearview mirror as she backed out to the road.

"Yeah, here."

She dialed it one-handed and then tucked it between her ear and her shoulder. "Sidney? It's Rachel. Pack yourself and your mother up, and meet us at grandmother's house and we'll decide what to do next." She folded the phone closed and handed it back to me. "We've got a long drive ahead of us," she said. "Anybody else hungry?"

· · · ·

Acknowledgements

FOR JIM, MY HUSBAND, my love, it means so much to me that you're so proud of me that I'm published

To Jazzi, for loving my characters as much as I do, if not more.

To Tori, look, the werewolves! It sure took me long enough.

Thank you to Premee, this publishing journey sure is something! At all times!

Thank you to Lennon, for proofreading, and for being there for my writing, and for so long!

Thank you to my patrons, Brian, Heather, Kelly, Sheryl, and Wendy. I'm so glad that you signed up and stuck with me.

• • • •

About the Author

JENNIFER R. DONOHUE grew up at the Jersey Shore and now lives in central New York with her husband and their Doberman. She works at her local public library where she also facilitates a writing workshop. Her work has appeared in *Apex Magazine, Escape Pod, Fantasy, Fusion Fragment*, and elsewhere. Her Run With the Hunted novella series is available in paperback and eBook, and her debut novel, Exit Ghost, is available in eBook and hardcover. She tweets @AuthorizedMusin and you can subscribe to her Patreon for a new short story every month: https://www.patreon.com/JenniferRDonohue

• • • •

Other Works by Jennifer R. Donohue:
Exit Ghost
The Drowned Heir
Between the Blood and the Sun
Run With the Hunted (series)
Run With the Hunted
Run With the Hunted 2: Ctrl Alt Delete
Run With the Hunted 3: Standard Operating Procedure
Run With the Hunted 4: VIP
Run With the Hunted 5: Insert Coin to Play